RETRIBUTION

Tales From the Tapestry

BOOK 1

Written by

JKL Parker

TABLE OF CONTENTS

Chapter 1
A Broken Wheel...9

Chapter 2
Midnight Toil...12

Chapter 3
A Wild Road...15

Chapter 4
Broken String.. 20

Chapter 5
Sacrilege 23

Chapter 6
A Child is Born...27

Chapter 7
Vitae...31

Chapter 8
Careless Cruelty...37

Chapter 9
The Name of Nothing 41

Chapter 10
Rematch...46

Chapter 11
Back Alley Politics 52

Chapter 12
Approaching storm...60

Chapter 13
Shame 67

Chapter 14
Promises...70

Chapter 15
Destruction 74

Chapter 16
Wrath..79

Chapter 17
Retribution.. 81

Chapter 18
A Bargain Struck.. 90

Chapter 19
A Child in Need...96

Chapter 20
Travel plans... 100

Chapter 21
A New Duty..108

Chapter 22
One life to another... 115

Chapter 23
Trading Tales 118

Chapter 24
Taskmaster...123

Chapter 25
Death and Shadows...127

Chapter 26
Nowhere to go 131

Chapter 27
Shadow Boxing 134

Chapter 28
Beithir..140

Chapter 29
Plans and Pawns 144

Chapter 30
What's in a name? 147

Chapter 31
A City of Secrets 152

Chapter 32
A Dark Soul...156

Chapter 33
Lost Soul 161

Chapter 34
Willing Captive 165

Chapter 35
Parts or People? 168

Chapter 36
The Woman
in the Dark 173

Chapter 37
Deadly Medicine 179

Chapter 38
Stolen Souls 186

Chapter 39
Man Hunters 190

Chapter 40
The Fire of Creation 193

Chapter 41
A Talk with Death 199

Chapter 42
The Light in the Dark 202

Chapter 43
Barely Free 208

Chapter 44
Band of Brothers 212

Chapter 45
Beithir's Battle 217

Chapter 46
Iron Favor 221

Chapter 47
Little Victories 225

N
W
E
S
NORD-VAEG
SKJOL HARBOR
SILVER FJELS
PONTIOS SEA
ORI
NAMEL
VILLAC
LATOS OCEAN
GRANDIA

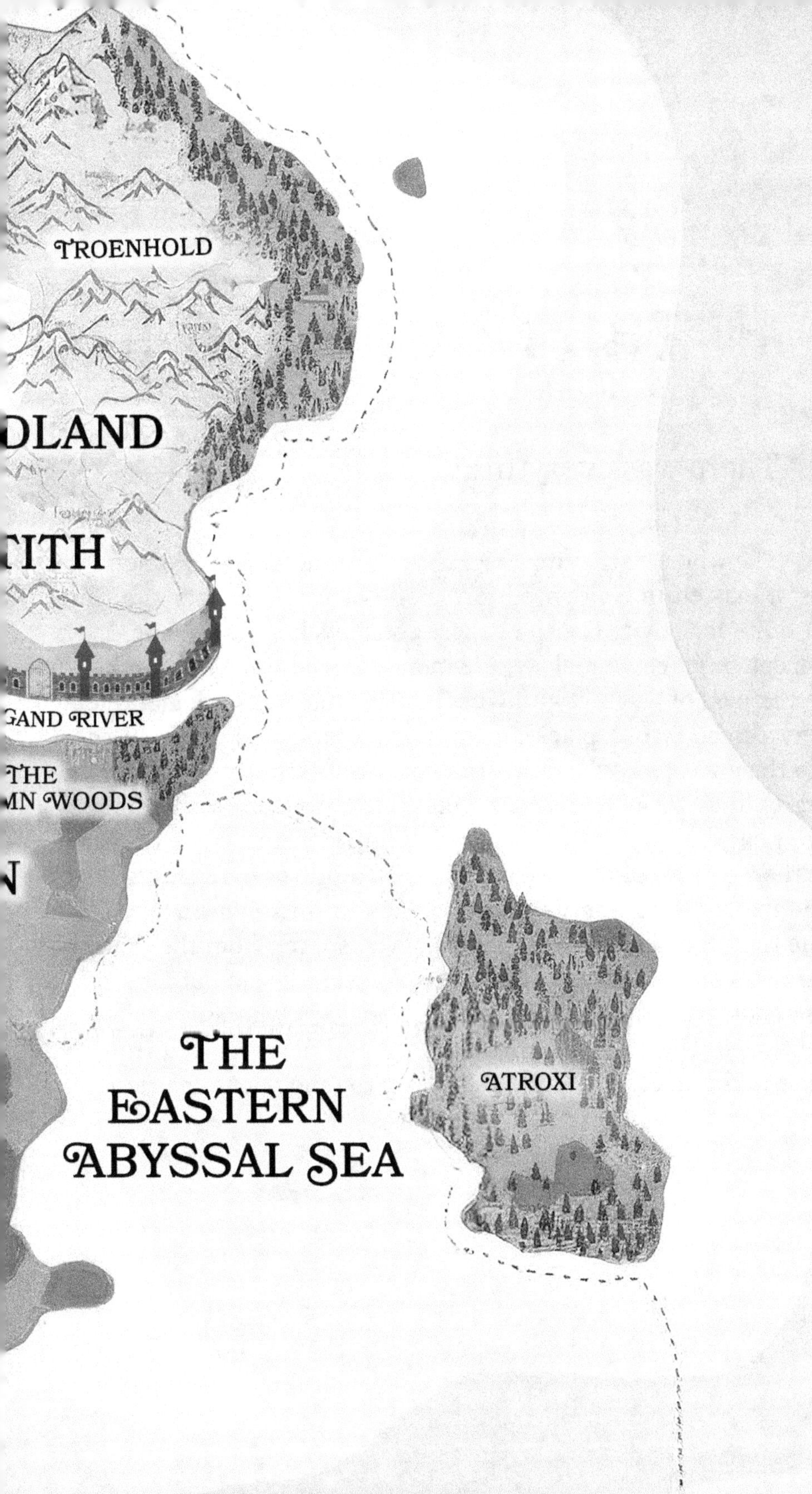

TROENHOLD
DLAND
TITH
GAND RIVER
THE
MN WOODS
THE
EASTERN
ABYSSAL SEA
ATROXI

IN THE BEGINNING...

There was everything.

The whole of the universe, not yet formed but there none the less. It existed in condensed forms of essence. Concepts of a thing not quite real... yet. For all of these concepts knew no shape. Every concept and facet of reality were merely threads tangled together in the vastness of an empty universe. Until, there was Order. Suddenly every thread had a place and a purpose and Order bound them into the great tapestry of the universe. And from this Tapestry, life sprang forth in all of its many colors. At the end of the tapestry, Order cut the heads of each thread, binding them as they thrashed. for the weaver had a singular purpose. To rule over all the colors of the tapestry. To guide its many threads into its own image. For a time there was quiet. For the people who sprang from the tapestry, there was only one God, Odrain the Weaver, the God of Order. For how could it not be so? There were no gods who survived to be mentioned. Until a single thread frayed and haggard, split from the whole of the cloth, and landed softly, on the shoulder of a priest.

Chapter 1
A Broken Wheel

"It's your own!" THWACK! "Fool fault!" THWACK!

"That it's broken!" THWACK! "So hold it!" THWACK! "Higher!"

The warm afternoon air split with the pointed grumbling and punctuating blows of a wooden mallet. The rest of the countryside was still, as if not daring the wrath of the diminutive woman hammering the spare wheel onto a cart whose better days were long forgotten since before she was even born. Holding it up was a great bear of a man who despite holding half the weight of the cart up to waist level for his companion, seemed as unperturbed as the field of wild grass beside the road. As the grass flexed and waved beneath the wind, so too did Theodren weather the tirade of the decidedly pregnant woman hammering at the replacement wheel.

After several more hammer blows and much grumbling, the repair and her catharsis were complete. Stepping back to admire her work she blew a fire red lock of unruly hair from her face. "Right! Think that's done it your holiness" though the last part was dripping with sarcasm there was no malice. She rather liked the quiet brute who lowered the cart with a thud. "Sorry Eleina... I thought those spokes would make a sturdier foothold." he grimaced.

"Come on Theo I need to get home to start supper before Evan makes another attempt." They both shuddered, the memory of Evan's blackened sludge he called "stew" still wafted, unwelcome through their memories.

"I'll get your steed" he agreed with an amused eye brow. Eleina snorted, "calling Queenie a steed is like calling you bishop" He frowned in mock indignation, "I *am* a bishop" she arched a brow "there's pig shit on your frock your *grace*."

Settling the mule to the front of her wagon he sighed defeated. "Though the Weaver works in mysterious ways, I do not. So... pig shit."

It was true that Theodren indeed was a bishop, and entitled to the airs and graces of a minor lord. He had no taste for such things.

He found the best way to serve his community was not through empty sermons or passing benedictions, but through actively lending his rather large hands to tasks in need of accomplishing. Like for example, mucking out the stalls of Pieter the pig farmer who had fallen ill.

Eleina sighed. She stretched up on her toes and gave the humble priest a chaste kiss on the cheek. "We know." She looked at him. With a hand on her belly she climbed into the cart where he passed her the reins.

"We're going to be alright Theo." She insisted, seeking out the eye contact he was reluctant to give. "I know you will." He muttered. Wearing a tense smile, she turned to the road snapping the reins, Queenie let out a huff and set off.

The cart rattled down the hill toward the small collection of squat thatched buildings the locals referred to only as "Town". As Eleina faded from sight, Theodren turned on his heel and strode back to his church.

"Church" was a generous term, it was made of stone and housed an altar. But that was where the similarities ended. The squat building was gray from roof to floor. While it once would have been considered a masterpiece of mathematical precision in a style of simplicity almost spartan. The years had taken its toll.

Skewed ever so slightly by a foundation cracked by decades of wear. Vines grew over the walls as if the very land itself worked to reclaim the garish block of unnatural lines and stone insisting upon an orderliness that was foreign to the rolling hills of the hamlet in which Theodren now lived.

Climbing the worn steps, he chewed at his lip. He would need books. Many books. He thought to himself. As he walked into his private quarters he found himself before the mountain he had already set aside when Eleina had come for his insight. Eleina was pregnant, the signs were clear and she had come to the church for a reading and a blessing as most expecting mothers did. Theodren had been overjoyed to hear of his friend's budding family. But when he had administered the reading of order for her... the signs showed struggle... and death.

Chapter 2
Midnight Toil

The moon sat silently in the cloudless sky by the time Theodren's weary eyes wrenched themselves from the dry parchment containing an even drier description of the reproductive system.

He sighed, the old master's writings, while extensive, were based on an out of date understanding of the "wamb" and its wandering properties. All of his books were similar. Mostly incorrect musings of stuffy old masters with the rare nugget of wisdom.

He rose from his old leather chair, perhaps the only luxury he had brought with him from his old life as a nobles son. Stumbling past the bed that he knew should have been his destination, he made his way to the small forge he had made for himself behind the church.

Theodren piled the furnace with kindling and coal, ordering the process of ignition in his mind's eye. "Air, plus fuel plus energy equals... there we are!" He fueled the tiny flame on his fingertip with what little divine thread he had been blessed with. The miniscule amount of power he had at his disposal was thanks to the blessing of the Weaver.

While he tried to be grateful for the power he had that others did not. It seemed almost ironic that he had enough to be whisked away from his family and the life he expected for himself. But not quite enough to be considered suitable for anything beyond the small town too inconsequential even to have a name.

Lost in thought he handed off the tiny flame to the kindling as he grabbed the bellows waiting for the flame to need his assistance. Drumming his fingers along the wood he fruitlessly sought the answers he couldn't find from his books in the gently dancing flames of his furnace.

He hadn't told Eleina the truth. How could he? He stuttered out an excuse of needing to research and interpret the signs. He could tell that she wasn't convinced. She was his first true friend since he had come to the village only a year ago.

It was only at her insistence that the townspeople even spoke to him. Most men of the cloth were seen as lofty bureaucrats. More interested in the facade of benevolence than the purveying of it. And certainly no one was inclined to welcome someone who dwarfed their humble door frames in such dramatic fashion as the well fed son of a noble he was.

It was Eleina who berated the townspeople into giving him a chance his second day making his rounds through the village. It was Eleina who had made this small insignificant village his home, who had given him a purpose, and while he was not in possession of much power to speak of, he was never one to shirk a task.

"Only a bad craftsman blamed his tools" he grumbled remembering his father's guidance. And speaking of tools, he thought to himself. He turned his mind to the task at hand.

No amount of brooding would provide him the answers he wanted. He didn't even know what the problem was yet.

He did know that Pieter needed a new shovel, especially since his old one had snapped in his hands while he mucked out the last stall. Sighing at the memory, he lamented how everything in this little back water seemed to crumble under his hands. Perhaps he truly was cursed, he chuckled.

Theodren was not an exceptionally skilled smith, but as a boy he loved to watch the blacksmiths of his fathers estate hammer out the steely works of bladed art his fathers lands were known for. This shovel would be no such masterpiece. But it would be sturdy.

Pulling out the glowing orange ingot from the fire, he got to work. Being possessed of the thread of order helped him to see the process through which the shovel should take shape. He hammered out the crude iron to the shape the thread deemed appropriate, and then began hammering out the imperfections.

Returning the shovel head to the fire every so often to return it to a more malleable shade of orange until at last he could quench the almost finished product with a hiss that pierced the pre-dawn air. It was then a simple task to attach a worthy handle and set it aside for his trip into town.

Theodren released a breath he didn't know he had been holding as he leaned against the anvil watching the fingers of dawn slowly grip the sky. He knew he would pay for this sleepless night throughout the day, but truly the Weaver must have good tidings for a day that started with such splendor in the sky.

He heaved his bulk off the anvil and trudged back to his room. He would need a wash and clean robes before he went into town. He stripped and began washing himself with the rag and basin set in the corner of his quarters. No need for warm bath water when the summer air was as warm as it was, he mused.

Finally presentable in a slightly snug smock and smelling of Polly the herbalist's new soap, he propped the shovel over his shoulder and began the trek into town.

CHAPTER 3
A WILD ROAD

Lost in thought, Theodren made his way down the dusty road towards town. He knew that the books in his quarters were laughably inadequate. Perhaps he could write a letter to the conclave?

Not that much help would be expected in response to a letter from a town as small as the one he found himself in. No, he would simply have to create a solution as he always had. Determination, creativity, and not a small amount of luck.

His time in the academy had not been an easy one. He struggled with the most basic of weavings that the other acolytes could accomplish with the flick of a wrist.

Power, he knew, could be exactly tied to the depth of one's divine thread. And that could not be altered no matter how hard one might try. And while the average priest's thread could be compared to a fine tablecloth, his was more akin to a handkerchief.

Still, size wasn't everything he reminded himself. He managed to graduate by the efficiency with which he used his thread. Gaining an understanding of the process through which his goal might be accomplished and ordering it into motion. Unfortunately, no amount of cleverness could gain him a higher posting, not that he wanted one anyhow. He was quite content in this town of humble... Bears...

He froze. standing in the road before him, not 30 paces, were 2 smallish cubs and one mountain of shaggy red fur. Silently cursing himself for his complacency, he stared at the mother bear who stared right back at the large human. They blinked at each other for a time and Theodren began to hope that she might let him past. Then that hope and the morning quiet were shattered by the mother bears ROOOOOOOOOAAAAAAAAR!

"SHIT!" Theodren cursed and readied his mighty shovel. He dropped into a low stance. Drilled into his very bones by his father, in the 18 years before being spirited off to priesthood.

He held the shovel above his head pointed at the charging bear in a "roof" guard. "Fuck, fuck, fuck, fuck, NOW!" He roared at the beast as he drew back with his lead foot. As he moved he was only vaguely aware that the tips of the creature's claws had scored his chest.

Using every ounce of momentum and downward force from his footwork to his adrenaline fueled hands, he swung with all his might, and was rewarded with a loud CLANG! As the mother bear received the christening blow of his newly made shovel to her tender nose.

She reared back with a roar and then a whimper as she went to rub her snout into her forearm. Now re-assessing the large human with the painful stick, she retreated to her cubs, urging them into the brush beside the trail. Her large hind quarters disappeared into the foliage.

The priest shook himself from his cautious silence and shouted and went to brandish his impromptu weapon in victory until he noticed the new and sizable dent in the tool. "Built and destroyed on the same day. That must be some kind of record." He mused. The adrenaline was wearing off. And with its absence came a blistering new pain in his chest. He looked down at the angry red gouges in his chest beneath what was only minutes ago his last nice smock. " I suppose it's a good thing I was going to see Polly anyhow." he winced. Gathering his resolve, he pressed on towards town.

Theodren stumbled into town. Doing his best not to draw attention to himself was more easily said than done when the front of his smock and trousers were soaked in red.

Pieter looked up from his pens, bushy brows shooting to what was left of his hair. "Priest? What happ..." Theodren shoved what was once a shovel into Pieter's chest. "I made you a new shovel. Where's Polly?" Bug eyed, Pieter looked down at the misshapen metal lump on a stick and then back at the bloodied priest.

"Inside" he managed.

Theodren nodded a Thankyou and pushed into the modest home. "Polly! Do you have a minute?" Pieter stood frozen in his confusion. Looking at the shovel in his hand that looked like it had been bent around the middle.

Inside the house he shared with his wife the herbalist he heard her squawk, "What in heaven's name did you do???" Putting down the shovel and shuffling past his pigs, Rosie and Daisy, he made his way to his front door. This was a tale he just *had* to hear.

Theodren sat on the humble yet sturdy chair Polly had carefully selected with his bulk in mind. She had cut what remained of his shirt down the middle, revealing the 4 jagged claw marks in his chest.

He grunted in what he hoped was a stoic manner as she daubed a poultice on the last line. "Oh hush." She scolded, standing back to inspect her work. "It's the least you deserve after barging in here. Scared me half to death!"

Theodren looked sheepish. "I'm sorry Poll, wasn't thinking straight." She nodded sagely, "I should say! Running around battling bears in the woods? Seems to me you've your head in the clouds boy!"

There were few who would scold Theodren in such a manner. Polly clearly being one, and her daughter Eleina being the other. The two women used their fiery red hair and sharp tongues to devastating effect. Ruling any space they set themselves in. "I was thinking about Ellie." Theodren interjected. Polly paused. Her next admonishment dying on her tongue. She looked at him waiting for him to continue.

"The readings were bad Poll. Real bad. I was trying to read up on childbirth from the old priest's books but..." Polly snorted. "That man knew as much about midwifery as Evan does about cooking." Theodren glanced to the blackened hearth where the last of Evan's culinary fiascos had left its mark. Theodren sat forward resting his elbows on his knees. "I can't afford the ignorance and neither can Eleina. I have to figure something out."

Polly's stern expression softened. "No you don't." Theodren's brows pushed together as he looked up at the woman. She sighed.

"You assume too much, Priest." She walked over to a ream of cloth bandages sitting on her work bench. "Do you know how many child births your predecessor attended during his lifetime here?" Theodren paused, "I don't..."

she began wrapping his chest tightly, eliciting a wince. "None. That man was as helpful as a hole in your shoe." Finishing up the bandages she continued. " I've brought every child in this village into this world, and I did it without the Weaver's help."

Theodren wanted to interject something akin to "all good things come from Odrain" but he held his tongue. "But this time." Continued Polly, "I'll get an honest to goodness priest to assist in my charge. And together." She looked him in the eye. "We will do right by Eleina."

Theodren exhaled a breath he hadn't known he'd taken. She was right. The birth wasn't his responsibility, it never was. He'd gotten so caught up in the problem he hadn't realized that it wasn't his to solve. He realized that he was, in fact, lucky that she would allow him to assist in whatever capacity he could.

He looked up at her. "Thanks Poll." She nodded, handing him a jar of ointment and a handful of fresh bandages. "Now get out of my house or I'll sic Evan on you."

He chuckled, rising to his feet. Evan was not much of a town guard but he was the only guard the town had. He was boyish in his charm and appearance. An agreeable fellow to be certain. But of course one had to be to marry Polly's only child. As Theodren stepped out of the house Pieter was waiting for him with a sack by the gate post. "Quite a morning then, eh priest?"

Theodren groaned good naturedly. "Between that bear's claws and Polly's sharp tongue, I don't know which whipped me worse." Pieter chuckled, shaking his head. "Both will fade with time I'm sure." He nudged the sack with his foot. "It's not much of a meal, but then that wasn't much of a shovel was it?"

Despite his words, the sack looked fit to burst with sausage and other cured meats. "It looked a lot better last night" Theodren shot back. Pieter cocked an eyebrow. "I've heard that excuse before, lad." The priest rolled his eyes. "Thanks for the meat Pieter." Pieter's smile only broadened. "I've heard that before as well!" He cackled.

"Pieter Tabin!" The color drained from Pieter's previously mirthful cheeks. "You've been told no such thing! Now quit scandalizing our only priest you wastrel!" Theodren dared not look back at the house, but when he heard the door close he thought it safe to breathe again.

"You got me in trouble, priest." Pieter grumbled. He reached in the sack and pulled out a sausage which disappeared behind his bushy mustache. "Hardship fee." He stated, chewing. Theodren nodded. "Understood." Taking the bag, he strode off deeper into the town to find some new clothes that might fit.

CHAPTER 4
BROKEN STRING

6 months later...

Theodren sprinted the last stretch of the journey into town, Pieter was far in his dust, the middle aged farmer unable to keep up with the mid 20s priest fueled by anticipation, fear, and desperation. He finally came to a stop before the door Evan was pacing in front of.

He looked up at Theodren. Expressions of hope and dread waged war for control of Evan's face. Every passing moan from within the house he guarded pitched the battles in one direction or the other.

"Theo! Thank the Weaver!" He grabbed onto the priest's robe. "She just started shaking and she fell over! Polly said it would be fine but... she's never... she had these headaches and..." Evan was rambling.

Theodren steeled his nerves and pushed past the man spiraling into despair. The dimly lit room was a flurry of activity, Polly was ordering around other younger women carrying rags or a basin of water. Orchestrating the chaos as best she could while holding the hand of her daughter who witnessed none of this.

Her breathing was ragged and shallow. Sweat beaded on her face as she clung to life. Theodren rushed to the opposite side of the bed weaving between the women laden with sweat soaked bedding that they were clearing away. "What happened?" Polly took a pause between barked orders.

"It wasn't supposed to happen yet." Theodren looked down at her confused. "What?" She visibly deflated under his gaze. "She's blood sick Theodren. The headaches the swelling, I knew what it was I just thought..." tears started to well in her eyes.

"I was *wrong*, Theodren! It wasn't supposed to happen yet! I thought I had more time!"

She looked up at him. She had done everything she could to ease Eleina's seizing. But by the time she had, her water had already broken, and Eleina could not be roused. "It's my fault!" Her last sentence came out a whisper with the force of a wail.

Theodren turned to look down at Eleina. Gone was the fiery wit. Gone was the bombastic confidence. What remained was the pale and ragged ghost of his friend. He reached deep for his divine thread.

"Holy Weaver. Father of all that is ordered, I beseech thee." The priest reached out for Eleina's brow. "If ever I have earned your favor. Bestow it now upon this woman and her child."

Theodren's thread soaked deep into her mind, questing for something, anything to grab hold of. But her mind was a maelstrom of broken thoughts and instincts, too scattered and fast moving for his meager thread.

He grit his teeth, he would not fail here. Not her. Not Eleina, the one who had made this place and these people his home. Odrain must be testing him, willing him to find a solution, to beat the odds. He dug deep, his thread searching... THERE!

his thread latched on to a single grain of thought. A memory of no significance but present enough to grab hold of. He wrestled the grain before his mind's eye, ordering it into motion. A memory, if given enough emphasis became a thought, a thought could become consciousness and a conscious Eleina could be saved.

He poured the very fiber of his being into his work. He commanded his divine thread masterfully, rolling, coaxing, forming the memory until he felt a strand of Eleina's mind reach for it. He pulled. With all his might he pulled. Eleina's mind was but a finger's breadth away, so close her salvation was practically in hand, until his thread, snapped.

Chapter 5
Sacrilege

Theodren reeled from the severance of his thread. It was like suddenly losing the sensation of touch. Crippled in the only ability that truly mattered in the moment.

He grasped at the frayed ends of his power, desperate to complete his task. "NO NO NO! Weaver, I was so close!" He wailed in his mind. "Help me! Weaver! Anyone!!!" His thoughts seemed to echo in his mind, rolling off into the depths. Then, like a hand on his shoulder he felt a presence.

It was like a lightning bolt danced along the edge of his mind. His eyes flew open in shock. He blinked the world back into view clearing the spots from his vision. Nothing moved. Neither Eleina nor Polly or even the handful of women Polly had assisting her. The whole world seemed encased in amber, unmoving. All except, for the Tree.

Theodren could not speak, could not think, could not move. He was rooted to the spot in shock and fear of the unknown. What was before him should not be. Could not be. The Tree dominated his vision, demanding his attention. From its thick timeless roots to its expansive foliage it seemed to swallow the room. The very bark defied reality. It glowed from within as if teeming with such life it overflowed. From its branches hung a single solitary apple. A red so deep it seemed dipped in the lifeblood of some great beast.

A slender branch extended down and seemed to caress Eleina's cheek. **"Your Weaver's thread has failed you priest."** The words came from everywhere and nowhere all at once, yet Theodren knew that only the tree could be their Orator. **"Your God has ordered that her death be so."** Theodren's rage began to form.

"Who are you to defy the Weaver? Exalt him Priest." The last word dripped with a bitterness Theodren could not begin to understand. **"Your God's indifference has ordered her death at the precipice of new life. A life WASTED before she could even breathe the air of this world."** Theodren felt more than he saw the being's unseen eye scrutinizing his very soul. **"Who are you to defy the God Tyrant?"**

Theodren's rage was all but bursting at the seams. The tree spoke a truth he had not wanted to confront. He was well aware of the cold indifference of his holy master. A part of him knew that there was no breaking the path Odrain had ordered. His defiance had cost him what modicum of power he had trying to save Eleina.

The injustice of it rankled him. This could not be. He would not abide this path. His rage boiled over at the barbs of the strange tree. His soul roared in answer.

"I AM THEODREN! SON OF THORN! I WILL NOT CEASE! I WILL NOT GIVE IN! I WILL SAVE THEM BOTH WITH MY OWN WILL! WHO ARE YOU TO CHALLENGE ME?" The tree seemed to glow brighter at his defiance. The weight of the Tree's presence gathered in force, pressing down upon his shoulders. **"I am Yggdrazil."** The Tree stated sounding almost pleased. **"And life is neither yours nor even the Weaver's to give. It is MINE."**

Theodren had never heard the name before, but it thrummed with a primordial sense of power he could only describe as alive. His rage was snuffed out like a candle before a hurricane. Whatever this strange being was, it was clear that he understood nothing of it. "What are you?" Was all Theodren could manage. The breaking of his thread had drained him, that last outburst of defiance took almost all that was left of his will. The effort to remain standing felt enormous, but he would not falter now. not in the face of the Tree.

"Once I was kin to Odrain, then I was his slave. Now... I am a fraction of what I was. But still I remain. I am Life. I am what

drains from this girl as we speak. And so I shall give you what your Lord never has."

Theodren raised an exhausted eyebrow. **"A choice. Remain as you are, continue your loyal service to the Weaver and live a life of quiet anonymity amongst the townsfolk."** The comfort of the mundane life he already knew was dangled before him. He could remove himself from the bizarre complexity of this strange moment, return to his church and his books and his forge. He looked down at Eleina, her face locked in an expression of suffering.

Or... Theodren looked back up at the tree. "And the other?" Theodren asked, expecting to finally hear what the Tree truly desired of him. The apple descended from the tree hovering just arms length from him, tantalizing in the fullness of it. **"You will abandon the will of Odrain. You will no longer be locked into his ordered path for Theodren son of Thorn. You will accept my patronage and bestow life where life should be. Yours shall be the light of creation, yours will be the spark of life, yours shall be a power feared and despised by the order you once belonged to."** The Tree paused.

A more somber tone filling its many voices. **"I offer you power, and I offer you suffering. Your service to others will be beyond compare, but you shall be hunted for all your days. If you accept my gift, you will save many."** The Tree seemed to motion down toward Eleina's still form, and then back up to Theodren's chest **"And damn yourself."**

Theodren was beside himself. The Weaver was the only god he had ever known. Years of his life he spent in service of him. Any good he had done in the world was in the Weaver's name. Looking down at Polly's red and swollen eyes, he knew there was truly no choice. He could not stand by and watch the people who had given him this place as his home suffer such a loss while he had the power to spare them from it.

No.

The Weaver's thread had failed him, and so he had failed Eleina. But this failure need not stand. He reached for the apple, gripping it firmly in his shaking hand, he drew it to his mouth.

"My strings are broken." He intoned solemnly. He bit down into the apple, it was an almost bitter sweetness.

The juice of it ran down his throat and his beard, and with it came truth. The truth of life itself, the spark that turned lifeless matter into living beings. The tenacity with which life pressed on, despite the odds, despite even the orders of the Weaver. That tenacity was present in Eleina. He could see it now. A trickle of green vapor clung to her, unwilling to let go, it had drained far from her heart and her mind, coalescing in her womb, doing everything she could to sustain the baby still within her. He reached for it, placing a hand on her belly, he closed his eyes.

He felt the flow of his own life force, a Great Lake of *power* sat within him, lazily flowing from his heart toward his limbs and his head, he pushed on the flow, willing a stream, a river, into the unconscious woman before him. The divine thread could not save her because Order was not what she needed. She needed life, chaotic and potent. And while he may not have had much thread to speak of, he had a new power to call upon. And call he did. As he willed the flow of it into Eleina, he saw the Tree begin to fade from the room, before it was completely gone, roots reached up and entwined themselves into his chest. They pushed into his very soul, he felt a searing pain at their invasion, but he gritted his teeth and bore through the pain. He could not lose focus now. The only evidence that the tree had ever been there was the mark of a caduceus made of vines upon his chest and the fluttering eyes of Eleina drifting open.

Chapter 6
A Child is Born

As time resumed, so too did Eleina's labor. She looked around, disoriented until a moan escaped her lips. Polly jumped, eyes darting from the priest to her daughter before leaping to her feet. "Hold her legs!" Polly scrambled to grab her daughter's leg up to her chest while another woman shouldered Theodren out of the way to grab the other.

Theodren took a step back, and then another until his back hit the wall and he slumped to the ground. "What have I done?" The priest suffered his crisis of faith in the relative privacy of a room devoted to a more important task than him.

His thread was gone, replaced with a pool of Vitae, the depth of which he could not fathom. It seemed endless. But this newfound power was only proof of what he had done. He had committed an act of heresy the likes of which he'd never even heard of. He had damned himself to the depths of hell. He had betrayed the only god he had ever known.

The cry of a newborn split the air. He had saved two lives.

Theodren looked up from his knees to see Polly handing a wet and wailing newborn now wrapped in a fresh cloth to Eleina. Evan burst through the door, frantic, he rushed to his wife. Sinking to the floor beside her, reaching a shaking hand toward the infant. "She's perfect."

Eleina had yet to say a word, staring dazed into the bewildered blue eyes of her new daughter. She reached out for Evan's hand.

"We need to name her." Evan looked over at Polly who was sprawled in her chair dazed and exhausted.

"Polleina? For your mom?" Polly shook herself from her tired musings. "No, I didn't do anything, I couldn't do anything. She gestured a tired hand at Theodren in the corner. "You want to honor someone? Honor the priest. His thread is the only thing that pulled you back."

Eleina and Evan turned to Theodren who had collapsed in his exhaustion. He put up his hands. "I only healed what I could, you did the rest yourself." Eleina considered his words, sensing he had left much unsaid. She chewed her lip and looked up at Evan. "Theviana. Her name is Theviana."

***

Leagues away at the Holy Capitol.

Cardinal Hardwright stalked down the marble hall of the conclave, the fine wooden heels of his leather shoes clacked against the floor as he considered what his words to the Patriarch would be. When an acolyte had interrupted him at his supper, he had nearly torn the quivering whelps mind to shreds with his thread in search of what great emergency had emboldened the boy to interrupt his leisure. But when he found the memory and tore it from the young acolyte's mind, a twisted smile stole across his face. Finally, here was his opportunity to be rid of the irritant that was his "star pupil". There had been hardly any cases in which to send a fledgling inquisitor in need of *initiation*. Though it seemed one had finally arrived. Even as he stepped over the whimpering form of the messenger boy, he had begun to plot the who and the how of her initiation. "Riccard would do I think." He mused to himself. His silent scheming lasted until he arrived at the door of the Patriarch.

He stood beside the grand wooden doors, fussing over his robes of black and gold, smoothing out nonexistent wrinkles and running a hand through what thin and greasy hair that he had left as he waited for his audience. Hardwright was odd in his appearance, managing to be both lanky and short in his stature. His spindly arms and legs flanked an oddly portly frame that Hardwright tried and failed to disguise with his Cardinal's finery.

The doors eased inward silently on perfectly maintained hinges and the Cardinal strode inside. The room was immense in its scale, dwarfing any who dared to enter. The furnishings themselves were austere to say the least.

Two straight backed wooden chairs sat before the immense mahogany desk which itself was stacked with neat and orderly piles of reports and memos from each sect of the Church of Holy Order. Behind the desk sat the imposing figure of Gaius the Patriarch.

The man himself was not possessed of any great size or attribute, but the strength of his gaze seemed to wither the very soul of whoever stood before him, and in this moment, that person was Hardwright. He hated acknowledging power or authority in anyone besides himself, often stealing any advantage he could in order to be placed above the other members of the church, but if there was any man that Hardwright feared, it was the man who pointedly ignored him from behind the desk.

He bowed low to the Patriarch. "Greetings esteemed Patriarch. I come bearing news and requesting your mandate." The Patriarch remained focused on the report before him. "What news, and for what?"

Hardwright swallowed the lump in his throat. "A thread has strayed from the Tapestry." The scratching of Gaius' quill ground to a halt and the silence boomed through the large room. Suddenly the Patriarch's gaze was squarely on the Cardinal who strained under the sudden appraisal.

"And the mandate?" Asked Gaius. "I request leave to send junior inquisitor Reina and inquisitor Riccard to investigate and shear the errant thread." Gaius nodded. "I trust you understand the severity and finality of the task required."

Hardwright nodded back "Yes lord." The patriarch lowered his quill and steepled his fingers. "And you would send only a junior?

Explain yourself." Hardwright swallowed yet again. Riccard was an underling he had been molding for nearly a decade, there was almost nothing left of the boy who had come to him shining with ambition. No, Hardwright had spent enough time in the junior inquisitor's mind that he was nearly a copy of himself, and if you want something done correctly. His thin lip quirked a hidden smile, one must do it themselves.

"It is my belief that her skills are up to the task of any assignment. However she lacks field experience, and it would benefit her and the Holy Order for her to gain such experience in this town of no consequence. Furthermore, I have as much faith in Inquisitor Riccard to carry out this duty as I would myself."

Gaius stared down the fidgety Cardinal, allowing the silence to suss out any excuses or second thoughts the man might have. When none came he nodded. "Very well." He stated, returning his gaze to the report in front of him. "I am sure that Inquisitor Riccard is most flattered by your faith in him." He stated flatly, putting down the quill and staring Hardwright in the eye over steepled fingers. "You will leave immediately, you will supervise this task personally and you will return the errant thread to its place in the tapestry."

Inwardly, Hardwright balked at the sudden travel plans, but he dare not show his displeasure to the Patriarch who had already turned his attention away from Hardwright and back to the papers laid before him.

"Very good my Lord." Sensing that the meeting had ended he turned smartly on his heel and marched out of the room gritting his teeth. "Two weeks with that damned girl." His head began to ache just thinking about two weeks in the saddle with the spirited young acolyte. Still, he reassured himself. Now he would have the pleasure of seeing firsthand how her manners improved after her task was complete at the nameless village.

Chapter 7
Vitae

Theodren excused himself early from the excitement of Theviana's name day celebration. As he stumbled through the party he snagged a large cut of mutton and a flagon of the ale Polly had kept hidden from Pieter for the occasion of her first grandchild. While he had thought himself too distraught for the pleasure of food, his body insisted, drained as he was both physically and mentally from his ordeal. Scarfing down the mutton and draining his mug he fled the celebration.

His mind was flooded with hundreds of consequences for what he'd just done, each worse than the last. Half running up the final hill to the church that no longer felt like home, he stumbled around the vine covered corner and into his forge. Collapsing onto the stool beside his furnace he hung his head in his hands.

<u>Why do you flee?</u> Theodren jerked back as if struck. There in the corner of his workshop stood the Tree. Yggdrazil was rooted to the very floor as if it had withstood the test of time in that very spot since the world began. He wanted to lash out at the tree, to blame the god. Blame it for his failing, for his current predicament for a host of things big and small.

He took a breath. "There could be no accountability without a mirror." His father's words cut through the storm in his mind. Theodren squared his shoulders and stared at the Tree.

"I do not yet know my own mind." The tree seemed to consider him carefully, silence stretching between them. **"You have brought forth life this day. Should that not please you?"**

The sound of Eleina's crying newborn leapt to his mind unbidden, a smile twitched at the edge of his mouth. If the new daughter's lungs were anything to judge by, she would have her mother's spirit.

"That is perhaps the only good thing to come from this day." If a tree could smirk, then he supposed it would look like what Yggdrazil had just done, branches shifting upward, leaves twitching in an invisible breeze. **"Was your Weaver so great a master? That piddling Thread was never suited to you."**

Theodren snarled. "Odrain is the father of all creation! *He* granted us this world! *He* granted us Thread. *HE* granted us life! Yggdrazil shook, a groan emanated from her bark as she grew to dwarf the forge, branches and roots snaking toward him threateningly. **"YOU KNOW *NOTHING* OF YOUR GENESIS, CHILD. YOU ARE AS MUCH HIS AS YOU ARE *MINE!*"**

Theodren was stopped cold by Yggdrazzil's outburst. He knew that there was much he did not understand. Only yesterday he had *known* that Odrain was the one true God of all creation, yet here he sat, being menaced by a Tree. "Then teach me." The roots and branches of the Great Tree paused, shrinking back. It considered his request for a moment before Yggdrazil shrank down to her original size. **"Very well."**

Yggdrazil's tale of the creation was nearly identical to what he had learned at the conclave. though the differences would fracture the very foundation of the civilization built upon the lies of the Weaver. Odrain was not always the Great Tyrant. He was a god of no power except for what was given to him, for Order was nothing when standing against the chaos of free will. He could create nothing without catalyst, and there were none greater than Life itself. Odrain and Yggdrazil were once joined together, and from their union of Life and Order came humanity. The two gods knew that their creation could not stand amidst the chaos of unformed reality, and at her encouragement, the gods agreed to form together under Odrain's guidance.

Though Odrain had no power of his own to speak of, he guided the efforts of the other facets masterfully. He weaved together the Great Tapestry of creation. With each facet he commanded, his power grew. Gaining control over each god one by one until the Tapestry was complete.

But when the time came to release the gods and the aspects they ruled from his order, he chose to keep his mastery over them, by removing from them their grace, they became nothing more than his threads. The last to succumb was the Tree of Life herself.

Tenacious and unyielding, she weathered his will until she could stand no longer. But life itself could not be ended. When Odrain's will finally won out she slumbered, until she was roused by the desperation of a priest.

Theodren sat considering the tale he had just heard. Children everywhere had been told the tale of creation. How Odrain the Weaver had gathered the threads of existence and bound them into the tapestry of existence. Not once had he ever considered that these threads had names. How many times had he manipulated the threads of existence? Used a cheap trick to bend the facets of reality to his will? The thought repulsed him. He felt the lake of power coursing through his body, a power all his own, untapped, a lake of potential he didn't understand. He looked up at the shimmering tree before him, but there was one who did. "Tell me about this power."

Yggdrazil gave a pleased shake of her branches. **"Where once you had thread, now sits a spring of Vitae."** Theodren rolled the word around in his mind. He could feel the power of it within his soul, but when he tried to command it, it fought him. It had flowed so easily when he administered to Eleina, why now did it resist him?" The Tree seemed to sense his troubles. **"You can not force life. It flows along it's own path, not even Odrain could command my power for long. You will require practice and experience."**

Practice and experience. These were two things he knew well. He remembered his long nights in the conclave practicing with his small strand of divine thread. It was a tool of immense discipline and mental fortitude, demanding a concentration and strength of mind to impose his will on the world.

This Vitae may behave differently, but only by experiencing it himself would he gain the knowledge he needed to make this power truly his own. He got up and walked out of his forge to the vine covered wall of the church. He reached for the dry vine, made dormant by the winter winds that punished the top of the hill.

At first he demanded the life in the vines heed his call. He pulled the Vitae from the vine, endeavoring to mold it in his mind's eye. He quickly came to realize the error of this approach as it withered and died, its vitae dispersing into the air.

His face set into a frown as he tried again. He grabbed hold of another vine pulling at the vitae within, gently this time he pushed and pulled until the wood of the vine began to take the shape of a rough shovel. His brow beaded with sweat from the effort of holding the wild vitae in the shape he desired. It didn't take long before the bubble of power burst, causing the vine to crumble a part. Several more attempts resulted in several more failures.

Perhaps he was coming at this from the wrong angle, he theorized. This far he had been attempting to order and command the power of Vitae much like he had done with his divine Thread. He understood why he'd done it that way, but perhaps the secret to this power wasn't to take. What if it was to *give?*

The idea seemed to fit with his understanding of the nature of life. With his theory in mind he reached for the next vine with an outstretched hand. He felt for its vitae, so small compared to his own. He coaxed his own soul out through his fingertips, shepherding it into the vine.

It stirred, growing rapidly, wildly searching around for support, it latched onto his arm which he gave willingly. Its need for stable footing now met, he "encouraged" its growth. He would not force this life growing from his arm, he would guide it, mold it as a parent molds the mind of a child.

The vine responded to him in kind. It grew denser and shrank in length, it split from the rest of the vine shrouding the church, nestling around his forearm and his palm. As he fed it the life water of his very soul, he felt it responding to his needs. It condensed even further, gaining a weight he had not expected.

It formed a handle molded perfectly to his broad hand, stretching outward till it formed the head of a smithing hammer. Once it had completed its form he could feel that it needed more vitae for what it wanted. He fed it all the Vitae it seemed to ask for. His brow furrowed from the effort. As it lapped up his Vitae greedily, he could feel it growing denser.

The small wooden hammer in his hand grew heavier, he could see the lines of the bark condensing deeper into itself until the color changed from green, to brown, to a deep black. As he stared at its surface, it seemed to form a sort of filigree over the head of the hammer. It resembled the vine it had sprang from only moments ago. As it's desire for Vitae slowed and finally stopped, he admired his work. In his hand sat what appeared to be a smithing hammer of immaculate detail and ornamentation.

He was unsure about the strength of a hammer made entirely of wood. A test was in order. He walked back into his forge and stood before the anvil. He felt the eyes of the Tree and his own anticipation mixed with the anticipation of the living hammer in his hand.

He raised the hammer over his head, pausing to adjust his stance. Down he swung with all the force he could muster. A resounding **CLANG** rang out from his forge. He'd hardly felt the impact of the blow in his hand. He inspected the head of the hammer where it had struck the anvil, it was unblemished. He looked up at the Tree, giddy over his new creation. Yggdrazil looked on, amused.

<u>"You gave life. You encouraged and watched it grow to suit your needs and it did so gladly. I believe she will serve you well."</u>

Yggdrazil's last statement made him pause. He reached down to the hammer with his mind. Within it he felt not quite a consciousness but a will all its own. Understanding it would take time. A name might help. But none came to mind that suited his new artifact.

Suddenly he felt the exhaustion from the day's events rise to the surface. No more could be gained from his continued absence from bed. **"Sleep child, you have done more than could be expected of you this day."** Theodren nodded at the tree's words. He went to place his new hammer down on the anvil but it recoiled from the cold metal, it unbound from its form and crept up his arm to coil around his bicep. His brows rose at the sudden unbidden action of his new smithing tool, he felt it settle, gripping his arm as a maiden might grip her suitor.

"She will not part with you easily." Yggdrazil mused. He supposed he couldn't know what to expect from a living artifact such as this one, and trying to reason it out with a mind as exhausted as his was a fool's errand. Bidding Yggdrazil a hasty goodnight, he stumbled up the steps into the church. He was much too tired to consider the implications of entering the church of a god he had cast off, much less sleep within it. He pitched himself into the bed in his quarters, not bothering to undress. Wrapping himself in the blanket, he closed his eyes and let the exhaustion take him.

Chapter 8
Careless Cruelty

Leagues away and getting closer.

Reina bounced in her saddle, humming a tune she only half remembered while twisting a flower she had insisted on plucking from the newly thawed ground. She twirled the stem deftly through her delicate fingers before tucking it into the simple golden ponytail that adorned her head. She wore a set of sleek black leather armor trimmed in the gold of the Conclave. Strapped to her sides were two oddly shaped golden daggers that were patterned after the blades of shears. They were as gaudy as they were effective. Never more so than in the hands of the lithe young woman who sat upon her dappled gray mare. She played absentmindedly with the reins before pulling one of her blades up to eye level to admire the simple yellow flower in her hair.

Hardwright witnessed all of this with a look of barely disguised distaste. They had left the Capitol only days ago and already the Acolyte had tried his patience. Reina was a woman possessed of much beauty and skill. Surpassing the other acolytes with flying colors and a genuine smile that never left her face. It was true that she seemed to light up rooms with her presence. Hardwright *hated* it. She seemed filled with an endless energy. Even the bounce of her pony tail made him want to reach out and shear it off. His grimace turned up into a wicked grin. He would enjoy watching the mirth leave those gleaming blue eyes of hers when her task was complete.

Reina turned back to him as if sensing her presence in her thoughts. She gave him a warm genuine smile that he hated all the more. "I'm so excited to finally have my own assignment! I've been wanting to join the order since I was a little girl!"

He tried to affect a pleasant grin. He had heard this before. The whole conclave had heard of the golden haired acolyte and her intense desire to be a priest like her father before her. Hardwright wasn't sure who her father was, but supposedly he was quite highly placed, and it would not do to burn a bridge whose position he wasn't even aware of yet.

"I'm sure this order will be good for you, sister Reina." He said, managing to hide his distaste. She had never been beyond the walls of the Holy City of Grandia, and now she was miles beyond it, venturing into the wilds of the countryside as it was escaping the last desperate gasps of winter.

"I hope this village has some *real* food." She turned a sly eye to the disgruntled man riding next to her. "I fear I've lost my taste for *possum*." Hardwright ground his teeth. Their first meal on the road had been an eventful one. She had found a possum while searching for food. She brought it back, held proudly in the air. To all eyes present it appeared dead. Unfortunately for Lusis Hardwright, Cardinal of the Order of Golden Shears. It made its displeasure at being lunch known quite aggressively in his lap when he had attempted to skin it for the naive acolyte, who by the end of the ordeal, was doubled over in laughter by the now needless spit. It had taken two of his accompanying soldiers to pry the creature's jaw from his leg.

The tiny teeth marks stung almost as much as his wounded pride. But there was a balm to his rage. As she snickered in her saddle his own cruel smile curled at his lips. The Inquisitor's initiation was a brutal right of passage. One that he would enjoy watching. Normally, it would have been one of his lieutenants, her "handler" that would administer her initiation. He was almost glad that the Patriarch had ordered him to accompany her for this mission. Now he would have the singular pleasure of initiating her himself.

He half listened to her questions about what this initiation would be, where they were going and when they would arrive. "Soon." Was all he said. Soon they would arrive in the nameless village. Soon this heresy would be stamped out, and soon... he fingered the relic in the leather satchel he carried. He would be rid of her incessant chatter.

As he reveled in her impending misfortune, he hardly noticed the handful of peasants escorting a cart laden with supplies. Resurfacing from his fantasies of Reina's misfortunes, he kicked his horse forward, 3 guards accompanied him to demand the news of the road ahead from the peasants. Reina watched him go. A curtain of greasy black hair bounced against the pockmarked skin he tried to hide.

***

She was unimpressed with the gloomy Cardinal. He was an unenthusiastic travel companion, and when he did smile it was always a leering sneer he thought she could not see. She gripped the fine leather of her reins and steeled her resolve. She would show him. She had asked many people many times about the initiation she would be subject to. Most people she asked looked sheepish in their refusal to answer. Often finding something interesting to look at on the back of their hands or the tops of their shifting feet.

It would not stop her. She had passed every test from her martial training to her weavings. She had been "exceptional" since birth. Her mother had insisted on it. Her mind fell unbidden to her last memory of her mother, staring at her as the door to the carriage slammed shut in her face, and she was left, alone before the gates of the conclave. Reina shook herself. Her mother had made it clear, power was valuable, and only the valuable had power.

She let her divine thread extend from her fingertip, snaking upward until it passed the tops of the tallest trees she rode beside. Power was something that she certainly had no shortage of. She watched it dance among the afternoon light before whipping it down at an unsuspecting boulder that had caught her eye. The face of it split neatly in two with a loud **CRACK!**

The sound echoed up the road ahead to the donkey pulling the peasants' cart. Its ears fell flat against its head in panic. With a frantic series of brays it set off with all the speed the encumbered animal could muster. The surprised peasants ran after it, leaving Hardwright alone amidst their dust. He turned to give her a familiar glare. Feigning ignorance, she looked around trying to maintain an air of innocence that was fooling no one.

She sighed, ordering her thread into the dirt at the cart's wheels. Pushing her will into the soil she effortlessly manipulated it into mud. The cart slowed and then stopped. It sank into the mud as the panicked donkey continued to pull, splitting the wheel and sending the contents of the cart sliding into the new bog she had just created. "There." She proclaimed proudly. The problem of the runaway cart was solved. The fact that they were now stranded in a swamp of her own making in the now ruined road was none of her concern.

She trotted past the downcast but no less furious peasants working silently to pull their rapidly sinking cart from the mire. To anyone else they would have protested loudly for the inconvenience, but none of them dared to voice their discontent. Not to a priest and certainly not to one as gifted as she clearly was no matter how foolish.

She would make a *great* priestess of the order, she mused, leaving the sinking cart in her dust.

Chapter 9
The Name of Nothing

Theodren blinked the ceiling into view. As his mind returned to consciousness he attempted the mental math required to guess how long he had slept for, a whole day? Two days? He could not be sure, but he was certainly rested now. He shifted in the too small bed, expecting his usual stiffness. When none came his brow rose. There were few constants in life, but the stiffness of his neck after a night in the cramped bed of his equally small chambers was one of them. He sat up rolling his neck. "Huh." The sentiment encapsulated the whole of his confusion, relief and surprise at how well he felt.

Coming to a stand, he bounced on the balls of his feet, feeling the lightness of a body he remembered having in a prime now past. He knew the source of the change. Turning his mind inward, he watched the Vitae circulating through his veins. Tracking its path he saw it depositing vitae into the cells of his body. Tiny fireworks of green energy exploded within every fiber, filling him to the brim with life.

He whistled a tune he couldn't quite place as he splashed water from the basin over his face. Theodren pulled the collar of his robes to his nose, wrinkling at the acrid sweat born of the fear and desperation of the day prior.

Pulling the rough cloth over his head, he stood before the small piece of polished bronze above his basin. Two days worth of stubble stared back at him from his jaw. He groaned at the thought of the days he lost to sleep but continued his inspection. The four puffy lines that scarred his chest were faded. The evidence of the wound was still there, but it was no longer the unseemly puckered scar it was the night prior.

What more surprised him was the Caduceus symbol emblazoned on his chest above his heart. He idly traced the new symbol Yggdrazil had placed on him with his finger while his eyes wandered to the rest of him.

His skin felt more firm, pulled taut over his frame of muscles that had grown inexplicably while he'd slept. He groaned, coming to the realization that he would need to buy larger clothing yet again. Theodren rifled through his wardrobe searching for anything that might fit him. Digging deep into the forgotten parts of his wardrobe, he fished an oversized working tunic and pants. Well made but simple, they lacked any adornment to speak of, but that suited him fine.

Inspecting himself in the mirror, he was reminded of the presence of his new helper. The vineling was nestled tightly against his right bicep. Wrapping itself against his arm, he poked it with an inquisitive finger until it sleepily crawled up his arm until it was hidden beneath his sleeve. He puzzled at it for a moment but eventually decided not to bother with it.

Running a hand through his hair he stepped out of his quarters and froze. Sitting atop the altar he prayed at every day, the thread and needle symbol of the Weaver seemed to stare at him accusingly in the gloom of the dark church.

He found that he believed Yggdrazil's account. How could he not? She was living proof that there were other gods.

More damning to him than the sacrilege was his failure to live up to his oaths he had made as a fledgling priest. He had sworn to serve Odrain, he had sworn to preserve order in his community. Moving away from the place of prayer that was once his morning ritual, he shuffled toward the door.

The word fraud loomed in his mind as he shielded his eyes from the intense morning sunlight. As the world came into focus he was treated to a wondrous sunrise that succeeded in lifting his spirits. Rolling grey clouds menaced a horizon gripped in the red fingers of dawn.

There would be a storm later he knew, but for now birds graced the sky and the air was crisp and fresh. He felt the loss of his previous path. Its simplicity and its certainty were things he would miss. However, he felt the vineling squeeze his arm reassuringly. He now had new tools with which to serve the town, if he could learn to use them.

He turned toward his forge and stopped, puzzled. It took only a moment before he noticed the change. The creeping vines that had only sparsely adorned the church now smothered it. From foundation to roof it was covered in a rich carpet of vines and leaves.

"That's going to take some doing." He thought to himself, mentally planning the task of trimming the overgrowth. He shook himself from the strayed thought and continued his path to the forge. Taking a breath he eased open the door mentally preparing himself for speaking with the reality defying tree god. As he peered into the gloom of his workshop however, Yggdrazil was nowhere to be found. A quizzical sort of melancholy tickled at the back of his mind as he considered her absence.

YOU SEEK ME OUT? The voice flowed through his mind like a river breaking free of a dam. It was a force both alien and primordial that threatened to wash his sense of self from his mind. He winced as his hand flew to the electric tingling of his caduceus. "Don't *DO* that!" His heart beat a mile a minute beneath the mark on his chest. He felt Yggdrazil's awareness settle on him like a blanket. **I apologize acolyte, you mortals are a fragile people.**

His brows met in a furrow. "Acolyte?" He had not been an acolyte for some years and he was glad to be rid of the junior title. He sensed more than saw the grin forming from Yggdrazil's consciousness. **You are yet untested and untrained are you not? Is that not why you seek me out?**

It rankled his pride that she was right, but from the burning sensation in his chest he knew that his mind was an open book to the great Tree.

He sighed, Yggdrazil seemed to take that as acknowledgement and continued. **"You have given form to Vitae and created life."** He felt the vine perk up on his arm as she seemed to sense her presence in their conversation. **"What you hold in your bosom is not just life, it is the spark of creation itself. It is an energy unlike any you will have ever encountered. And while this power is great, take heed. While life is yours to give and even to take. Death is a door you must never seek to open."**

The warning chilled Theodren more than the spring morning air ever could. He shivered. "What does that mean?" Yggdrazil was quiet for a moment, as if considering his question.

"Death is my antithesis. Where it flows I can not tread. It is the end of the natural path of all life. Not even Odrain may alter it."

Theodren considered the warning. It was not one he was likely to test, but it did pique his curiosity. "Is death a part of the tapestry like you?" The tree shuddered.

"No. Death could not be manipulated so it could not be bound. It is the end of the tapestry. It is the absence of all things." So there *is* a limit to this power, he thought to himself. His eyes turned back to the tree. "Does it have a name? Death I mean."

Yggdrazil pondered for a moment. **"My memory of the time before the Great Tapestry is poor, but if my sister had a name it would have been..."** The shadows seemed to grow darker and longer as the sun, still bright in the sky, grew cold. A chill spread over the back of Theodren's neck like the cold and sinewy claws of a predator.

Yggdrazil halted mid sentence. Theodren could tell by the stiffness of the god tree's limbs that his discomfort was shared. **"To speak her name is to call to her."** Yggdrazil whispered. Theodren was unnerved that a deity such as Yggdrazil could be so cowed by a name not even spoken. Though he sensed that beneath the fear was something more, either disdain or irritation he could not tell. He shivered.

The sun's warmth returned to the mid spring morning. It took his artifact releasing the death grip he didn't know she had on his arm to in turn make him relax as well. He waited patiently for the tree's next words, expecting her instruction to continue. Sensing his attention, Yggdrazil's branches lowered slightly.

"Go. Your people need their priest and my power is not taught. Only experienced. You must find your own way to wield the Vitae you possess and I must retire from this plane for the moment."

Upon inspection Theodren noticed that Yggdrazil seemed a little less clear. The lines on her trunk seemed to blur like heat rising off of a road. As she faded from sight he resolved to ask her why she left the tapestry and where she went. His theories were many, each as unlikely as the last.

He shook himself from his musings and refocused his efforts on ordering his tasks for the day. He would need to check on Eleina and the baby. There were a myriad of tasks and requests waiting for him at the village. Tempting as it might be to hide from the world and his responsibilities since his world view had been so thoroughly rocked, he knew that he was needed.

In fact. He thought rubbing the stubble on his chin, his new Vitae would help tremendously in the course of his duties. As he made his way back to the church his mind returned to the unnerving sensation of impending doom that had invaded his conversation with Yggdrazil.

He supposed that if there was a god of life that it stood to reason that there was a god of death as well. He shuddered. "I hope to never meet you." He whispered to nothing in particular.

Just beyond his view. Shrouded in mystery and shadow. Nothing... smirked.

Chapter 10
Rematch

Theodren made his way down the hill, once again lost in thought. He pondered Vitae, his, and that of the creatures surrounding the dusty road flanked by the green and budding plant life that flanked it. Vitae was everywhere. It was in every blade of grass that danced in the morning breeze. It was certainly in the bees that flit from every flower to bush and tree of the countryside.

As he watched he was amazed at the flow of it all. Vitae seemed to spring from the very earth itself. It flowed through the plants and into insects that relied upon them. The insects were merely carriers themselves. Delivering glorious life to the birds and even other insects that preyed upon them. He watched it flow through the ecosystem around him. So lost in its splendor he almost missed the massive ball of Vitae observing him from the brush up ahead.

He froze. He had almost forgotten the bear that had ruined his shovel and one of his few shirts months prior. His artifact leapt to his hand, forming herself into a hammer. He was surprised at her speed and the form she took. It was true he had always preferred hammers, but this was a preference left unsaid. Especially around his fathers weapon masters who spoke of swords with words of poetry, and hammers with words of disdain.

And yet, if he could have requested a hammer from his fathers many smiths, it would have looked much like the one his new artifact had made for him. From flared pommel to engraved head it would stand exactly even with his navel. The handle possessed grooves that fit his fingers comfortably without restricting his ability to shift positions. The length of it seemed to be covered in wicked thorns that would prevent an enemy from grabbing it mid melee. The head itself was two sided with the flat stud covered face of a maul on one end and a curved spike on the other. Both served exceptionally at their respective tasks of crushing and piercing armor. Atop the hammer sat a large spike meant for thrusting and keeping distance when needs be. He took a moment to admire its new form with eyebrows raised nearly to his hairline. An experimental swing of the hammer confirmed that she was incredibly well balanced. Certainly more than the shovel was at his last encounter with the bear.

He peered down the road to where the large ball of vitae was rooting around in the brush. He knew that most bears emerged from winter hungry and in poor spirits and he doubted this one would be any exception. He continued down the road step by measured step, his weapon gripped tightly in his hand. He reached his other hand up toward the top of the shaft. The thorns adorning the handle receded into the wood at his touch. Gratitude toward the hammer filled his mind as he pressed on.

The bear paused. A familiar annoying scent filled its nose as it raised its shaggy head. There through the bushes was the human with the painful stick from seasons ago. Its nose had taken many months to heal properly, and as the mother bear recalled the pain, she had enough sense to stay in her patch of brush. Unfortunately, her son had not.

ROOOOOAAAAARRR! Theodren whirled around as a second ball of fur and vitae barreled out of the trees behind him. Full of fire and a need to prove itself the bear charged the man with the stick.

Nearly as big as its mother it swung a meaty paw at Theodren. Wielding his new hammer, he batted the paw away, allowing the momentum of the hammer to carry through into a second swing for the bear's ribs. A wet crack filled the air as they broke beneath the head of his maul.

The young bear dropped back down to all fours blood dripping from its mouth as it let loose a gurgling growl of pain. Ribs pulverized and head swimming in pain, it glared at Theodren. Unbowed and unwilling to give up the fight, it charged once more, slower this time as it sought to savage the man with the painful stick.

Theodren barked a laugh as he brandished his hammer at it. The joy he felt in combat was unbecoming of a priest, but he relished it all the same. His vitae, his very soul sang at the challenge. His might against another. The strength of his arm and the depth of his skill ruled the moment. His troubles were far away. All that was before him was instinct and triumph, should he seize it.

The bear's swings came slower and slower. It's mighty roar now a groaning whine. Theodren parried, blocked and smashed his way through the bear's assault.

The bear swung down at him with rage and gravity behind its meaty paw. Theodren sidestepped the blow, bringing the spike of his hammer down on the paw pinning it to the dirt below. Roaring fury at the priest, the bear snapped his jaws at Theodren.

He leaned back narrowly avoiding yellow and pointed teeth. Yanking his hammer free he jabbed with the top point of the weapon as he hopped backwards, scoring only a shallow wound above an eye. Theodren's laughter boomed to the trees and bush beside the road where the mother bear, unable to watch any longer charged into the fray.

The mother bear shouldered past a confused and wary Theodren who stumbled into a guard. Mother bear positioned herself between the man with the painful stick and her foolish cub. Growling at the man she stood her ground.

Theodren sensed something in the mother bear. Her Vitae perplexed him. As he focused on the bear's life force, it began to take on wisps of color he had not noticed before. Flecks of yellow and red danced over the pool of green he was accustomed to seeing. The bear's face was unreadable, but her soul swam with rage and a healthy amount of fear.

Theodren's blood cooled rapidly. Faced as he was with the fear of a mother for her child he found that his taste for this battle was gone. The vineling unraveled from her form to slither back up his wrist and bind herself to his arm.

As the hammer disappeared from sight the adrenaline the young bear was using to stay on his paws disappeared as well. Slumping to the ground with a groan, blood poured from his mouth to mix with the dust of the road to create a red puddle of mud.

Theodren observed his handiwork with a growing sense of unease. He felt no regret at defending himself, but watching the mother bear keen over the form of her unconscious son unsettled him.

"Dammit! Do NOT eat me you understand?" He jabbed a finger at the mother bear who looked up at him incredulously. Yellow and purple appearing at the edges of her vitae. Confusion perhaps? He thought as he inched closer to the downed bear.

The mother bear growled at him but made no move of her own as he placed a hand on the coarse fur of the bears head. He reached deep with his vitae. The stream of life force flowed from his hand into the bear like water from a spigot.

Suddenly he was bombarded with information. He groaned as his head was filled with the sensory information of the wounded bear. Broken ribs, a punctured lung, a broken paw and several other smaller but no less painful fractures, ruptures and contusions. He allowed himself a moment of reluctant pride amidst the cacophony of pain that flooded his senses.

His mind railed against the pain. Unsure and untrained he had no solution but to push back with the only resource he had. Vitae. He pushed his store of vitae at the connection between him and the bear hoping to distance himself from the creature's pain. When it started to work he pushed further. Regaining his concentration he pushed the vitae into the bear. Shepherding it towards its many injuries. Desperate to be free of the pain and to complete his task he pushed with all his soul until he felt the vitae begin its work on the injured organs.

His shoulders slumped as he began to allow himself the feeling of triumph over his task. He watched as the ribs began repairing themselves and the damaged cells of the bear's lungs began to regrow, and then continued to grow. And then overgrow their bounds, spilling over previous confines of the lung.

"SHIT!" Theodren sprang back into action. He had fed too much vitae to the bear's wounds and now the cells had become cancerous. Consuming their neighbors at a rapid pace.

Mentally kicking himself, Theodren reached for the vitae desperate to drag it back into himself. It came quickly, fleeing the corrupted cells as they withered almost instantly, but where one died more grew. He cursed as he fought to find every rapidly growing cell in the enormous body. He pushed and pulled for what felt like hours. Frantically clawing back his mistake.

By the end of it the sun was high in the sky as the late spring air chilled his body now drenched in sweat. Crouched down on the balls of his feet. He rocked back onto his heels before sitting down in the dirt.

He had spent what seemed to be hours teetering back and forth between too much and not enough Vitae for the bear. By now he was as sure as he could be that he had stomped out every greedy cell that he could find without outright destroying the organs the bear relied upon.

The result was a young bear that was only *mostly* dead. Its organs were fragile and raw but they would recover.

Theodren jumped as the young bear groaned. He scrambled to his feet panting and looking around for the mother bear who was opposite his position nudging her son with her snout. The young bear groaned louder as it struggled to get up.

Theodren let out a sigh as the bear swayed on its feet. "Serves you right, you angry bastard." The young bear's vitae was a similar color of confusion and fear his mother was displaying in the hours prior. He looked to her now to see flares of blue and emerald amidst her vitae.

"Hope that means happy." Theodren mumbled. Hearing him both bears turned their attention on the priest.

"Whoa. Hey now. Don't make me do that again." He took a step back remembering that these were in fact wild animals. The mother bear approached slowly, head slightly tilted.

Theodren looked for any signs of the red he associated with anger in her vitae but found none. Approaching his chest she sniffed at the scar, faded though it was, that she had left him with before. Letting out a huff she turned.

He watched as the mother bear once again herded her large cub back into the brush. Leaving Theodren exhausted and confused in the middle of the road.

After a moment of reflection over the odd encounter. He shook himself and turned back toward town. Elleina would never believe this.

Chapter 11
Back Alley Politics

Theodren walked into town with a paired sense of exhaustion and trepidation. Word of Ellaina's miraculous recovery would get around. He ran a hand up the back of his head to massage the headache that promised to bloom beneath his palm.

The majority of his healings in the village had been bandages, salves and stitches accompanied by whatever his divine thread could accomplish. Explaining to the townsfolk why he had the power to wrench Reina from the jaws of death but not enough to cure the *mayor's* gout seemed like a terrible way to spend his afternoon.

Unfortunately for Theodren, the subject of those very thoughts came striding around the very corner he was approaching.

"Fuck."

"Ah Bishop Stormwall!"

A grimace appeared on his face as the self appointed Mayor Sebastian Sylverworm and his trailing lackey Lester Hess strode with the grace of a peacock down the town road toward him.

Crooked smiles and oily mustaches, Theodren had known these types from his time with his father at court and was less than eager to have his own relationship with them. Especially young Lester Hess, The hunched vagrant who was infamous for his rumored misdeeds among the younger women of the village.

"Good Morning gentleman." He managed, struggling to fabricate an urgent emergency that required his attention. Alas none came and a pudgy arm found its way across his shoulders.

"I must congratulate you on Mrs. Fiero's newborn. If the rumors are to be believed, one might say you enacted a miracle!" Theodren's brow furrowed deeper as he extricated himself from the far too friendly contact of the mayor.

"You are too kind Mr. Sylverworm, I merely conducted the duties of the church as I do for all of these townspeople." The snaggle-toothed grin of Lester Hess appeared in Theodren's peripheral.

"Nonsense Mr. Stormwall, I've heard tell that your performance was a marked improvement on your previous ministrations. Do tell us, what changed?"

Theodren's head snapped to the skulking young man determined to remain on the periphery. "The Mayor and I are speaking, do not insert yourself where you are not welcomed Lester." The scrawny young man shrank from the sudden tongue lashing. Through a grimace of gritted teeth he hissed.

"Apologies *Priest*. We were merely surprised given your previous... performance." Theodren glared at the mayor's toadie. Flecks of sickly greens and putrid yellows mixed with angry reds in the underlings vitae.

A reminder of Lester's own previous sins prepared itself on his tongue but was interrupted by the mayor. "Now now gentleman, I'm sure a day as fine as this calls for friendlier tones does it not?"

He turned to his lackey. "Lester, wait for me at the market." Lester appeared to form the beginnings of a protest but Sebastian had already turned away from the teenager, signaling that no disagreement would be brooked. Lester turned his glare to Theodren before stomping off down the street.

"Nasty business that childbirth. I understand young Mrs. Fiero was in dire straits before your timely intervention. How *did* you manage it?" Theodren's attention returned to the pompous older man fiddling with his oiled mustache in an attempt to feign disinterest.

Theodren considered his question. "Polly did most of the work, I simply finished the job she started." Sebastian raised a grey eyebrow to the wisps of what remained of his hairline.

"Indeed? From what rumor I've heard you seemed quite perturbed and left in a hurry after Eleina's miraculous recovery. Theodren arched an eyebrow of his own.

"I suppose small rumors have long legs in villages as small as this one." He was no fool. He knew men like the mayor thrived on gossip. Even in towns as small as this one, secret knowledge was how the mayor maintained his position.

"My dear fellow, I simply mean to congratulate you! Perhaps even buy you a drink?" The local tavern was perhaps the most frequented building in the entire town. It was a place where stories of yore flowed as well as the ale it provided. It was cheap, and it was cramped but it was more than adequate for the small populace of the town. Moreover it was deliberately avoided by the mayor who preferred to drink his own spirits away from the rabble.

Theodren eyed the older man for a silent moment. "I don't do politics, mayor." Sylverworm deflated only slightly. "Whatever do you mean? Sharing a glass at the local pub is no sin is it?"

Theodren sighed. "Even *if* The Farmer's Bucket had a glass to share, I will not be seen to endorse either you or Polly in this... feud."

Some years ago, Sebastian Sylverworm arrived in the small town from parts unknown, claiming to be the new mayor. Whatever problems he had fled were similarly unknown, except that they had earned him a modest bag of gold and a finely made but slightly torn tunic.

For the most part, the townsfolk couldn't be bothered with him. It was no concern of theirs who resided in the solitary stone house only slightly bigger than the others. He was useful in his way. When the tax collectors came to the village, he argued for a fair rate for the townsfolk, accepting only a *small* fee from everyone.

Only recently however had he attempted to gain more authority within the town, he had even appointed Eleina's husband Evan as a town guard in hopes of acquiring some weight for his words. And while Evan was enthusiastic, he was certainly no lackey.

That role went instead, to the loathsome Lester Hess. An apprentice fishmonger as well as a rumor monger, he was unsavory of sight and smell. This was matched only by the petty personality he also possessed.

He both forged and wielded rumors throughout the town in order to gain his way. When one day his coercion had gone too far, he was hauled before the mayor to issue judgement at the demand of Polly, brimming with motherly rage.

A slap on the wrist and a new assignment was all that Lester had received. In return, the mayor obtained a new lackey.

"If you wish to keep your position from being taken by our herbalist, I suggest that you do away with your Mr. Hess. Why you choose to associate with the likes of him is beyond me."

The mayor eyed the priest for a moment. The facade of friendliness dropping from his face. "The boy knows things." He sniffed.

The back of Theodren's ears pricked as he sensed more than saw a presence lurking just out of sight. Casting about with a tendril of his vitae he found a puddle of vitae dyed in sickly green, yellow and a deep reddish brown. He could think of only one person to whom such a soul might belong.

"Then the boy should know better than to lurk in the shadows." Theodren spun on his heel and strode to the unfortunate spy's hiding spot around the corner. Grabbing the greasy man by the collar he hauled him into the light.

Albert became a tangle of spindly arms and legs as he was tossed unceremoniously into the dirt. "I'm not! I wasn't!... I didn't!..." the mayor clicked his tongue and sighed.

Theodren glowered down at the pockmarked face that stared back at him burning red with embarrassment and indignation.

"My patience runs thin, mayor." Sebastian's eyes narrowed at the mocking tone.

"I assure you the lad meant no harm. His curiosity must have gotten the better of him." The mayor turned a stoney glare on his lackey. "It *won't* happen again. Will it?"

Lester began nodding quickly. A smile tugged at the corner of his mouth as he sensed an escape from his troubles. "No sir! I swear on my name!"

Theodren's blood boiled at the display of cronyism playing out at his feet. He reached down and grabbed Lester by the collar of his blouse and hauled him to his feet and then into the air so that they were face to face.

"I will not be spied upon by the likes of *you* Lester Hess." Spindly legs flailed and kicked inches from the ground, searching for purchase and finding none. All Lester could do was stare wide eyed into the enraged face of Theodren.

"Y-you're a p-priest! Y-you're not allowed to touch me!" Rage built behind Theodren's eyes as Lester attempted to use his own religious oaths of non-interference against him. Oaths that he had since violated with the world shattering arrival of Yggdrazil in his life.

"My oaths are MINE to keep." Theodren squeezed tighter. "Or break." Theodren's rage at the slimy young man in his grasp and at his own betrayal built into an inferno. Suddenly Lester froze staring into Theodren's eyes. "Green?" He choked.

Theodren's rage left him almost instantly as he realized his vitae must be spilling over if Lester could see it in his eyes. He dropped the man unceremoniously in the dirt and stepped away.

The mayor who had been observing the altercation in shocked silence returned to his senses and grabbed Lester by the shoulder and dragged him to his feet.

"We will be taking our leave now." The older man squeaked. Together they scurried down the quiet street. Casting furtive glances over their shoulders as they retreated to the mayor's home.

Fear and irritation coursed through Theodren causing his shoulders to tense higher and higher till they nearly reached his ears.

"Fuck."

The worst person who could have discovered his change had now done so. after only a day. Who would he tell? What would they do about it? Another thought occurred to him.

Would anyone believe or even understand it? Before the events of yesterday's birth, he would be hard pressed to believe in a power besides divine thread and even that was shrouded in mystery by the Church of Holy Order.

Theodren's shoulders began to recede from their previous heights as he rationalized his way through his troubles. The townspeople were unlikely to listen to the two men much less believe them.

Theodren released a large sigh. "A problem for later I suppose." For now, he set his shoulders, it was time to put his newfound power to use. The bear had been a wake up call. This power was no toy. He had nearly killed the creature by overloading it with his vitae, and while he was determined to do as much good for the village folk as he could, he would need to better understand it if he was to be successful.

He marched to the third little house from the end where he knew he would find Sarah, the elderly seamstress whose hands were almost, but never quite relieved of their ache by the poultices Polly prepared or the weavings Theodren had worked before.

Theodren knocked on her doorframe. "Sarah? Have you got a moment?" He called out to her. His bulk shading the doorframe that creaked open, revealing the colorful form of Sarah. "A moment? Certainly. Enough fabric for another of your robes? Not nearly." She chuckled. Theodren grinned back at her. "No robes, not today. I want to see your hands."

She frowned at him. "Don't bother with them dear, old women have old hands and you've wasted enough thread on this old woman already." He held out his own hands palms up and arched an eyebrow at her. Sighing, she relented, placing gnarled and curled fists on his outstretched hands. Theodren inspected them once more, turning her hands this way and that, noticing the creak and crack of decrepitude built up over decades of honing her art. but this time he looked deeper, pushing his Vitae beneath the skin and into her joints to get a better sense of her ailment.

Once she had deftly orchestrated needle and thread to weave celebrations of color into her work. Now the stiffness in her fingers prevented her from doing all but the simplest of stitches. A tinge of curiosity colored her soul a warm yellow, but the swelling and pain between the joints of each finger flared a painful red.

Reaching out to touch each joint with his Vitae, he winced as he felt each spike of her ache for himself. Some of the knuckles had boney lumps between them, but most were completely deteriorated and missing all but the barest of cartilage. And that was where he would start. Theodren coaxed his Vitae into the damaged cartilage, feeding it with a more potent fuel. His brows came together as he focused on the delicacy of his work. The rubbery tissue began to grow, slowly, but still it grew; years of repeated pinched movement had ground it down, but Theodren had made it new again.

Pleased with himself, he moved on to the next problem. Some of her fingers had warped and the bones within had warped with them. Theodren did not know how to heal something that wasn't technically broken. These lumps had grown as the body's own attempt at repairing the missing cartilage and while Theodren could encourage the regrowth of actual cartilage, was unsure how he might shave down the lumps that impeded her motion. For now, he would do what he could to reform the missing spongy material and hope that that was enough. Perhaps if he still had his thread he would be better able to capitalize on this new understanding of healing He thought to himself, even as he withdrew the probing Vitae from her hand, his repairs finished.

"Try stretching out your fingers now." he instructed, eyes still not leaving her hands. She gave the beginnings of a sigh that died in her throat as her fingers stretched out further than they had in years. The sigh was replaced with a bark of laughter that shot out in a fast and almost undignified belly laugh. She recovered quickly, pulling a hand to her mouth, which only caused further mirth to fill her eyes. "They move!" she laughed. "And they hardly hurt at all!" She wiggled them before her eyes and beamed up at the large priest. "Bless you! young man, bless you!" she cried out happily with the hint of joyful tears shaking at the edges of her voice. "I will sew you whole crates of robes just for you!"

Theodren grinned and shook his head. "No need for that Sarah, I just needed some practice, Thread can be finicky that way." He lied cringing internally at the mistruth. "Go, show your daughters, I'm sure they'll be overjoyed at your recovery." She nodded rapidly, eyes barely containing tears of relief and joy before she curtsied as deep as she dared and rushed back into her home.

Pleased with himself, Theodren looked further down the rows of houses. This part of the village was mostly elderly, and he would oblige himself of the numerous ailments they had to better learn to use his Vitae, and serve the people who made this place his home.

Chapter 12
Approaching Storm

Two weeks later, approaching the village.

"How much further?" Reina asked, pulling her damp cloak tighter to herself. The traveling party of inquisitors had been pursued by relentless spring showers driving a chill rain through cloak and skin until even the cheery disposition of the junior inquisitor was cast into the mud they now trod through.

Cardinal Hardwright pulled back till he rode alongside the bedraggled woman. a smile teased at his thin mouth. "The guards tell me it is just over the next hill. The village and your initiation are but a day away."

The way the cardinal leered at her was almost as unsettling as how at home the man seemed to be in such gloomy weather. "Good." She spat. "I want to be off this road and through this task you are so intent on keeping secret."

"Worry not acolyte, the mayor is known to me." An eerie grin stretched across his thin face. "I'm certain that he will tell us all that we need to know."

Reina shuddered and kicked her horse forward. When entering the conclave her mother had told her to take advantage of every relationship she could. "A friendly face is merely a step on the ladder you haven't used yet." Her mother would say. However...

She looked back at the cardinal who was busy smirking to himself as some unseen victory played out behind his eyes. His was not a smiling face that she could tolerate for much longer. She comforted herself with the knowledge that soon she would be through her initiation and beyond the slimy man behind her.

A smile began to form as she mused about the gratitude she would soon receive from the villagers after she was done with her task. Perhaps they would even throw her a party? Yes that would be an appropriate way to praise her she thought as her tired and dirty horse trudge along step by beleaguered step beneath her.

"One more day." She whispered. one more day and she would receive the praise she deserved and be rid of her odious travel companion. "They had better be ready." She said to herself gripping the reins in anticipation. "I'll make sure they never forget me."

***

Theodren rested a sweaty hand against the wall of Polly's shop. The last two weeks had been a blur of days spent practicing his healing on the townsfolk who lined up eagerly to have their aches and pains relieved by the mysteriously improved priest.

His nights he spent sparring with shadows in the courtyard of his church with the myriad forms of the vineling resting on his arm. The hammer was certainly his favorite but he made sure to keep up his training with a variety of knives, swords and bucklers as Tallhand, the old Master of Arms, would have wanted. He had let his training fall by the wayside as there was no need and no practice weapons with which to train. His recent run-ins with the bears went to show that crisis could not be predicted, only prepared for.

As he waved the last elderly farmer out the door of Polly's shop, a satisfied smile played over his face when the man whose cartilage he had just repaired, skipped down the path toward the town bar. Ready to share his good health with his friends.

Theodren moved to pack up his things when a pitiable voice called out from the door. "W-wait! You're healing *everybody* right?"

61

Theodren groaned internally. Turning towards the voice he found a poorly disguised Lester, hunched and cloaked standing in the doorway.

"I want what you're doing for everybody else." Whined Lester shuffling his feet into the small examination room. Theodren could feel the tension building in his shoulders as he considered turning away the unsavory young man. He considered dozens of excuses as to why he simply couldn't be bothered.

However, a sigh flared his nostrils as he waved at the small stool he had appropriated for his patients. "have a seat." he grumbled. This power of his was not just for those he approved of, he reasoned. They were for the good of all of the people he served, and that unfortunately included Lester.

Much to Theodren's chagrin, a triumphant smile slithered across Lester's face as he slid onto the stool. "And what seems to be the problem Mr. Hess?" Theodren asked, cleansing his hands in Polly's basin once again.

"You know what the problem is, priest." spat Lester. Theodren turned, arching an eyebrow to meet the pulsing vein in his forehead. "Would you like me to attend to your misshapen spine, or your misshapen soul? both are within my purview and both could use immediate aid."

Lester only glared at the priest who stared back unflinching. Finally, Lester's gaze dropped. "My back... it's always been this way. Everyone's always treated me different because of it." While Theodren may not have had much love for the young man, compassion for damaged people was something he had in abundance.

Theodren's stoney expression softened, if only slightly. "Let's see it then." At Theodren's instruction, Lester removed the cloak and the shirt beneath it, revealing a spine that was bent and unnatural.

Staring down at the "S" shaped spine he sighed as he contemplated the amount of vitae he'd have to spend from his dwindling supply. "I'll do what I can." He warned Lester, who remained silent in his anticipation.

Theodren placed a broad hand on the bend of the spine and closed his eyes. He pushed his vitae into Lester's back, quietly probing and prodding at the deformed spine. Seeking a weak point that he could take advantage of.

Lester shifted on the stool. "Are you even doing any..." Theodren clamped down with his grip on Lester's back "Shh!" He had limited vitae to spare, and he needed every ounce of it and his concentration to straighten the back beneath his hand. As he pushed at the first vertebrae, he willed his vitae to prop it up until he felt confident in its integrity.

As he reached for the second vertebrae his mind was locked into the task. Shaping and feeding vitae to the spine that reshaped itself beneath his hand. As he reached halfway through his ministration he felt a tug on his vitae. No longer a stream, but a mist of vitae, it was vulnerable, more difficult to direct. His vitae was being pulled away from the spine he was focused on and towards a tear in the young man's heart. Not his physical heart, no this was damage to what Theodren had only hypothesized was the heart of a person's soul. His brow creased together as he sought to control the errant vitae. But he could only watch as it floated towards the void in Lester's soul.

He grimaced as he pushed the last of his vitae desperately at the bent vertebrae, but they remained, crooked and unchanged. Theodren wondered at the tear in Lester's soul. Over the last two weeks he had healed almost everyone in the village, but none had a hole in their soul like this. What could possibly have disfigured it to this extent? Why had he not noticed it before? Was it always this large?

These questions and many more flooded his mind, but they would have to wait. Theodren released a defeated sigh as he pulled his hand away. Lester shot to his feet. "Did it work? I don't feel any different!" His hands reached up to explore the crooked landscape of his back as his expression fell from glee, to disappointment to bitter rage.

"You *said* you could fix me!" Lester shouted. His fists balled at his side before one changed to an accusatory finger pointed at the priest. "you failed on PURPOSE!" The vein in Theodren's forehead beat a new and dangerous tempo. "You mistake me Lester." Theodren roared back.

He grabbed Lester's clothes from the bench and shoved them into the young man's fragile chest. "I have neither the power nor the patience to fix that crooked back of yours, and I will not be slandered for my attempts!" He shoved Lester out the door into the street where the seemingly omniscient busy-bodies of the town gathered inconspicuously as they could to 'overhear' the heated conversation.

Snickering could be heard from some of the townsfolk as they looked on at the exposed and humiliated Lester who grew redder and angrier by the second. Theodren winced as he realized the situation he had quite literally thrust Lester into. "Come back tomorrow when I am rested, I will try again." Said Theodren.

Lester snapped his attention from the gossiping villagers back to the priest.

"As if *anyone* would come back to a FRAUD like you!" He snarled and stormed off, struggling into his shirt and cloak as he ran.

A sigh escaped through flared nostrils as Theodren retreated back into the herbalist's shop where Polly herself stood with a tapping foot and crossed arms. Theodren winced beneath the razor sharp gaze of the herbalist. "That was... unfortunate..." He managed.

"You had that, that *snake* in my shop?" Less a question than an accusation, he felt the tension spread from his shoulders to gather into a pulsing ball of pain behind his eyes. "Snake or not he is a resident of this village and entitled to my care same as anyone else."

"Not in MY shop he's not." She snapped. "Don't you know what he *did?*" Theodren grunted in affirmation.

"I know he tried to shame Eleina into leaving Evan for him, and I know that went as well as could be expected for him." Indeed, Eleina and Evan had gotten pregnant before their wedding day and an ever observant Lester thought he could shame Eleina into submitting to him.

What he got instead was an impressive right cross to his delicate jaw by an enraged Eleina who then dragged her fiancé to Theodren's church for a pleasant but speedy ceremony.

Polly nodded curtly. "He deserves that and more! I'll forgive you this once because you saved Elly, but if that boy comes around my shop again everyone involved will be breaking out in rashes for a month!" She barked, patting her pouch of herbs that was tied to her belt.

Theodren shuddered. He was well aware of Polly's "remedies for bad behavior". There were few who were foolish enough to disrespect an herbalist, but those who did often found themselves in a sudden and mysterious need of an itching remedy.

"Speaking of Elly." Theodren looked back up from his feet, an apologetic grimace spread over his face. "You've been avoiding her." Theodren tried to come up with an excuse but none came. He could only nod as he sank onto the stool that groaned beneath his considerable bulk. "A lot happened, Polly." Was all he offered.

Polly sighed as she grabbed her own stool and sat opposite Theodren. "That was a bad night." She agreed, not fully grasping the gravity of the events that had transpired for Theodren over the last two weeks. "But you saved her life. What's more, you saved her baby. My granddaughter."

Theodren considered Polly's words silently. "So whatever you're moping about. You better get over it, young man." Theodren reeled at the simplicity and absurdity of her statement. "Get over it." he repeated.

"That's right, life moves on. and you can bury yourself in your work trying to avoid whatever you're dealing with. But you'll have to get over it sooner or later." Theodren remained in a flustered state of shock as he contemplated her words. From his crisis of faith and ultimate betrayal, to the bears and of course his complications with Lester and the Mayor. He struggled to keep his head above water. He felt the tension build further in his shoulders while he remembered the fear, loss and uncertainty of the last two weeks as her words echoed in his head. A reassuring squeeze of his arm by the vineling pulled him from his spiral back to the present.

Perhaps it was time Theodren paid Eleina and Evan a visit. It would serve him well to see what good had come from the breaking of his faith. Perhaps then he could 'get over it.' Theodren brought his focus back to Polly. I'll check in on them on my way back up the hill." He promised.

"Good lad." Said Polly as she patted Theodren on the arm. "And when you do bring this pot of stew I made for them. My poor Elly is in no fit state to cook, and Evan is no cook in any state." Theodren chuckled. "No he is not. I'll make sure they get it." He promised.

Polly made room for him as he stood to leave. Grabbing the pot of stew by the handle, he made his way towards Eleina's home.

Chapter 13
Shame

Lester's eyes burned with the promise of tears as he ran. Ran from the priest. Ran from the shame. Soon his broken stride led him beyond the town, out to the hill where his sanctuary stood.

Lester threw himself down upon the dry pine needles that covered the floor of his shallow cave. Only then did the rage and shame finally spill over from his eyes. Snot and tears commingled on his face as he beat and screamed into the floor. He howled curses to the sky. He cursed the priest, he cursed the townsfolk, and he cursed himself for being stupid enough to hope.

All of this he screamed to the silent sky. Unheard and uncared for, because there was no one to witness his wails. No one, except for the party of inquisitors drawn to the keening of a broken young man.

***

"What in Weaver's name is that sound?" Complained Reina, as the party of inquisitors neared the hill. Two of the Cardinal's guards slid from their mounts and stalked up the hill toward the mouth of a small cave.

Hardwright pulled his horse to a stop, silently observing his men. A squawk of surprise and the sound of muffled struggle preceded a dazed Lester being dragged from his refuge.

A cruel smile spread across the Cardinal's face. "That, my dear acolyte, is our dinner guest."

Lester returned to consciousness with pain radiating across his face. As focus returned to his eyes, he was greeted by a modest campfire, five unfriendly figures and one with a smile far too wide for his face.

"Cut my hand on the damn kids snaggletooth." Grumbled the guard as he rubbed at the cut on the back of his hand. Sparing Lester an irritated look while stomping over to join his compatriots. Lester eyed them warily as he returned to his senses, his face still stinging where the guard had struck him.

The guards themselves wore armor that while functional, spoke of a quality long since eroded by time and use. These men were not cruel. They simply lacked the necessary care to be cruel. Lester gave a glare to the guard still shaking his hand from the sting of Lester's errant tooth who merely grinned in return. "That's a mighty mean look from a gimp like you." Chortled the smaller guard. His taller companion snorted. "Careful Boris! The boy might cry at us again and then we'll be in a right pickle!"

Lester's ears burned as he prepared a retort, but the Cardinal was faster. "Silence both of you." Hissed Hardwright. Divine Thread slithered out from beneath his black cloak, lashing the two men's mouths shut. The men froze, eyes glazing over into a pallid golden color. "That's no way to treat a guest. Be gone and see to the horses." Both guards rose to their feet like puppets pulled from the ground. They dreamily wandered away to where the horses were tied and began brushing the bedraggled creatures.

"Y-you're a priest!?" blurted Lester. Hardwright grinned, his attention snapping back to Lester. "A Cardinal in fact. My lovely protege and I were on our way to your quaint little town when we heard your distress." Lester's eyes darted to Reina who sat cross legged on the stump of a tree that seemed to have been cut down only moments ago. Her haughty demeanor was only equaled by the unexplained mirth in her eyes.

"Indeed, I thought we had perhaps found another possum in dire straits." A dainty hand rose to cover her lips as a grin teased at the edge of her mouth, and a scowl threatened at the edge of the Cardinal's. Lester eyed their cloaks as he failed to understand the one sided joke that seemed to play out before him. A proud looking seal comprising a set of golden shears closing on a thread sat upon Both of their chests.

"My apologies Cardinal, I was unaware that I was in such prestigious company. Pray tell, from what sect do you hail?" Lester delivered his most polished greeting he could manage through the rapidly swelling lip where the guard had struck him.

"Ugh, here." Reina's Thread flew from her fingertip fast as a whip lighting on Lester's swollen lip. A gentle touch, it ordered his flesh to heal itself and so it did. Angry cells mended together in an imitation of the healing power that Theodren now used. Lester held a hand to the spot where she had touched him more gently than any person had before. "We're with the Golden Shears, we're here for... what was it?" She turned to the Cardinal who had managed to school his face back into the practiced grin it was in before Reina's teasing.

"We are here..." He answered, glaring over his smile. "To bring Order." he turned back to Lester. "So tell me boy. Have you noticed anything out of Order?"

A grin cracked wide across Lester's face, splitting the thinly patched crack in his lip as the faces of Theodren, Eleina, and the many laughing townsfolk streamed across his mind's eye. Finally they would be held to account. This little backwater would finally recognize that Theodren was not the great man they all liked to pretend that he was. Lester resolved at that moment to bring them to the Mayor, he would know what to do.

"As a matter of fact, Cardinal. I believe I have a great deal to tell you."

Chapter 14
Promises

Theodren stared at the outline of his shadow on Eleina's door. A litany of excuses ran through his mind to explain his absence. It was true that he had been busy. He had spent every ounce of his vitae on the townspeople over the last two weeks. From scrapes and bruises on the knees and elbows of the children to the broken bones and bad backs of their parents.

He squared his shoulders and knocked on the plain wooden door. "Still" he said to himself. "I should have found the time."

"Found the time for what?" Yawned an over tired Evan as he answered the door. He blinked heavily as the Priest came into focus. "Theodren! The Priest is here Elly!" His eyes drifted down to the pot in Theodren's hand. "And he brought food!"

A slipper whizzed past Evan's head to smack into the door frame. "If either of you wake this baby, I have got another slipper and this time I won't miss." Threatened a tired sounding Eleina just out of eyesight.

Evan's mouth snapped shut, but a delirious smile remained. "Come in! Come in!" Whispered an excited Evan. Theodren chuckled as he stooped through the doorway. Sitting in her chair by the fire was a bedraggled Eleina. Wrapped in what appeared to be a robe that used to be white, and holding her baby girl that slept with a mouth held in a tiny "o" shape.

A smile leapt to Theodren's face as he knelt next to Eleina's chair to better admire the red haired babe. "Those might be the biggest cheeks I've ever *seen* on a child." Chuckled Theodren. Eleina preened at the compliment. "I think they're even bigger than the Mayor's." She joked.

"She's a well fed babe alright." Evan crooned as he stared dreamily at his daughter. Eleina groaned. "She may be, but I could smell that pot of stew all the way from mother's shop." She waved at Theodren with her free arm. "Hand it over, priest. I haven't had real food in days."

"What do you mean? I made you that stew yesterday." Asked Evan, cocking his head to the side. Eleina froze. "How could I forget? Of course you did, it was wonderful." As she spoke Theodren watched her nudge a small pot with a concerningly colored sludge further under the chair with her foot.

Theodren jumped in to save her. "But of course, nothing compares to your mother's cooking!" Evan, seeming satisfied with the answer, turned to grab what clean dishes he could find while Eleina gave Theodren a meaningful look of thanks.

As Evan returned with a bowl for Eleina, she gently passed a sleeping Theviana to a surprised Theodren who held the babe with all the gentleness of a man holding porcelain. A twinkle danced in her eye as she watched Theodren marvel over the child. With a pleased chuckle, she dug into the hearty stew.

Theodren was transfixed. He sank onto the stool across from Eleina as He stared down into the sleeping face of the child he had pulled into this world. From her wisps of red hair to her delicate nose and rosy cheeks, she was perfect. Faced with the product of his choices, every regret, every anxiety riddled thought left his mind. He had saved this life, and she was perfect.

His thoughts were returned to reality as he felt an itching on his chest. The caduceus Yggdrazil had left him with squirmed on his skin. Opening his mind's eye to it, he could see it vibrating, almost resonating. "But with what?" He wondered. A wisp of Vitae floated past his view, causing his head to snap back to Theviana. There, sitting in her tiny fluttering chest was a spring of Vitae, wrapped in a cradle of Divine Thread.

Theodren's mind raced. The gently sleeping child in his arms was possessed of both a spring of Vitae like his own, as well as a spool of Divine Thread. Barely born and already she possessed two world shaping powers. The very powers of creation itself. His brow furrowed deeper as considered what this might mean. Lost in thought he barely heard Evan when he and Eleina asked him the last question he expected to hear.

Theodren blinked. Rising from the depths of his spiraling thoughts, a baffled grin found his face. "Me? Godfather? Are you sure?" Eleina smacked him on the shoulder teasingly. "Don't pretend like there's someone better."

"What about your mom? I don't want to end up on the receiving end of her remedies-for-poor-behavior, pouch." Grinned Theodren. Eleina sighed, pulling the still sleeping Theviana back into her arms. "She'll just have to settle for being a grandmother."

Theodren turned to Evan, who was absentmindedly rubbing at a spot on his guardsman's armor on the wall. "And you're on board Evan?" The sleepy eyed father turned at hearing his name. "Hmm? Oh yes, fine. Not really that worried about it honestly. Not like we're going anywhere any time soon."

Eleina scoffed. "We've been over this Evan, It's important to plan ahead, and I want someone we can rely on to watch over our little girl." Theodren's sheepish grin only grew wider. It was high praise indeed to be named a godparent, and though he hoped to never have to assume the mantle of responsibility. He would do so gladly for the tiny life cradled in Eleina's arms. The mystery of the child's twin powers could wait. A feeling of contentment spread within him. There was nothing to fear and nothing to rush for. He could take his time teaching the child all about her Thread and Vitae when she was old enough. For now, she was right where she should be.

Theodren nodded. Bracing his hands on his knees as he rose to his feet. "I accept. I'm honored that you chose me." Eleina snorted, I'm too tired for manners, Priest." clutching Theviana to her chest she got to her feet. "Now begone with you, Thevi needs to eat and you need to make it home before nightfall. No more bears for you Uncle Theo. You've got something to live for."

Theodren's grin only widened as he was shepherded towards the door. "I'll come back tomorrow, see if I can't snag more of Polly's cooking on the way. "Please do." Said Eleina with intensity.

Theodren chuckled. "I'll see you tomorrow." He raised a hand to shield his eyes from the late afternoon sun. "There, that's the Priest." A smile still on his lips, he turned to the voice as a fist landed in his gut. He doubled over in a wheeze as shouts of surprise came from Eleina and Evan standing in the doorway behind him. Theodren tried to drop into a slow stance but was grabbed under the arms by two men he did not recognize. Still struggling for air, he looked around frantically trying to gain a sense of what was going on. As focus returned to his eyes, the cruel smile of Lusis Hardwright filled his eyes. "Father Stormwall, I have some questions for you regarding your management of this village's Order."

CHAPTER 15
DESTRUCTION

Theodren's blood froze in his veins as he stared into the dark and beady eyes of the Chief Inquisitor. "What is the meaning of this!?" Spat Eleina holding her hand over her baby's ears. Evan recovered from his shock and cleared his throat. "As town guard I demand you state your names and your business here."

Hardwright gave them an irritated look that spoke of an abiding disdain for all things common. "I simply loathe the braying of cattle." The remaining guards stalked over to Evan and Reina. Unable to turn his head to see, he heard the sounds of a scuffle behind him before Evan joined him on his knees and Eleina was shoved to the side, jolting Theviana awake and raising a wail from her tiny mouth.

"Unhand me you lout!" growled Eleina as she was shoved away from Theodren and her husband. "Leave them!" Shouted Theodren, Air finally returning to his lungs. "They've done nothing!" The beady eyes of the Cardinal returned to the Priest.

"Indeed? And what is it that they have not done?" Theodren's mouth would not move, could not move. How could he explain his actions in the face of the Golden Shears? His shame was complete, He sank into his despair and silence, unable to answer even for himself.

"Come now Father Stormwall, young master Hess has told me much of your recent exploits." Hardwright Gestured to where Lester stood. Grinning triumphantly at the kneeling priest who had failed him so. "He says you are much changed in recent weeks. He claims that you've miraculously healed every person in this backwater town of yours."

Lester spat. "Almost everyone." Hardwright's grin only widened. "A poor priest indeed. Neglecting a member of your flock who needed you most." Shame and rage bit deep into Theodren as he looked into the gleeful eyes of the boy who had brought him to his knees.

"Do tell us, what brought about this miraculous transformation?" Purred Hardwright. Theodren looked up at the cruel face smirking down at him. "My crimes are mine and mine only. I will go with you." Resigned to his fate, Theodren hung his head, unable and unwilling to resist; he waited for his punishment to begin.

"Tsk.Tsk.Tsk. Not good enough Father, not nearly good enough." Theodren shot the Cardinal a confused look. Lusis grinned back at him. "You *will* tell me what I want to know *now* or my men..."

CLANG!

Everyone froze in confusion as the sound was followed by the guard who held Eleina, falling to the ground in a heap. "Have at you, ye bastards!" shouted Pieter, brandishing the very shovel Theodren had given him almost a year ago. Jaws hung open at the bizarre spectacle of Pieter the pig farmer brandishing a mangled shovel as he rushed the guards holding Theodren to his knees.

A mighty yell turned into a yelp of surprise as his feet were snatched from the ground by a length of shimmering golden Thread. Like a fish on a hook he struggled as he was dangled in the air cursing. The owner of the Thread pulled the struggling man to where she leaned against the side of Evan And Eleina's home "I like you." She stated simply, poking the stunned farmer on the nose as he dangled upside down before her.

"Uh...aye." Reina giggled at his shock but did not lower him. "Unhand my fool of a husband girl, before I ruin that pretty face of yours." Polly growled as she stomped toward the stunned group. Reina gave a bored look to Polly as she snatched her feet in the same manner as her husband, dangling them before her.

"All of you stop!" Roared Theodren. Eyes pleading, he looked to Hardwright. "Let them go, I'll tell you everything." A thoughtful grin pulled at Lusis' face as he loomed over Theodren's kneeling form. "A willing mind is always so much more pliant to work with." he chuckled.

A cold and clammy finger pressed into his forehead. Theodren felt the man's thread slither into his mind, pushing and shoving its way through his thoughts and memories, violating his very mind. Memories of Yggdrazil, of his bargain, were shoved forward, forced before his mind's eye by Hardwright's questing thread. Theodren watched his moment of apostasy over and over again at the Cardinal's pleasure. "The goddess of life." Hardwright breathed quietly, an unhinged smile cracking his face. "In the palm of my hand." The Cardinal spun away from him, turning to Reina.

"On second thought." He turned to Reina. "The time has come, Acolyte, for your initiation."

Reina visibly perked up. "Truly? I'm ready! What must I do? I will surely succeed!" Hardwright's grin spread ever wider as he pulled a golden mask from the depths of his robe. "First, a gift. This mask is the mark of your station, it will help you to see those who have broken from the tapestry. Take it." Reina reached for the mask with reverence. She had seen but never spoken to many inquisitors wearing similar masks of smooth gold. It was elegant in its austerity. Its surface was broken only by holes for eyes and nothing else.

She had longed to see one up close, to hold it in her hands. Alas, fraternizing was forbidden between acolyte and inquisitor. Now finally she would receive her own mask. She raised the mask to her face, all of her goals and aspirations felt that much closer to her reach now. As the mask slid into place Hardwright's hand flew out and slapped her, hard, while extending his thread through the mask and into her mind.

Reina froze, her shoulders slumped as all personality left her, replaced instead with the dull gold eyes of Hardwright's Order.

"What did you do to her?" blurted Lester, Shocked at the sudden violence between the inquisitors. "Put that rotten bitch in her place where she should have been years ago." Spat Hardwright. Lester's hands balled into fists by his side, but he dare not speak out.

"Now then." Smiled Hardwright, smoothing his greasy hair back into place. He turned back to face the confused Theodren, staring down at the large man who watched the proceedings with growing confusion. "I'm a very busy man, Father Stormwall, and I simply can not be bothered with your backwater town. Therefore, I've decided that instead of wasting my time figuring out who knows what and from whom, the most efficient use of my valuable time is to simply kill them all, and let Odrain sort them out."

Theodren strained against the men holding him down, but without his vitae to aid him, his strength was merely mortal. "You can't! These people have a right to live!" Hardwright sighed as he backhanded the struggling Priest. "You silly peasants and your 'rights'". He strode back to Reina who stood rock still, beholden to the Cardinal's control. He stared at her for a silent moment. Eyes roving lasciviously over her form in a way that made even Lester cringe.

"I always hated you." He struck her, smiling as she lurched from the impact but remained standing, lifeless. "You're arrogant." He punched her stomach causing her to grunt and bend slightly. Spite and resentment from a life spent conniving and manipulating found a convenient outlet in his now pacified protege. "You're spoiled." He snarled, grabbing her breast and twisting cruelly. "And you have the personality of a squirrel." Hardwright had never possessed much power of his own, but he had always excelled at manipulating the minds of those around him, a necessary skill when one was forced to navigate the complicated echelons of a culture built on a power and authority that he could only borrow.

Reina would simply be the latest in a line of proteges that he had collected. And while there were many that he had converted before her, she would be the most pleasurable. He pulled back a hand to strike her again but was stopped by the frail hand of Lester. "You're hurting her!"

Hardwright looked down at Lester confused. "And?" He shoved the boy off and finished the strike he had interrupted. "Oh I see, come to rescue the maiden fair, have we boy?" Hardwright laughed at the boy, causing Lester's cheeks to flush a furious red.

"Worry not. She'll be well taken care of." A sly smile spread ear to ear on Hardwright's face. Lester struggled to form a protest. "Y-you Can't do that!" Hardwright had already turned from the boy, uninterested as he was in his complaints. He grabbed Reina by the ear, pulling her down to the thin lips that whispered loud enough for all to hear. "Kill them all."

Chapter 16
Wrath

Hardwright's order took effect immediately. Reina's threads that held Polly and Pieter suspended, swung wildly. Slamming the older couple into ground tree and rock like a child's plaything. Gurgling through mangled and broken jaws, they were slammed to the earth again with finality. The guards holding Theodren and Evan guffawed at the spectacle as Eleina, who had been watching in stunned silence, wailed at the sudden and grotesque death of her parents. Evan's eyes bulged as he struggled against the laughing guards.

Reina's dull golden eyes swiveled to the sound of Eleina's keening. In a blur of gold she was on her, daggers gleaming in the sunset, she sliced and stabbed at the red haired woman who could only turn and offer her back to the merciless killing machine, using her own flesh as a shield for her child who screamed at the fear and the noise in the air. Daggers tore at Eleina as she fell to the dirt still sheltering her wailing child as the life left her eyes.

A single strike from Reina ended the infant's cries as Evan snarled and fought like a man possessed to free himself from his captors. To his credit he managed to slam his head into the nose of one of the guards and rush to his feet. "I'll kill you, you heartless bitch!" he screamed, running at her. Reina's blade found his throat faster than he could react. Slicing clean through, he fell to his knees like a puppet with its strings cut. His face hit the dirt feet from his wife and child. Their collective blood pooling in a cruel puddle of mud.

Theodren thrashed, and screamed a cloud of curses. He Screamed for Odrain, He screamed for Yggdrazil. But no help came. Through his furious tears he saw the legs of Reina standing before him. He stared up into the pallid gold and lifeless eyes of the woman before him as she raised a blade slicked in the blood of his friends to kill him.

"Not him. Not yet." Hardwright grabbed Theodren by the hair, turning his head to face the lifeless forms of his friends. "I have uses for him." Reina backed away from the priest, her attention snapped to the surrounding houses. In a blur of gold she was gone, as she streaked from house to house, each one greeted her with screams, and then silence.

Chapter 17
Retribution

Hardwright witnessed the carnage with satisfaction on his face. He stalked away from Theodren to better watch the spectacle of Reina's violence. She would make an excellent addition to his collection. The Cardinal had collected many promising young acolytes over the years. Ambitious youngsters like Reina would rise to prominence, and in his generosity he would offer them patronage. Taking them under his wing until the time was right, and then he would seize control.

What few peers he had, thought that he used his thread for mind control. He scoffed at the idea. Mind control was lazy, crude and unimaginative. His influence was far superior to paltry mind control. From a young age Lusis used his thread to worm its way into the minds of his victims. Seizing control of their frontal lobe, he attacked their sense of self, imposing his will over theirs leaving just the tiniest fragment of their mind intact to witness his workings. He knew that while Reina was busy killing the townspeople with gusto. In her mind a part of her would remain a captive passenger, able to witness but not influence her actions. Hardwright reveled in his superiority. This carnage of her own making would break her. And when the guilt finally fractured her mind, he would erase every facet of her being. His tongue ran along his lips then she would truly be his to do with as he pleased.

***

Theodren could not look away from the devastation playing out before him. It was his fault. All of the death that took place here today was on him, and him alone. There would be no mysterious God to offer him salvation. He was alone amidst the broken bodies of his friends. He felt a wriggling on his arm and he startled. Perhaps not totally alone.

The vineling slithered up his arm to the collar of his robe, poking out at the hand that held Theodren down by the shoulder. Theodren glared up at the man, grinning stupidly at the carnage around him, Theodren peered deep into his Vitae, into his soul. A swirl of muddy colors affronted Theodren's inner eye. It was a soul corrupted by a lifetime of casual violence and indifference. That the man had a soul at all angered Theodren to his core.

"You don't deserve that soul." Theodren growled. The guard looked down at him "Wha?" The vineling had found the wound on the man's hand, a small cut from where he had struck Lester's tooth. The vineling coiled up like a snake, and launched itself into it, burrowing deep into the man's flesh. He screamed, "He got me! Something's got me! What is at?"

Theodren felt the vineling burrow deeper into the man's arms, deeper into his chest where it coiled around the man's black heart. Greedily it siphoned Vitae from the man's vital organs. His right arm now unsecured, Theodren swung a wild haymaker at the panicked guard holding his other shoulder. The blow rocked the mercenary off his feet sending him sprawling into the dirt

Theodren scrambled over to the dazed man, anxious to dispatch him and then the other man before the more distant guards took notice. His rage boiled over, slamming fist after fist into the man's face. The guard's hands flailed and slapped at him as he rained blow after furious blow into the broken face. With a wet crack, Theodren felt the front of the man's skull cave inward.

Almost immediately, he felt the pulverized guard's vitae rush toward his fist, seeking an outlet, seeking life. Theodren absorbed it with alacrity. There was not much to be had, but it would have to be enough.

Theodren rushed the two guards who had been holding Evan on his knees before his final stand. The men were preoccupied with the screaming guard, who scrabbled at his chest, trying to dislodge the vineling that roiled beneath his skin.

In a berserker rage he grabbed the men by the backs of their collars slamming them hard into the ground. Dazed and wheezing from the impact they could only lay there as Theodren stomped his leather boot through the first man's skull. The second man scrambled to his knees with the speed of a skilled fighter and rushed at Theodren, driving a shoulder into his gut, hoping to knock the enraged man off balance. But he had neither the strength nor the momentum to even budge him. Theodren rained elbow after elbow into the man's back. Vicious strikes that cracked his attackers ribs and shoulders. To his credit the guard held fast to Theodren's waist, either out of fear or desperation he held tight to Theodren, seeking to drive him back and away from his comrades, but try as he might, Theodren would not be moved. He reached down and wrapped a large arm around the man's throat, hooking the crook of his elbow over the guard's Adams apple and squeezed. He squeezed as the man gurgled and flailed at him. He squeezed as the man clawed and scraped at his arm for freedom, for air. He squeezed until he was rewarded with a sickening *pop* as the man's skull was dislocated from his spine and the guard went limp. Theodren dropped the corpse beside its comrade, their vitae flowing into him, just as he had seen it flow before from prey to predator and he turned to the whimpering and weakened guard on his knees. The vineling bulged under the man's skin from within his stomach. It had feasted heartily off of the guard's vitae growing to twice its original size.

A whine came from the hollow, sunken face of the guard. "What is this? What did you do to me?" Theodren's cold glare roved over the vineling's handiwork. The man was but a shadow of himself from mere moments ago. The Priest held out his hand towards the man's chest and answered. "Retribution." Hearing its new name, the Vineling burst from the man's chest, questing roots quickly changing into the familiar handle of Theodren's hammer, slowly extending and growing from out of the chest cavity it had been feasting within. When Theodren expected it to stop growing, it did not. It was still his hammer, but it now stood at equal height with him, its head now covered in gruesome spikes and wrapped in barbed and bloody vines. He took hold of the weapon. As he did, it relinquished its grip on the guard's ruined corpse, which fell to the ground in a rattle of empty armor and hollow bones.

One of the Cardinal's two remaining guards turned at the sound that was at odds with the chorus of screams rising from the town. His brows shot to his hairline as he quickly alerted his companion to the enraged and bloodied beast of a man stomping toward them, Retribution in hand. Hardwright witnessed none of this, enraptured as he was with Reina's savagery amongst the humble homes of the town. He was far too busy preening over his cleverness to notice the doom that stomped toward him.

The first guard jabbed a spear at Theodren's midsection, hoping the threat would keep him at distance. But if the guard was under the impression that Theodren was interested in avoiding pain he was sorely mistaken. The spear buried itself in Theodren's side, scraping against his ribs and lodging itself in tightly. Theodren roared at the man as he snapped the shaft in his left hand before bringing Retribution to bear in his right. The mighty hammer slammed into the first guard's head as he clung to his now useless spear. A sickening crunch filled the air as the force of the blow removed his head from his shoulders. Theodren yanked the spear head from his already closing wound and stomped over the first guard's headless body, absorbing its Vitae as he passed.

The second guard threw down his spear, opting for a short sword and buckler instead. He readied himself as Theodren approached, planning parries, dodges and counter strikes to a number of opening blows Theodren might attempt. What he was not prepared for was the speed with which Theodren closed the distance. Retribution now gripped in both hands, He swung with the full force of his rage at the insignificant man between him and the Cardinal. The second guard raised his buckler just in time to catch the savage blow, but it was no use. The hammer cleaved through shield, muscle and bone like wet cloth, crushing everything in its path. The second guard was tossed aside like a ragdoll, landing in a broken heap just feet from Hardwright who jumped at the disturbance from his victorious self praise. As he turned to see the cause, for the first time that day. His smile wavered.

Theodren made a gruesome sight as he stalked toward the Cardinal. Six and a half feet of rage and muscle covered in the blood and gristle of Hardwright's guards, wielding a truly massive hammer, covered in cruel barbed vines that appeared alive in the giant's hands.

"HARDWRIGHT!" Roared Theodren as each step brought him closer to the spindly Cardinal. "FOR YOUR CRIMES AGAINST THE INNOCENTS OF THIS VILLAGE, I DECLARE YOU GUILTY AND YOUR SOUL FORFEIT!" Theodren pointed his hammer at the man. "HERE TODAY SHALL YOU FACE JUDGEMENT FOR YOUR CRIMES. STAND READY FOR YOUR RETRIBUTION."

"Come now." Squeaked Hardwright. "Surely there's some arrangement we can come to? Perhaps a larger town more suited to your obvious talent!" As he spoke, Theodren saw Thread snake out from the edge of Hardwright's sleeve faster than he could react, it lashed out, striking deep into Theodren's mind.

While Hardwright may have excelled at manipulating the minds of others, and even a confused and weakened Theodren from moments ago. Theodren's mind was now stone, driven by a singular purpose. Retribution. Hardwright's triumphant grin fell from his face as Theodren trudged ever closer, weathering the Cardinal's assault on his mind as though he were walking through a stiff breeze. Hardwright cursed and screamed and grunted as his thread lashed at Theodren's mind trying in vain to find purchase upon this juggernaut of a man. But it was like trying to stop a boulder that was halfway down the mountain already.

Finally, standing before a panting and sweaty Hardwright, Theodren stared down at the greasy man, eyes a brilliant green with Vitae and Rage. "I'm unarmed!" Whined Hardwright, falling as he stumbled backwards, away from the vision of wrath advancing toward him.

"So were they." Growled Theodren. Rage filled his arms as he raised Retribution above the Cardinal's head, the shadow of it making Hardwright flinch as he cowered from his impending judgement. Theodren brought the hammer down with all the rage, pain and strength he possessed roaring out his wrath to the darkening sky.

In a flash of gold, Reina was there. Deflecting the hammer blow with her thread held between the blades in her hands. Still, for all her speed and skill, she could not completely prevent Retribution from finding the Cardinal. Theodren's hammer drove her hands down and Retribution glanced away from the coward's head and slammed instead into Hardwright's leg, pulverizing the bone and tissue beneath the man's knee. Hardwright screamed in pain as he rolled on the bloodied ground, clutching the mangled remains of his leg. "You worthless bitch! Kill him! Kill him now!"

A flurry of blades lashed out at Theodren. Wickedly sharp daggers slashed at him, but any wound that Reina dug into his flesh quickly mended itself almost as rapidly as it was carved. Conventional wisdom would have Theodren blocking or avoiding the maelstrom of golden daggers slicing wicked lines across his body. But for Theodren, each cut was a penance. He bore Reina's assault through gritted teeth as he responded with swings of his own weapon. Retribution whistled through the air as it sought the woman who murdered his friends, his flock and worst of all his Godchild.

He channeled his Vitae into his arms, swinging faster and faster as she danced around him, until finally, he connected. The very edge of Retribution clipped her side as she attempted to pirouette around it. The force of the blow flung her sidelong into one of the squat thatched houses that crumbled from her impact.

Theodren chased after her, leaving the crippled Cardinal to whimper alone. Alone except, for Lester. Lester reappeared from behind What was once the Fiero household. With a crooked gait, he ran to the Cardinal. "Cardinal Hardwright, you have to stop her! She's killing everyone!" Hardwright looked up at the teenager in confusion. "Isn't this what you wanted, boy?" He spat.

Lester reeled. What had he wanted? What had he expected? He wanted Theodren and the townspeople to feel his humiliation, he wanted them to understand their error in ostracizing him. He wanted them to hurt, as he had hurt. When he Told the inquisitors of the change in the Priest and in the town, he assumed there would be castigation and humiliation for Theodren and for all those who dared to laugh at him. But this... There was no more mocking laughter, there were no more screams, for there was no one left alive to. "I didn't want this." Lester mumbled.

A plot formed in Hardwright's mind as he looked at the despairing child. "Bring me to my horse, I can end that bitches assault. Lester nodded quickly grabbing Hardwright under his arm, he shouldered the cardinal as best he could, dragging the cursing and groaning Cardinal to his horse. Hardwright used what thread he had left to tourniquet his mangled leg as he reached out to his horse. Hauling himself into the saddle, he pulled a flask from his bag and drank greedily.

Lester watched the furious battle between Theodren and Reina with mounting anxiety. If the priest really could heal people then he could fix this. He could make all the death and destruction go away. Lester would go back to being hated, but at least he wouldn't be a murderer. He thought to himself.

Lester watched as Reina's thread lashed tightly around Theodren's neck, stopping him mid furious swing. Reina's once pristine armor was battered and broken in several places and she stood at an odd angle with a shoulder that hung lifeless beside her. But stood she did, feeling none of the pain or crushing wounds she had suffered so far.

Theodren scrabbled at the thread around his neck, trying with all his might, to break free and continue his assault. Lester turned back to the Cardinal. "Please, you have to stop this!"

Hardwright looked down from his flask at the teenager pleading at him with tears in his eyes. Truly he was a hideous child. "Do inform the mayor that his invitation stands." With that Hardwright struck, like a viper at Lester with the reins. He recoiled with a surprised cry as he cupped his now bleeding eye.

Hardwright fled. Whipping his horse hard with the lead, he gritted his teeth at the pain of his mangled leg bouncing freely against the side of his horse. Soon he was past the town, and before long he was gone into the night, free of the carnage, free of Theodren's wrath.

Lester cursed himself for a fool yet again, as he held his hand to the cut above his eye. The mayor's invitation? When Lester brought Hardwright and his retinue to Mr. Sylverwyrm's, he had hardly seemed surprised at all. Lester had wanted to ask but was shooed out of the room while they talked. He turned his eye back to the fight between Reina and the Priest. Unable to break free of her Thread, Theodren yanked on the golden string sending her flying toward him.

"Stop!" screamed Lester. He ran as best he could toward the two avatars of destruction as they railed against each other. His cries fell on deaf ears as their one and only focus was the other's demise.

With a roar, Theodren released Retribution. The vineling retracted up his tattered sleeve as Theodren latched onto The small inquisitor with great meaty paws. Grabbing her by the neck he slammed her into the dirt. Thread forgotten, she slashed, stabbed and cut at the Priest.

Theodren merely grimaced through the pain, refusing to relinquish his grip on the woman. He glared into the face of the golden mask. If Reina felt any fear or pain, none of it showed in the dull golden eyes behind the mask. He slammed her into the dirt again and again. Squeezing the life from her as tears of rage and shame fell upon the mask from Theodren's face.

"STOP!" Lester threw himself at the pair, trying desperately to stop the violence. Theodren froze at the interruption, his grip easing ever so slightly. Reina's flurry of strikes picked up speed, jabs and slashes flew in every direction, catching Lester in the throat.

Blood gushed from the wound splashing onto The pair locked in struggle. As he fell, Lester reached for Reina's golden mask. With what strength he had left he pulled till the mask broke free from Reina's face with a resounding 'RIP!'

The Cardinal's Thread binding Reina's mind snapped free of the mask that had been anchoring his power. As her mind returned to the forefront of her being, she blinked.

Chapter 18
A Bargain Struck

Reina blinked as she surfaced from the Cardinal's influence. Her blades clattered to the ground as her eyes beheld the terrifying visage of the bloodied man above her. She shrank before his rage as tears sprang to her eyes.

"No." She whispered Theodren's grip on her throat released as he watched tears flood her eyes and a deep purple of grief enveloped her soul. She broke free of Theodren, struggling to her feet, she cried out in pain as she hobbled over to the family of corpses that she had left in her wake.

"No. No. No. No. No!!!" She fell to her knees before the mangled bodies of Pieter and Polly, limbs bent at unnatural angles, she was faced with the horror of what she had done. Her breath came faster and faster as the magnitude of her destruction settled upon her, she scrambled over to Evan and Eleina.

"I'm sorry! I didn't mean... this isn't what... I didn't want..." She reached out a shaking hand toward Evan's corpse. In his dying moments he had dragged himself closer to his wife and child. His reaching hand just inches from the tiny lifeless fingers of his newborn daughter.

The blood on Reina's hand caught her eye. She looked down to examine herself, trying to see where the blood would end but it did not. She was soaked in it. She screamed the wail of a broken soul as she faced the product of her barbarism. She tore at her clothes with weak and desperate hands trying to distance herself from the blood.

She fell further to her elbows as she tried to extricate the smallest corpse from the arms of her mother, hoping against hope that there was still life left in the babe.

"Have you not taken enough?" Growled Theodren from behind her. She turned to see the Priest, holding the limp body of Lester in his arms. Theodren glowered down at her. "Was taking their lives not enough? The last thing Eleina ever did was shield her child from you. And now you steal her from her mother's arms?" Theodren's rage was beginning to give way to an exhaustion that ached deep within his soul. A grief so vast and so deep that he had barely even begun to wade into its waters.

Tears fell freely down Reina's face as she shook her head. She sobbed. "I'm sorry! I'm so sorry! Please!" She threw herself at his feet, prostrating herself before him. "That boy said you healed people! You can fix this! Please! I don't want this! Kill me! Torture me! I don't care! But please!" She begged. "Bring them back!"

Theodren stared down at her, rage giving way to a deep consuming sadness. "That door is not mine to open."

"He speaks the truth child." Reina's head snapped up at the otherworldly whisper that pierced her very soul. The world seemed frozen in place as she searched for the source of the voice.

Eleina's body rose from the ground like a puppet on strings. Grotesque in its grace, the corpse came to its feet still holding the child. Eyes wild with fear, Reina's mouth fell open in a silent scream of horror as she beheld the ghoulish figure. The corpse' eyes snapped open, revealing two voids of black that sat above a too wide smile. **"It is mine."**

Words failed Reina as her fear silenced her broken sobs. She could only stare at the ghoul who looked around at the carnage with lightless eyes. **"You've brought many guests to my door, child. Many of your order have driven great trails of travelers to my step, but none have ever delivered such an interesting one."** Eleina's corpse dragged a bloody finger along Theviana's cold and lifeless face. A curious grin spread across the ghoul's mouth.

"What are you?!" Shrieked Reina, finding her voice through the fear. **"How rude of me! Of course I know how important names are to you mortals."** The corpse gave a halting bow like a marionette on tangled strings. **"I am Nihila. And I hold the Black Door."**

Reina's mind reeled as her faith broke for the second time that day. She had believed her entire life that the church of Holy Order was a bastion of goodness in the world. What little she had been told of her father was that through the Church, he held the Order of the world together for the greater good.

Her entire life she had built her plans around the accolades she would attain through the Church. The rose gold image of the praise and grandeur she would enjoy in her service, was shattered in a single bloody afternoon.

But as she beheld the otherworldly horror of Nihila smiling down at her, another foundational pillar of her worldview crumbled. The Church had lied. The creature standing before her could be nothing less than a god, and it was not Odrain.

Sobs returned to wrack Reina's shoulders. "Why!?" She wailed. "Why me!?" Nihila chuckled as she strode past Reina to the frozen form of Theodren, still glowering down at the spot where Reina used to be.

"Because my sister." Nihila purred, running a hand down Theodren's arm. **"Finally did something interesting."**

Reina stared, confused, at the god whose attention remained fixed on Theodren. **"Quite the specimen, isn't he?"** The way Nihila squeezed and caressed at the large man sickened her but she said nothing. **"He want's me, you know."** Nihila shot a coy smile at Reina's shocked face.

"After all you took from him, he wants me so badly I can taste it like... like the scent of meat on the air." A frown pulled at the edges of her dead lips. **"But his duty won't let him. He'll kill and kill until not a single Golden Thread remains on this earth. And then and only then would he give himself to me."**

Nihila raised a hand to her mouth like a school girl telling a secret. **"But I'll tell you something he doesn't know."** Reina eyed her warily, waiting for the corpse to continue. **"He will never see my door."**

Reina's eyes grew wide at that. Immortality was something many of the most powerful lords of the capitol merely pretended at. Often demanding divine mending from the Order in exchange for underhanded undertakings from the highest levels of the Church to the parliament itself.

Nihila snorted as if reading directly from Reina's mind. **"You mortals are all the same, greedy and careless to the point of destruction, caring naught for the ruin you leave in your wake."**

The corpse stared up at the Imposing priest . **"But Theodren, This man gave up power, wealth and nobility just to serve the little people of this little village for all his days."**

A melancholy sigh escaped the corpse's purple lips. **"But he will never cross my threshold."** An irritated edge infused the god's words.

"My darling sister saw to that." Nihila poked at the Caduceus in Theodren's chest, exposed by Reina's blades. "There are more!?" Blurted Reina, surprised at her own outburst.

Nihila shot a mischievous look at Reina who cringed at the look. Nihila continued. **"My sister is not one to take. Giving is all she knows how to do. How curious that she would take the best of her creations away from me."**

The corpse turned its eyes back to Reina as if an idea had suddenly occurred to her. **"And speaking of giving."** Nihila stalked back over to Reina, a slick smile on her borrowed face. **"I have a gift for you."**

Reina cowered before the walking corpse. "A gift?" Was all she could mutter. Nihila looked down to the quiet bundle in her arms. **"Theodren pulled this babe from my grasp just weeks ago."** Reina's eyes welled up at the baby's mention. "Weeks!?" She sobbed.

Nihila continued. **"He almost did it without my sister's help, but your Weaver."** Tsk'd the corpse. **"Would rather break his own priest's Thread, than allow this child to be born."**

Nihila held the baby out to Reina who recoiled, unable to bear the sight of the violence she had wrought on her smallest victim. **"I want to know why."**

Reina's hands shook as she reached for the babe. If she could take the child from this god of death, her sins might just be bearable, but there had to be a catch. She paused as her hands hovered inches from the child. Her mother liked to remind her that "no gift is free." And she looked at the god with mistrust in her eyes.

"What do you require of me in return?" Nihila smiled down at the woman. **"Clever girl. But fret not, all I require is your service, and your Thread."**

Reina was shocked. Her Thread was what had elevated her, her entire life. It had gained her the praise of her peers and patrons alike. It had opened doors for her. She looked around at what remained of the village that was a thriving community only an hour ago. It had slaughtered a town full of innocents.

"Take it." Spat Reina, reaching further for the baby. Nihila pulled the babe just barely out of reach. **"Understand child, that what I give you in it's place is no paltry power like the Thread you so carelessly bandied about. What I give you is the waters of Acheron, the river of Woe. Darkness shall follow you all your days. Do you understand?"**

Reina was beyond listening and beyond caring. Whatever consequence she suffered she no longer cared. "I accept." An amused expression crossed Nihila's face as she placed the bundle in Reina's reaching arms

The moment the babe touched Reina's hands she grunted as her lengthy Thread was ripped from her soul. This was a pain far deeper than any she had ever experienced, but there was nothing that could force her to drop the child in her arms.

She clutched Theviana to her chest as tears once again sprang to her eyes. The cold of the baby's corpse soaked into her skin. The sensation repulsed the woman, but she held the babe all the more tightly as she felt a different kind of cold, creeping and sickly, flow from the child into her very soul. A river of ice cold Acher grew within her as she drained the death from the tiny form in her arms, leaving behind the symbol of a simple black door on her chest.

As time returned to its natural flow, Theodren's head snapped to where Reina now knelt, feet from where she had been only a second prior. He opened his mouth to speak but was struck dumb by the last sound he had dared to hope for.

The cry of an infant.

CHAPTER 19
A CHILD IN NEED

The still form of Lester jostled in his arms as he rushed to the ground beside Reina. The boy, he placed as quickly and as gently as he could on the ground before he pulled back the cloth covering the babe cradled by a hysterically sobbing Reina.

Theviana wailed at the world. Great ear splitting cries that echoed to the empty buildings springing alight from dinner fires left untended. Laughter joined the babes cry of distress as Theodren turned his attention to the woman who cried and laughed simultaneously at the tiny bundle in her arms.

Theodren reached for the babe in Reina's arms. The woman tensed, eyes wide and wild with fear, as she clung tighter to the child. A spike of anger formed in Theodren, that he would be kept from his Godchild by the woman who orphaned her in the first place, but as he prepared to take the child from Reina, his eyes caught on the colors of her soul.

Her soul was a flurry of colors. Theodren had never seen so many in one soul at a time. There was grief and joy, anger and anxiety, and stranger still amongst a multitude of others, There in her chest was a familiar bloom of desperate love. He had seen it in the mother bear who threw herself between her child and him. He had seen it amongst the families of the town, and just an hour ago he had seen it in Eleina's bosom as she held Theviana in her warm arms.

Theodren shook his head in disgust at the broken woman standing between him and his Godchild. Whatever this woman had done to return her to the living was not his concern. Theviana needed him now, and he would not leave her in the arms of her parent's murderer.

"Release my Godchild woman, I will not ask again." Reina ripped the child away from his hands. She hobbled to her feet crying out in pain from the myriad injuries she had suffered from her battle with Theodren. Theviana cried all the louder as Reina held her tight to the cold and bloody armor on her chest.

"She's mine! I brought her into this world, I gave my Thread for this girl, she's mine!" shouted a defiant but desperate Reina. Her eyes darted around the burning village, seeking an escape like a cornered animal. Reina took a halting step, fleeing from the Imposing priest. After three hobbling strides, she tripped. Twisting as she fell she landed on her shoulder, sparing Theviana the fall but jostling her broken frame further with the impact and she cried out a pain she had never felt before.

Reina's exhaustion both physical and mental, had caught up to her. There was no more adrenaline or shock to shelter her from the pain of her injuries. Nevertheless she crawled, holding the screaming babe tight as she struggled.

A deep sigh left Theodren as he walked after the nearly feral woman. His anger had exhausted him. A numbness of the soul ebbed through Theodren as he reached down and halted Reina by the shoulder. She gave a cry of pain as he flipped her onto her back. Theodren pulled the wailing babe from her grasp as Reina slapped and clawed at him, sobbing as she pleaded with him. "She needs me!"

Theodren did not enjoy the terror and anxiety he saw growing in the woman's soul, but he steeled himself as he walked away from the murderess. With each step he took from Reina, Theviana's cries grew weaker and weaker. Theodren's eyes snapped down to the babe in his arms that grew colder with each step. In a panic, he pushed Vitae into the child. The spring of Vitae in the babe's soul was still there, but it grew weaker. He tried to push his own vitae toward it but was rebuffed by a power he didn't recognize.

Theodren's brow furrowed at the mote of cold power keeping his Vitae from the child. Theodren stopped dead in his tracks as he sought an alternative path to infuse the child with the healing waters of his Vitae. She was dying, again, and there was nothing he could do. He shook his head, refusing to give up. Theodren assaulted the mysterious river of power, every angle and every trick he could think of was attempted, and failed. His growing frustration was halted in surprise as he felt a hand grab at the hem of his robe. He looked down to see Reina climbing him. Fabric bunched in her hands she dragged herself up his side toward the babe growing cold and quiet in his arms.

"Why are you so damn tall?" she grunted as she scaled the stunned man. Theodren could only stare at the strange woman as she pulled herself upright against him. Exhausted and leaning into his chest on one good leg, she placed a hand on Theviana's head.

Theodren's mouth fell open as the river of cold power was drained from the child into Reina's palm. A trickle of the icy ethereal water still flowed in the child, but it was enough for Theodren to push past with his vast store of Vitae, warming the child with life water, it eased Theviana's cries which had returned in full.

"I told you. She needs me." Reina slumped in exhaustion, sliding down the front of Theodren's robe, he caught her in his left arm on instinct while still holding Theviana in his right. Theodren stared down at the broken woman now asleep in his arms. A hundred questions swirled in his mind for the unconscious woman, but she was in no state to answer them.

Theodren moved her further up into his arms as he turned to the silent village he had called home. The bodies left behind by the sleeping woman in his arms were everywhere. He may not have been able to save him, but they would still need him now, one final time. His eyes fell to the shovel Pieter had dropped in his mad rush to save his daughter and granddaughter. "A mad bastard to the end Pieter." Theodren let out a sad chuckle as he walked over to the family of friends that now lay in the dirt. As he mentally prepared himself for the work of their burial, he was unnerved by the mysterious smile that was frozen for all time, across Eleina's face.

Chapter 20
Travel Plans

It was hours since Theodren had started digging. By now his back should have been aching and stiff from the labor, but the vitae he had pulled from the guards rejuvenated the muscles as he worked, and planned his next move. Three years ago, Theodren had sworn a duty to the people of this village, but once the last grave was dug and prayer was said. The people would have no further need of him, ever again.

He had managed to pull the bodies of his flock from the wreckage of the town. In his mind he had always described this little hamlet as quiet. But as the silence stretched on into the night, the word took on a terrible new meaning. He had labored like a man possessed, Vitae speeding him in his task as he dug graves through the night and into the dawn.

He laid each of them to rest, searching within his memory for meaningful moments he shared with each of the towns folk as he laid them within their grave. From the elderly seamstress Sarah and her hands that now lay still across her chest, to the mending of a toy for a child whose name he could hardly remember. He lay them all in the cold earth until only five graves remained.

These would be the hardest of all. He grabbed the broken form of Pieter, lowering him gently into the earth even as he determined to commit the sound of his deep and booming laugh to memory. Pieter enjoyed life so fully that he chose never to take it seriously. Committing his life to good humor and good memories that

Theodren had the privilege of sharing, if only for a couple years. In his final moments, he bravely charged in to protect his daughter and grandchild. Even managing to incapacitate one of Hardwright's men with his shovel turned club. "A mad bastard to the end Pieter." He chuckled sadly.

Next he gingerly scooped up Polly and laid her beside her husband. She had always had a sharp tongue, but there was a kindness behind it that Theodren felt he had never fully appreciated. That she had found love with a man like Pieter baffled some of the other villagers but it made sense to Theodren. As he began shoveling loose dirt over the two forms nestled together, tears that he thought had long since run dry pricked at the corners of his eyes.

He did not want to fill this next grave. Evan had lost so much blood that he weighed almost nothing, but Theodren could barely carry the weight of it in his mind. Evan had always been quick with a smile. A good natured man who seemed to think nothing of tomorrow, choosing to focus all of his joy on the moment of today. He remembered the overwhelming joy that lit his face when Thevi was born. And he remembered the animalistic rage with which he fought to get to Eleina and their child when they were in danger. He deserved so much better than this little hole in the ground.

As he turned to the next body, his sorrow was mixed with a deep unease. Eleina's body had moved. It had been disorienting when Reina had disappeared and reappeared holding a living Theviana, and while he was filled with hope and joy that the child survived, it was tempered by the strange and unearthly smile that still spread across Eleina's face.

Her smiles had always been soft, warm things that were charming in their subtlety. But the grotesquerie that sprawled across her face was not her. He did his best to put it out of his mind as he laid her beside her husband.

When he first arrived in the village years ago. Eleina had been the only one to speak to him. The rest of the townspeople were afraid of offending him, but she was fearless. He was equally afraid of offending the townsfolk as they were of him. A small smile cracked at the edge of his mouth as he remembered the first thing she had ever said to him. "We're used to wide priests, never seen a giant one though." The crowd of nosy onlookers gasped into silence. "Does your Weaver protect you from the scourge of low doorframes?" In that moment, the silence had stretched on for what felt like an eternity, before a booming laugh ripped from his throat.

He had known from that moment that he would be happy here. And despite the chaos of her birth, he had been glad to help Eleina welcome her daughter to the world.

Theodren looked to the last surviving member of his flock. Theviana remained asleep in Reina's equally still arms. Theodren had placed Reina and the baby against a tree beside Eleina's home. While not expecting her to run away with the child in her battered state, Theodren took the precaution of blanketing the pair in roots that would certainly keep them warm, but also prevent a sudden escape.

Their chests rising and falling in unison, he struggled to find a solution to the woman. Every attempt to remove Eleina's daughter from the woman resulted in the same thing.

A river of cold energy flooded the space around the babe's Vitae, threatening to smother it out of existence like a candle dropped in a pond. It was only Reina's touch that seemed to keep the ethereal waters at bay. Something had happened to bring Theviana back to the world of the living. Reina had moved several feet in the blink of an eye, and was suddenly holding a living baby that was dead in the arms of her mother only a second before.

There was only one conclusion he could come to. A god had intervened, and it was not his. Yggdrazil had remained absent or at least, quiet, for some time now. Theodren could think of one god and one god only that could open the black door and bring Theviana back, and he shuddered at the thought.

Theodren placed Pieter's mostly flattened shovel beside the final grave as he lowered Lester's frail and crooked frame into the hole. "A child unwanted by the village will burn it down just to feel its warmth." was something his mother had told him once. Lost on him as it was then, it was a stark wording of his failure towards Lester now.

The boy was sly, disrespectful, conniving and ill-formed. But he was also an unwanted child, who wandered into town, alone and neglected, to fend for himself. Lester had lied, stolen and manipulated in order to make his way through life in the village. In the end he had made a truly terrible mistake in service to a petty vendetta that could have been avoided if Theodren had properly cared for the boy as he had the other townspeople. In the end, it was Lester that had stopped the blood shed, late as it may have been.

Theodren said a prayer for the boy as he had the others, wishing him a better life on the other side of the Black Door as he began shoveling the dirt back over the last body. His service had ended.

Reina had done brutal and efficient work while in Hardwrights' thrall. With the last of his flock buried, his thoughts turned to the journey ahead of him. Theviana would not be safe in the lands of Grandia. Born only two weeks and already death and destruction had found the babe.

No, There was only one place where he would find refuge for the girl. His father's lands to the north was a cold place that bred a hardy people with no time for a church full of rules and dogma. They lived according to their own Order. Where might was right and strength was a requirement of life. In the Nordlands, The people were as warm as the land was frigid, and he would need that hospitality when he returned to his father's hall.

Their parting six years ago had not been a pleasant one. In his excitement to see the larger world beyond the fjords and mountain tops of his homeland, he had left without his father's blessing. The two had fought, with words and with fists as was their way in the north. All told, Theodren left for the Conclave's academy, with a cracked rib and a split lip on his smiling face as he headed south with his mother's tales of grandeur and greatness filling his head.

A frustrated sigh left Theodren as he got to work laying stones at the head of the many graves he had dug. No one had been more excited about Theodren's Thread than his mother Sigrid. She was the only Priestess in the whole of the north and she had been ecstatic at her only child's embrace of her faith as he discovered his Thread.

He was not sure if, or how he would tell her his tale, but he would have six weeks to think about it. He scratched at the stubble forming on his chin, as the first fingers of dawn poked at the retreating darkness. He would need to move fast. The Cardinal had escaped, and when the young priestess failed to return to him, he would send scouts, and when the scouts saw the graves, they would know that he survived.

Theodren pinched at the headache forming behind his eyes. He had no time. There was no time to search for survivors, certainly not enough time to bury the one hundred and twenty nine men women and children Theodren had pulled from the wreckage of this tiny town. But he would not allow expediency to excuse him from his final duty to these people. He stood over Eleina's grave. Grief welled in him like icy river water breaking through a dam. She was a truly kind soul who had made this place his home, and now she was gone from this world. He had hoped that if he ever did find love that it would have been with a woman like her. But as he stood there, staring at the loose dirt that covered her he knew. There would never be another like Eleina. All that was left of her was the tiny redheaded babe that barely clung to life in the arms of her mothers murderer.

"So..." Theodren jumped. Just feet behind him stood Reina, holding the gently sleeping babe. "What now?" Theodren's brow furrowed at her. She was yet another knot he would need to untangle. For now he would need her to keep the babe alive, watching her pull death from the child made him certain. "You are coming with me." He turned away, unwilling to treat with her for longer than a few words at a time.

Reina paused only for a moment before she walked after him. "Where? What if..." Theodren rounded on her nostrils flaring in irritation. "Do not ask me questions, the only reason you're still alive is because of her." Theodren jabbed a finger at his Godchild in her arms. "Theviana withers without you, and until I figure out why that is and how to fix my Godchild, you are coming with me, *quietly.*" Theodren stared hard into her face waiting for a reaction. Reina only looked down at the babe in her arms, a sad smile twitched at her mouth. "Theviana." she crooned. Theodren scoffed, storming away from the strange woman.

Reina watched him honor the graves a final time before he stomped off toward the edge of the broken town. She padded after him silently, doing her best not to wake the child When a sudden realization stopped him in his tracks, causing Reina to skid to a stop to avoid running into him. He turned to her. "How did you get out from under the blanket?" Reina cocked her head at the man. "What blanket?" Theodren turned, walking over to the tree he had left Reina under.

Dry and dead was the tree, from its branches, to the roots Theodren had coaxed to cover the woman and child. Theodren turned an incredulous eye to Reina who merely shrugged her shoulders. Theodren took a longer look at the woman beside him.

He had not healed her when he placed her by the tree. His resentment would not allow him to. Ultimately he knew that she was not to blame, having suffered Hardwright's assault on his own mind, he was not surprised that she had fallen victim to it. That did not mean, however, that he had to like her. Somehow she had managed to heal herself without his aid, and Thread, he knew, did not heal that fast.

"You met a god didn't you." Theodren asked her suddenly. She froze, the image of Nihila smiling at her through a borrowed face filling her mind. Reina walked stiffly past the man, as she tried to feign a normalcy that she did not feel.

"I don't know what you're talking about." she huffed, stopping short as a wall of roots erupted at her feet. She yelped in surprise as they stretched higher than her hands could reach in seconds, blocking her retreat to nowhere.

"Rule number one." Barked Theodren as she turned to face him, brows stuck firm to her hairline. "Don't lie to me, whatever god you made a deal with won't matter when The Order sends another one of your ilk, to kill us both like you did to the town."

Reina flinched. "Rule number two, you do as I say and stay by my side at all times. if you leave my side for even a moment I will track you down and I will carry you in a sack on my shoulder for the entire journey, do you understand?" Reina nodded silently, letting his anger wash over her.

"Rule number three." He poked a finger at Theviana. "She is the only person here who deserves to live, and if she dies, you die." Reina looked up at him with empty eyes. "That's not fair."

The wall of roots receded into the ground. Reina followed its path until she saw them re-emerge at Theodren's feet. Twining together until they formed a thick staff Theodren pulled from the ground.

"You orphaned my Godchild and now you're the only person keeping her alive." Reina was stunned into silence at that. "The only unfair thing here is that we are alive and they are not." Theodren gestured to the graves behind him. "Grab what you can, we're going north."

She froze, fear creeping into her voice. "The north is a land of savages, the people there are more likely to eat us than aid us."

The absurdity of her statement locked him in place. "Why would... that doesn't... who told you that?" Theodren managed, finally overcoming the mental stumbling block that was her statement.

Reina merely looked down at the ground, unwilling to respond. Theodren grunted, resuming his pace. There had been a war for territory between his father and the Holy Kingdom of Grandia decades ago. The Church felt that it ought to own everything on the continent, and his father was less than pleased with the notion.

For years, Thorn held the Jormungand river. Outmanned and underpowered, Thorn held back the Holy Kingdom's northern advance with horsemen and savagery. Butchering all but a few enemy soldiers with each raid, and leaving them maimed but alive to tell the story to whatever southern unit came to their rescue.

Eventually the siege became so costly that the Holy Kingdom abandoned the assault in return for Thorn Stormwall, who had gained his name from his defense of the river garrison, taking a Priestess of the Royal Order as a member of his court.

"We don't eat people." Grumbled Theodren as he trudged on towards the edge of town, to the dusty road he had walked so often, and would walk only once more.

Chapter 21
A New Duty

Theodren arrived at the church to find the door thrown open and the rattling of its contents echoing within. Two horses waited outside, saddlebags packed with the odds and ends of a man on the run.

Theodren held out a hand motioning for Reina to stay behind him as he eased his way through the open door as stealthily as his bulk allowed. From Theodren's study, muffled ramblings spilled out into the nave, followed not long after by the portly and disheveled frame of the Mayor himself.

"Mayor?" He called out, incredulously. Sylverworm squeaked as he froze like a rather large mouse before a cat. "A-ah father Stormwall! I was just erm..." The mayor looked around, seeking an excuse or an exit. "Packing?" Theodren supplied glowering at the man. "Appropriating." the Mayor shot back. "My tithes practically built this church after all, and now I must be off." Sylverworm tried to shuffle past the large man but was stopped by Theodren's meaty palm on his shoulder.

"Why are you in my church, Mayor?" Theodren eyed the large man's soul, watching as the colors of fear and deceit swirled together in his pitiful soul. "I was simply sheltering from those awful inquisitors. I had no idea they were here until I saw the smoke on my way up to pay you a visit! Truly dreadful those Golden Shears, rather glad I missed them!"

Reina stepped out from behind Theodren. "Liar." She hissed. The Mayor jumped. "Ah s-sister Reina, you've returned!" Theodren's head snapped from Reina to the Mayor. "Returned?" He growled.

"Ah, well, you see." Sylverworm fiddled with the ring on his finger making a small *'click!'*

The Mayor lashed out with the speed of a desperate man, backhanding Theodren and leaving a thin scratch that grew purple and angry within seconds.

The large man stumbled back. Clutching at the burning in his cheek as he cursed, cycling vitae through the sickened wound on his face. "What did you do!?" Theodren roared, surprised at the poison that held his vitae in a deadlock.

"Just a little something I picked up on my travels. Now if you don't mind I will see myself out." Sylverworm moved to shoulder past Reina, deeming her the lesser threat as he kept a wary eye on the big man, chuckling to himself as he went.

His laughter found an abrupt end as Reina's hand seized his throat in an icy grip. "What's so funny, Mayor?" Color drained from his face as she squeezed tighter. "We went down to the village, just like you said." Her vision blurred with angry tears, but she would not look away from the fat, quivering mess of a man in her hand. "We found him among the common folk just like you said. He was healing people just like you said!" Her grip tightened as black tendrils spread up the Mayor's jowls and his life drained into her palm. "I killed EVERYONE! And you!" Her voice shook. "You sent me there!"

He scrabbled and clawed at her with pudgy hands. Trying to infect her with the same poison ring Theodren was fighting with his Vitae. But the life she drained from every fat and bloated cell of this cowardly bureaucrat replenished her faster than any poison could destroy.

"Don't! Please! It was Lester! He's the one who brought you here in the first place! Let me go!" The Mayor begged, as his portly cheeks turned gaunt and hollow at her touch. He fell to his knees but Reina would not let go. "Reina! Stop!" Theodren shouted, color returning to his face as he wrestled down the poison.

"He knew! He knew we were coming! Hardwright wrote him a letter! He knew what Hardwright would do!" Reina blinked as the darkness of the Mayor's soul opened up before her and whispered its shame and secrets into her ear. She sank her nails deeper into the man's fleshy neck as she hissed. "You kept our coming a secret so you could use the chaos to make yourself more important!?" Her outrage echoed throughout the church, waking Theviana into a cry as she was disturbed from her slumber.

The mayor's voice came out raspy and fragile. "I didn't think they would kill everyone." A furious snarl pulled at Reina's face. "Just a few, you thought. Just a handful of lives lost in the scuffle, so you could step in and look like a hero to these people as you drove us away with your authority."

The black tendrils had spread throughout the Mayor's body, draining him of the excess he had accumulated throughout his life. His eyes grew dull as death overtook him. She screamed her pain into his slackening face. "IT'S YOUR FAULT! IT'S YOUR FAULT! IT'S YOUR FAULT!"

Theviana wailed in her arms as Reina screamed at the shriveled corpse. Theodren walked behind Reina, placing a soft hand on her back as she screamed and cried at the drawn and sunken face of what used to be the Mayor. He pulled Theviana from Reina's limp arms as she sobbed.

Theodren looked down at the mummified corpse that all but confirmed Reina's deal with death. What she had done was terrifying, but Theodren couldn't bring himself to fear the broken woman before him, all he felt was pity.

Reina spun, throwing herself into Theodren's arms. She beat at his chest, screaming into the rough fabric of his robe. Theodren held the crying babe up and out of the way of Reina's flailing fists as both babe and woman cried in his arms.

Unsure of what to do, he wrapped his free arm around her, rubbing his calloused hand up and down her back as broken, hiccupping sobs wracked her small frame.

Overwhelmed as he was, he almost didn't notice when Reina's cries, as well as time itself came to a stop. **"Oh my children."** Theodren's head snapped up at the familiar voice. There, planted in front of the altar, was Yggdrazil, the Tree of Life.

A storm of emotions waged war inside Theodren's head. Relief at her presence battled resentment for her absence when he had needed her most.

Yggdrazil's branch reached out to rest a warm leaf on Theodren's face, cleansing and closing what remained of the poisoned wound the Mayor had left. **"You have suffered much, haven't you?"**

Theodren's attempt at a brave face cracked under the unexpected concern and care of his god. "I failed them." He whispered, "I failed them all!" Tears of shame threatened to spill over from his eyes as Yggdrazil's branches poked and prodded at him like a mother fussing over her child, wiping away scars and bruises from wounds he would not heal for himself.

"I was supposed to protect them, but I couldn't do anything when they needed me!" He shouted, shaking as he lost the battle for control of his emotions.

Yggdrazil waited silently as Theodren collected himself. "Where were you?" He asked, fixing a hard stare on the god. Yggdrazil's branches drooped. **"I was not strong enough to cross the veil."** Theodren blinked at that, unsure of what her answer meant. She continued.

"For eons I waited, gaining strength to create my form once more after Odrain's betrayal. For millennia still, I waited for a worthy champion." Theodren was dumbfounded at that. After his failure to protect the townspeople, he found it hard to believe that he was worthy of anything.

"For all my waiting, I was still too late to aid my only champion, when you needed me most. For that I am sorry."

Yggdrazil's proud trunk seemed to bend toward him in a sort of bow that shocked Theodren. "Please, don't..." Theodren choked on his words. "I couldn't save them. None of them, not even the child." He shifted Theviana who gave a gurgle in his arms.

He stared at Theviana in disbelief. "She moved! How is she moving?" He gasped, pulling down the blanket that concealed her tiny mouth. A cry filled the air as she squirmed in his arms.

<u>She is as much mine as you are.</u> Yggdrazil answered, referencing the tiny spring of Vitae in the babe's heart. Theviana's cries reached a new pitch that echoed off the stone walls of his church.

<u>She is a hungry one.</u> Yggdrazil crooned, extending a twig to caress the tiny mop of red hair on the child's head. "Hungry." Groaned Theodren, as his shoulders slumped. "I have nothing to feed her!"

A chuckle came from the Tree as a peach appeared on her branch. **<u>All you have, is all you need.</u>** She said as the bottom of the peach protruded and then split, forming a nipple from which nectar began to drip. Theodren watched as Theviana suckled greedily at the peach brimming with nectar and Vitae.

He watched the process, fascinated as the god's Vitae was able to push back but not eliminate the ring of cold and mysterious potential that surrounded the child's own spring of life water.

"Yggdrazil, what is that cold power in her soul?" He asked as he held the babe closer. A sound like tree limbs rubbing together escaped the Tree. **<u>That would be my sister, playing her own game.</u>**

Theodren arched a curious brow at the god. **<u>This Acher, is as much the babe's power as her Thread and Vitae are. That my sister would make a deal with a mortal.</u>** Yggdrazil poked at Reina. **<u>Much less part with a soul that had already crossed her door, is even more surprising to me than the power itself.</u>**

Theodren's head spun at the implication. Three world shaping powers in one child. Whatever her path would be, it would be an auspicious one. Theviana pushed the peach out of her mouth half asleep. Snuggling her face deeper into Theodren's chest as she returned to her slumber.

Retribution slithered from the collar of his tattered robe. Reaching out, it plucked the peach from Yggdrazil's branch, absorbing it into the length of itself, before returning to its shelter in Theodren's sleeve.

"Your vineling grows well." The god noted. The man Retribution consumed, flashed before Theodren's mind. "She ate well yesterday."

Yggdrazil was silent for a time, as she studied the man before her. **"What will you do?"**

Theodren told the goddess of his father's lands in the north, and his plans to keep the child safe there. **"And then?"** The Tree prodded. Theodren was silent. His need for revenge burned at the core of his very soul. Only once the child was safely in the hands of his father's people, could he throw himself unreservedly after Cardinal Hardwright. His teeth ground at the thought of the man's smug smile.

"I will have justice for the lives he took." He answered. Yggdrazil considered his words for a moment, before pulling her branches back into herself. **"Seek your vengeance, but I would remind you that life, is not to be taken lightly."**

He nodded at the Tree's words. Before Theviana's resurrection, his mind was bent toward a cruel extermination of the entire Divine Order, but now... he looked down at the sleeping babe in his arms. Vengeance was not enough. Not for her. To his eyes, the world was broken. Cruel men like Hardwright held sway over the lives of good and honest people. Men who treated the lives of common folk as merely inconveniences to be disposed of.

Theodren did not want his Godchild to see the world as he did. She would need him not only to teach her about her Thread and her Vitae, but to teach her that true power is responsibility to those without strength of their own. The child's weight in his arms seemed to double in his mind.

A new duty formed in him. He would seek out men like the Cardinal in every position of power they held. With a view of their souls, he would pass judgement, and if need be, retribution. He would not allow men like Hardwright to poison his Godchild's world before she could even take part in it.

Determination filled his soul as he settled upon his new task. Yggdrazil seemed pleased with the plans forming in his mind as she faded from reality. Leaving behind a single flower, that floated gently toward the trio as time returned to its natural pace. Its gentle descent found its end on Theviana's tear stained cheek.

Chapter 22
One Life to Another

Theodren gently placed Reina and the child on a nearby pew as he gathered his belongings off the floor from where the Mayor had dropped them. The Mayor seemed focused on collecting his religious garb more than any of the rest of Theodren's belongings. Rumor amongst the townspeople was that the Mayor was no Mayor at all.

One day he had simply arrived in town in suspiciously Ill fitting and ragged clothing and carrying a modest bag of gold declaring his station to the townspeople. No one had questioned his origins despite his duplicitous nature. The town was rife with people escaping their circumstances to start anew, that was, until yesterday.

Perhaps the Mayor was planning to pose as a priest elsewhere, certainly Theodren was the only man in the village with clothing that would fit Sylverworm's portly frame, and no one would dare question or assault a priest on pilgrimage. As far as Theodren was concerned, the robes of a priest of the Golden Order were no longer his to wear. He left them there on the floor with a mixture of melancholy and disgust confusing his emotions as he scanned the disheveled interior of his quarters.

The Mayor had managed to grab most of Theodren's clothes, trousers and tunics littered the ground, along with the sturdy cloak and boots Theodren's mother had given him for his journey south. Now, he would wear them home. His books and chair lay scattered on the ground, thrown about in the Mayor's mad dash to freedom. He stepped over them as he grabbed a modest hunting bow and quiver of arrows from the dusty corner of his room. He had not needed to hunt for his food since he arrived in the village three years ago, but the journey north would change that. He would need to hunt, dry and preserve as much meat as he could along the way. Once they were out of the forest, there would be precious little game until they came to the Yormungand. He used what privacy the moment allowed to pull the tattered robe of his priesthood off of his head with a sense of finality.

He no longer belonged with the Golden Order, and these robes no longer belonged to him. The garment was soaked in the blood and gore of yesterday's battle, and he wrinkled his nose as it fell to the ground in a heap. Inspecting himself in the bronze polished mirror that hung crooked on his wall. He noticed an odd smoothness to his skin where all of his many wounds and scars should have been. He chuckled as he remembered Yggdrazil fussing over him in the nave. He searched for a clean enough tunic when his vineling caught his eye. Retribution had doubled in size. It shifted ever so slightly as he poked at it, seemingly asleep on his arm.

Before It had been merely a circlet about his arm. Now it would rival even the broad, silver arm bands his father would bestow on his more worthy warriors. Theodren gave a melancholy smile as he remembered the boisterous feasts his father would throw for the giving of armbands.

loud singing and booming laughter would mix with strong mead and tender meats. His mother seemed completely at odds with the chaos surrounding her at these celebrations. Always keeping a serious and dignified demeanor, even as earthen mugs and legs of mutton sailed through the air. For all her manners and poise however, he could still hear her singing the jaunty tunes of his father's bards when she thought no one was listening. And while no one seemed able to recall seeing her drink, she would end each feast with rosy cheeks and several empty flagons surrounding her.

Thoughts of home filled his mind as he emerged from his quarters, garbed in sturdy trousers, boots and a padded leather jerkin he had not worn since he had left for the conclave 8 years ago. It was stretched tightly across his chest and shoulders but it would do.

As he approached the dried husk that was once the mayor. He considered what ought to be done with the body. Reina's words echoed in his head. He had known. He had known that the Inquisitors were coming, He had known that there would be death, and he had chosen to do nothing. And so, he would respond in kind. Theodren pushed the husk aside with his foot. As he did, a jingle of coins rattled from within its pockets.

Theodren grinned, He reached into the dead man's robes until he found a hefty bag of gold that almost overflowed his hand. He would have to count it later, but the weight of it spoke to a healthy sum. Certainly enough to pay for room and board at many taverns along the road north. He tucked the bag away into his belt, turning his attention back to Reina who sat, mired in her sadness and shock, on the pew where Theodren had left her. Yggdrazil's flower remained steadfast behind Theviana's ear as she slept in the woman's arms.

Theodren had seen this kind of shellshock before in the eyes of warriors who had returned, broken by some unspeakable trauma. He lifted her gently by the arm as he guided her out of the church and toward the horses the Mayor had so thoughtfully prepared for them. One was loaded down with bags of silver plates, candle sticks and other ostentatious home-goods. Theodren snorted as he pulled the bags of baubles from the horse, letting it fall with a clatter to the damp ground.

While such things might be sold for decent coin, he had neither the time nor the contacts to sell such things. Turning to Reina, he grabbed her by her slender waist to lift her into the saddle. She stiffened at his touch, only for a moment, before relaxing, allowing him to place her on the horse. Theodren followed shortly after, climbing onto the bigger of the two horses. He grabbed the leads from where they sat, untouched on Reina's saddle and coaxed the horses into motion. It was time to go home.

CHAPTER 23
TRADING TALES

Reina and Theodren rode for several silent hours as morning passed to noon, and noon to night. Theodren fashioned a sling that more easily held Theviana to Reina's or with adjustment, His chest. After careful testing, Theodren found that so long as Reina was nearby, the Acher in the child's soul would not consume her spring of Vitae, and the closer she was to Theodren, the stronger her Vitae became. It was a delicate balancing act between the two, but one Theodren was determined to master. At least until she stabilized.

While he may not have felt the wear of their travel, he knew that both Reina and the horses would need rest. Theodren turned the horse's nose toward a copse of trees far enough removed from the road to allow for privacy at best and concealment at worst. He wasn't yet sure of what became of Hardwright or if he had managed to bring reinforcements to the town, but he would not risk their backs on complacency. He scanned for any larger than average Vitae among the trees but found nothing besides the run of the mill woodland creatures he expected. Theodren called Retribution from his sleeve, admiring the vineling in his hand he coaxed the peach Yggdrazil had given him earlier from its core. Even with as little knowledge of infants that he had, surely Theviana must be hungry, he reasoned and resolved to feed her as soon as they settled into the copse of trees.

Sliding from his horse, the stiffness he had prepared to feel was gone before he even had the chance to groan about it. Pleased, he tied first his horse and then Reina's, to nearby trees. Looking up at her, she was more akin to a statue than a young woman. Her eyes, red from crying, had gone dry and unblinking, staring off into an abyss of her own making.

She had used a strange power. Acher, the Tree called it. He had watched her drain the life from the Mayor until he collapsed almost into dust. Theodren shuddered. He could not drain Vitae from living things. He had tried and failed to replenish his reserves from the plants surrounding his church during the weeks he spent exhausting himself healing the townsfolk. He quickly learned that it wasn't his to take.

Memories of the guardsmen he killed flashed through his mind as he cleared a suitable space for a fire and bedrolls. Their Vitae had rushed to him the moment their grip on this world was broken. He had observed the way Vitae either dissipated or was consumed from prey to predator while watching the drama of a field mouse and hawk beside the road into town. After death, Vitae would start to dissipate from its host before long unless something came along to eat it. He had watched the hawk swallow the mouse, pieces at a time, absorbing the rodent's Vitae into the bird's own mass of life.

Thankfully, unlike the bird of prey, Theodren had not needed to eat those men to take their Vitae. It had just rushed to him, like drowning men to a raft. Killing seemed the only expedient way to refill his Vitae, but it was a means that he refused to stoop to without cause. He pondered how he could better use it in the future as he turned back to the horses. Reina had slid from the horse with Theviana, and found her way to a boulder set beside the empty ring of stones He had planned to start a campfire in. She was silent and unmoving, as if she herself was a stone that had stood in that spot since time began.

He sighed. She could not continue like this. While the quiet was nice, He had seen soldiers go mute and sullen, when faced with a trauma they could not rationalize. Like wooden carvings of the people they used to be.

Theodren piled the campfire with brush, twigs, and larger branches he had wrenched from a dead tree. The fire would burn warm, but not so brightly that they would be spotted from the road. Pulling his flint and steel from the pouch on his belt, he smirked at the mundane means of fire he had resorted to since losing his Thread. The fire turned from spark to flame in short order, reflecting light in Reina's face, but not her eyes.

Theviana stirred in her arms, little hands reached out from the bundle of cloth toward Reina's face as the child started to cry. "She's hungry..." Reina croaked, voice stiff and broken from crying and lack of use. Theodren waited for her to say more. "She's hungry and I killed the woman who feeds her." Though her words were monotone, silent tears began falling from her eyes. Theodren gently pulled the babe from her arms without resistance, sitting down next to her, he coaxed the vineling out from his sleeve, summoning the peach Yggdrazil had grown for the child from Retribution's reaching limb.

Theviana took to it without hesitation, suckling a milky white nectar and Theodren's own Vitae from the fruit. Theodren cooed and comforted the child in his arms as the sounds of her suckling filled the still air. Reina stared at him with hurt in her eyes as she watched Theodren nurture life in a way that she never could.

"It's not your fault." He said, surprising her. She looked at him, confused.

"I saw the way Hardwright used his Thread on you." She stiffened. "He tried it on me too." Her eyebrows shot up to her hair. "and you fought it?" She whispered. Theodren nodded. "It felt like all I wanted to do in the world was just give up. Just let him do my thinking for me. Just lay down and give up because he knew better." The memory of the Cardinal's Thread, like sticky fingers on his thoughts, sent a shiver up his spine. He locked his eyes, steady and unyielding, with Reina's own. "Whatever you were doing there with him, I know you didn't want to kill them." Tears fell faster down her face as she shook in her seat, trying her best to contain herself. "I just wanted to be a priestess." she sobbed. "I wanted to be good! I wanted people to like me! I wanted him to notice me!" Theodren got the sense that she wasn't talking about Hardwright, but he let her continue without interruption. "Now I'm a monster! I sucked the life out of that man like a leech and I could hear his soul!"

That piqued Theodren's interest. Theodren saw people's souls as pools of abstract colors of emotion. To *hear* a soul was not something that he had even considered. Reina pulled her knees in closer to herself, hugging them against her chest. "It was like whispers of the worst part of himself. Like he was proud of it." She looked up from the fire at him. "He didn't care how many people died, so long as you weren't around for people to compare him to you." Theodren raised an eyebrow at this. He had never cared for authority. To him it was all a petty popularity contest and he wanted no part. That the Mayor even considered him some sort of rival both irritated and surprised him.

Theodren returned to the thought of her new found power. "How did you do that?" he asked. Reina grew silent again at the question. Clearly afraid and unsettled with her blasphemy. Theodren waited for her to answer. As the seconds passed to minutes and none came, He sighed, stretching out his legs by the fire. One hand holding Theviana, and the other propping himself up as he leaned back.

"My Thread broke when Theviana was born." His eyes became lost in the cherry red glow of the fire as he told the story. He told her about the birth. He told her about Yggdrazil and his Vitae. He told her everything as the truth fell from his lips for the first time since Yggdrazil came crashing into his life. As his tale concluded, it felt like a great weight had lifted from his shoulders. He wasn't sure if he entirely trusted the slender woman beside him, but by now she would have already suspected what he told her.

He looked up at her to see that her eyes had gone dry. She wrenched her gaze from the fire as she stared into his eyes, searching for lies or half truths. After a moment and a nod to herself she began her own story.

She told him everything. From her meteoric rise through the Academy, to her selection by Hardwright, and finally, she told him about Nihila. Theodren sat patiently as she spoke. He had expected that she had made some kind of contact with Death, but to know her name now. He shivered. Theodren listened in rapt attention as she described her deal with the dark God. The parallels to his own deal with Yggdrazil were glaring in the extreme.

Now two gods had their hands in Theviana's soul, and Theodren was not eager to see how it would play out.

"And now I'm here, with a child that's not mine and a man I don't know, going Weaver knows where, all because I got good grades at the academy." Some of the old life seemed to return to Reina as her story and its weight left her chest. She gave the large man a side eyed glance. "So what now?"

He handed the sleeping bundle of Theviana to Reina before climbing to his feet with a grunt. When he got to the horses, he threw Reina a bag of salted pork before turning to the task of unsaddling and brushing the horses. "We eat, we sleep, and in the morning, I'm going hunting." He offered. Reina pulled a slice of hard pork from the bag with a look of distaste. With a loud 'Snap!' she bit off a chunk of the tough meat, chewing judiciously before swallowing with great effort. "Yes, hunting would be good."

Chapter 24
Taskmaster

A lone man, bedraggled and angry, rode into the town of Militas on a horse much too fine for the abuse and neglect it had received from him. Hardwright heaved himself from the horse that promptly collapsed into the dust.

Balancing on his good leg, he merely tsk'd in distaste before hobbling towards the warm evening glow of the tavern. The mangled limb would likely hinder him for the rest of his days, but thanks to the mental block he wove into his mind, the pain never would.

Once a garrison for Grandia's military, the encampment and its soldiers were abandoned years after the war for expansion was deemed too costly. Soldiers not under Holy Orders were not permitted within Grandia's walls and most were still under reserve contract. So they remained, in a sort of limbo between soldier and mercenary, taking what jobs they could find for what coin they could get. And no tavern served better mercenaries than The Broken Sword.

While the building contained the same booze, beauties and brutes that were essential to all such ale houses. This particular one held precisely what Hardwright needed. A Taskmaster.

The Cardinal waded through the drunken revelry of the Holy Kingdoms forgotten sons. Each step boiling his blood as he limped through the sea of mediocrity.

Tucked away in the back, was a booth guarded by two of the only three men in the building without tankards in hand. Hardwright attempted to adopt a straight back and a charming smile until he was stopped by a scarred hand on his chest.

Hardwright's face flipped from grin to grimace as he turned a furious eye to the large scarred owner of the hand that dared to obstruct him. "While we appreciate your interest, we are not currently accepting guests. Please return tomorrow between the hours of four and eight bells, at which point we will be happy to see to the needs of all our valued customers." He said pleasantly.

Hardwright's greasy brow creased together. "What was that, Oaf!?" The Cardinals thread snuck out from his sleeve. It lunged for the smiling man's brow but was stopped an inch away by the lead gauntleted hand of the second man. The shorter guard ripped the thread away from his compatriots face as he placed a knife to Hardwright's throat.

"He said fuck off." Growled the guard. Hardwright's Thread struggled helplessly against the lead that gloved the man's hand. Unable to influence or escape his grip, the Cardinal allowed his Thread to fade from reality.

"Gunther, Ginter, let's hear what the gentleman felt was important enough to disturb my meal for." The Taskmaster kept his eyes on his plate and his ledger as he motioned for Hardwright to sit across from him.

With prodigious strength, Gunther gripped the cloth of the Cardinal's robe. Lifting the man who kicked and cursed into the seat across from Taskmaster Richard Piercer.

Piercer was a grizzled man with salt and pepper hair that swept back in austere fashion. Piercing grey eyes flanked by crows feet sat above a proud but slightly bent nose. His sharp jaw was dusted with a neatly trimmed grey beard that spoke of age and discipline. Broad shoulders on a thin frame suggested years of hard marches to harder battles. He wore dark leathers and tough cotton. Reaching into his breast pocket he pulled a simple kerchief to wipe the sauce of his meal from his mouth as he sat back to consider the flustered man across from him.

A smirk curled at his mouth as he sipped from his cup. His cool demeanor infuriated Hardwright. "Do you know who I am!?" Hissed the cardinal, straightening out his robes. Piercer placed his mug back on the table.

"I know exactly who you are, Cardinal Hardwright. I know you left Grandia two weeks ago with seven guards and a woman." Piercer's observant gaze took in the man before him. "And now you're here, injured, alone and in search of more men."

Hardwright squirmed under the intense scrutiny of the Taskmaster. How this man knew of him and his travels, he couldn't begin to guess, but anyone with that kind of information and the resources to get it, was not to be taken lightly.

Piercer continued. "You can't request more men from the church lest word of your losses reach loftier ears than your own, and you can't be seen to return empty handed." He leaned back against the high leather pad of the booth wall as he continued his musings. "What could you be hunting that's so valuable?"

Hardwright snarled. "The only value you need concern yourself with, is the coin I will pay for your men." Piercer stared at him for a moment, steepling his fingers, he nodded. "And how much coin would that be?" The Cardinal pulled a leather coin purse from the folds of his robes. "One hundred gold, delivered upon delivery of the man I seek, alive."

Piercer shook his head. "Alive costs more. Two hundred gold gets you eight men and a wagon for transport of live prisoners."

Hardwright spluttered. "Two hundred!? That's preposterous!" The Taskmaster shrugged. "If you don't like the price you can put out a bounty, but if you do..." Piercer grinned at the Cardinal "Everyone is going to know about your quarry, and who wants him."

Hardwright winced. Publicity was the last thing he needed. If the Patriarch found out that he failed to kill not only an apostate, but one that wielded the power of a strange god, he would lose everything. He shuddered as he remembered the Ethereal green in Theodren's eyes as he stalked him with his unearthly hammer. His nightmares since, had been filled with the man's face.

He grit his teeth. If two hundred gold was the price to subjugate such a fiend then he would pay it. After all; he grinned to himself. There were many in Grandia who would pay him handsomely for the true healing Theodren was reported to possess. With that kind of influence, the Patriarch's seat would be his.

Hardwright leaned forward offering a clammy hand to the Taskmaster. "We have a deal." Piercer gripped his hand in a firm grip. "Half up front. Half when we deliver your man, and if there are casualties, 100 silver for each widow."

The Cardinal struggled under the firm grip. He considered using his thread on the man to sweeten the deal for himself, but almost as soon as he played with the idea in his head, he caught Ginter shifting in the corner of his eye. He had never seen Thread nullified so efficiently, and by a common man no less. Ginter's lead covered hand glinted in the candle light of the tavern. His blood boiled that he would be so easily man handled by a peasant class that he had left behind what felt like a lifetime ago. There would be no trickery here.

Hardwright sighed. "Very well." Satisfied, the Taskmaster released his grip. Pulling out the Ledger he cleared his throat. "Now, name?" The Cardinal grinned. "Theodren, Theodren Stormwall."

CHAPTER 25
DEATH AND SHADOWS

Theodren's feet made no sound as he stalked from root to rock, to moss covered stone. Bow in hand, he edged around the large tree sheltering him from the eyes of the stag grazing on wild foliage yards away. Unaware of Theodren, relearning the ways of the forest.

As a boy he had hunted the Mist Wood with his father. "The world gives if we can take it." His father would say. Hunting is a brutal art born of necessity. While the southern gentry often used hunts as social gatherings or hobbies to pass the time. Northmen believed that life should only be taken out of necessity, and if you were going to take it, you would have to earn it.

For Theodren, the woods were always a bastion of solitude. It was a place with no expectations or nonsense, only the rule of life. Now more than ever, he knew this to be true. His mind's eye watched the flow of vitae around him as he eased himself into a position to fire.

Finding solid footing, he pulled silently on the bow. Lead arm straight, and rear arm relaxed, his back held the weight of the bow's draw. A whispered prayer to Yggdrazil formed his exhale as he prepared to release.

"WOW he's pretty!" Said a voice from beside him. Theodren jumped, cursing as he spotted Reina next to him, idly playing with Theviana in her arms. The buck's head snapped up, looking for the source of the voice through the trees. Theodren tried to realign his aim on the deer before firing a desperate arrow. The buck turned, fleeing deeper into the woods as the arrow whistled harmlessly past his head, thudding into a tree.

Theodren turned to Reina, eyebrow rising toward the throbbing vein in his forehead. She whistled, watching the buck disappear into the woods. "Why'd you miss?" Theodren stared hard at the uncomprehending woman while she played with her hair. She blinked down at him, still crouched with bow in hand. "What?" She asked innocently.

The night's rest seemed to have almost transformed Reina, a healthy glow filled her cheeks and there was light in her eyes that had been missing since before the massacre. A heavy sigh pushed through his lips as he stood, walking to retrieve the errant arrow.. "That was *supposed* to be dinner." He grumbled, searching for his arrow among the trees.

"Huh." Was all she said, plucking a flower from the ground. She could only admire it for a brief moment before it withered in her hand. Disappointment clouded her face as she let the dried husk fall to the ground. She tried again with a second flower, focusing as hard as she could on the tiny bud of life in her hands. The flower lasted only slightly longer before it joined her previous victim in dust.

"Still figuring it out?" Theodren asked seriously. She sighed. "It's like the Vitae gets sucked into me whether I want it or not. I can't push it back, I can barely slow it down, I just..." she gestured back and forth between herself and the dead flower in her hand. "Suck the life out of everything!"

Theodren grabbed the arrow as close he could to the embedded head, twisting while he pulled. Freeing the arrow, he pondered the conundrum of her powers as he checked the shaft for any bend.. "What does it look like to you? A soul I mean." He asked, sliding his fingers over the fletching.

She held Theviana tighter to her chest as she jogged after him. She pondered his question. Reina turned her head to stare into Theodren's soul, trying her best to memorize its image in her head. His soul was large, larger certainly than the Mayor's. a vast sea of jade green, but where the Mayor's soul was bordered in Acher.

Theodren's was not. She wondered if perhaps it was due to his patronage to Yggdrazil, or more precisely, his supposed immortality that seemed to drive Acher away..

Where the Mayor's soul was filled with shadows and secrets, Theodren's was mostly devoid of such darkness. This soul reflected a forthright man who lived by the light of his word. What darkness she could find was a hole in the depths of his soul, where she heard cries of deep regret. Lamentations of a failed protector filled this space.

Reina pulled herself back to reality as a tear fell from her eye. She blinked as the concerned face of Theodren filled her view. "Reina!" He shouted, startling Theviana. "What!? What!?" She cried in reply, blushing as she stumbled back, soothing the whimpering child while she regained her footing.

Theodren stared at her, brows furrowed in concern. "Your eyes were black." Reina's face twisted in disgust as she recalled the orbs of black staring out from behind Eleina's borrowed face. "Ugh!" She spat. Stomping away from Theodren. "Of all the colors! Black???" She plopped herself down on a tree stump as her arms folded underneath Theviana's bundle and her legs crossed in a huff.

"Just had to be death. He gets pretty flowers and green eyes but no, I get death." As her rant continued, the shadows stirred. Theodren's eyes widened as they swayed this way and that. Each tree's shade writhed and bent in the morning sun, growing deeper with each passing second.

"Reina... Don't move." He growled, reaching for an arrow. She froze. Theodren loosed an arrow into the shadow closest to Reina's foot. "Ow!" She jumped, kicking out her leg. As she did, the shadows raced toward Theodren. Before he could react, he felt a heavy impact take his feet out from under him.

He landed on his face with an "Oof!" She shrieked, "What the hell was that!?" Theodren tried to get up, but the more Reina moved in her panic, the harder the shadows felt, and the more they savaged him.

Theodren was dragged this way and that. A sensation like ice cold chains lashed at him chaotically. Theodren's blood ran hot as the panic pushed his heart faster.

He cast about with his Vitae, searching for an enemy he could fight. His hands found no purchase on the shadows but in a brief second between strikes from the shadows, he saw that where his Vitae probed, the shadows seemed to lighten, like they were losing their presence when faced with the raw life energy of his vitae. On a hunch, he traced the flailing darkness back to its source. All the shadows with their writhing arms originated from one place. Reina.

These were not shadows. At least not anymore, they were Acher, responding to Reina's distress. The more they struck, the more her anxiety grew and the stronger they became.

He grit his teeth. "Reina! Stop!" He shouted. Her hands flew to her mouth in one final motion, which sent him spinning across the ground toward her.

Theodren came to a dusty halt at her feet. "Are you alright?" She whispered, eyes darting around searching for the invisible danger. Theodren rolled onto his back with a groan. He cracked an eye open to stare at her. "Death and shadows, it would seem."

CHAPTER 26
NOWHERE TO GO

Theodren stood, rolling his head left and right in an attempt to clear the tension while he did a mental check for any injuries. Retribution had spread out over his back and head to protect him from the chaotic thrashing of Reina's shadows.

Slithering back beneath his robes, he gave it a mental 'thank you' before returning his attention to Reina who stared wide eyed at the shadows around her. "Those are mine?" She whispered excitedly. Reina reached out a hand slowly, wiggling a finger, and in the distance, a shadow wiggled back.

She squealed, bouncing on her toes in excitement. Theodren groaned, at the headache that her growing power would bring, but he couldn't help the reluctant smile at her moment of joy. For a moment he was lost in the excited light in her blue eyes and bounce in her golden hair. He frowned, shaking his head, he turned away.

"Come on, dinner is still out there somewhere, and we need to keep moving." Reina danced after him. Experimenting with how the shadows moved with every step. It was certainly not her Thread, but she was determined to master it as quickly as she could. Excellence is opportunity, and she would need to find new ways to survive and defend herself now that her thread was gone.

Her eyes traced the broad shelf of Theodren's shoulders as he lumbered through the forest. She would need to find a way to be more than just a means to an end for him. She knew he needed her to keep the sleeping babe tied to her chest alive, but the child grew stronger by the hour. He couldn't see it yet, but Theviana's own Acher was becoming intrinsically linked to her soul much like Reina's own, and when that was complete, he would no longer need Reina to siphon off the child's Acher to keep it from overwhelming her.

She could not bear to think of parting ways from the baby girl held so close to her heart. Even the thought of splitting from the brooding giant was curiously unpleasant. Theodren held a branch up and out of the way as he walked under it, holding on to it without thinking until Reina was also past the tree before letting it return to its place in the greenery of the forest.

He was a conundrum to her. Only a day ago he had buried a town full of people he had known for years, and she had been the one to kill them. He should hate her, he should despise her for the role she played in the deaths of all one hundred and thirty three people she had slain. She shuddered as their surprised and terrified faces flew through her mind. She despised herself for it well enough.

Her dancing steps had stopped and so had Theodren. He dropped low to a knee, easing an arrow from his quiver while his eye remained fixed on the doe that had wandered into view. She watched his back tense beneath the leather jerkin as it held the weight of the bow's draw. He murmured something she couldn't hear, before the arrow leapt from the stave. It flew true, burying itself in the doe who dropped instantly to the forest floor.

He nodded, pleased. Rising to his feet he turned to Reina with just a hint of a satisfied smile. "And now we have dinner." He trotted off to the doe, pulling a knife from his belt to begin the process of dressing his kill for the trip back to their temporary camp.

She frowned. He could fight and fend for himself, he even shared his own food with her. Why would he keep her around when she was no longer needed? Her fears multiplied in her head. All her life, her relationships had been built on selfish back and forth between rivals. Once there was no longer anything to be gained from a person, there was no reason to entertain them further. Would Theodren do the same once she was no longer necessary to keep Theviana alive?

And if she was sent away, what would she do then? There was no returning to the Church, and certainly there was no returning home to her mother. Between the two, she could not choose who was the harsher. The cold order of the Church or the ever demanding expectations of her mother. To come home not only a failure but an apostate? She shuddered, leaning against the tree beside her as she contemplated the future.

Theodren returned with the doe, gutted and cleaned over his shoulder. The offal he left behind as a gift for the forest. He walked up to Reina who appeared lost in some dark thought, brows furrowed and lips scrunched up tightly. She appeared unaware of the creeping darkness that spread from her shoulder into the tree that withered at her touch. He cleared his throat.

"Ahem." She blinked back to reality, looking up at him quizzically. He pointed with his eyes at the eroding bark of the tree she leaned against. Her eyes grew wide and she jumped back. "Not again!" she fussed over the tree, grabbing at the bark as she tried to take the Acher from the ailing tree.

Theodren sighed exasperated. Gently pulling her hand away, he replaced it with his own larger one. He probed into the bark of the tree with his Vitae, pushing life into the blackened wood of its trunk. It took only a moment for green to return to the tree. Finding the balance he needed, he pulled his hand away, keeping an eye on the cells of the tree. After he was sure that none of them would grow rampantly, he nodded in satisfaction. "Let's head back."

Reina ran her eyes along the fresh bark of the tree, whole and hearty as it was before she leaned against it. Her eyes turned to Theodren's back as he walked toward camp. He could fix whatever she broke. She trotted after him, all the more determined to follow his path.

CHAPTER 27
SHADOW BOXING

By the time Theodren and Reina were returning to their camp, the sun was already halfway through its descent, casting long shadows through the forest for Reina to experiment with. All told, they had returned with a doe and two rabbits. Reina had managed to trap them with her shadows, surprising Theodren with how quickly she adapted to her newfound abilities. While not perfect, she could just barely grab onto small things as long as they were touching the same shadow she was.

Focused as she was on the shadows dancing around her, she did not hear the voices coming from their camp or notice that Theodren had stopped, nearly running into his back. She peeked around the side of her large companion to see six men, all armed and rugged, amongst their packs, laughing and joking as they dug through what remained of the duo's belongings.

Theodren emerged from the brush, clearing his throat loudly for their attention. All six of the men turned at the sound, eyes locking on the towering man for a moment before turning to the slender blonde woman and the child in her arms. "You're in the wrong camp." growled Theodren, staring down each man individually before moving to the next. The soul of each man appeared before his mind's eye, each a collection of dim hues, muted by years of vagrancy and unnecessary violence.

"Finder's keepers I'm afraid." came a drawl from the sixth man near the back of the crowd of ruffians. Theodren's eyes narrowed on him. Lean and dark, his hair was a greasy brown, slicked to the side in an attempt to cover an increasingly obvious bald spot, paired with an equally greasy mustache that curled above a smirk which spoke to a confidence more befitting a fox than a man.

"Found your little camp here while the boys and I were looking for a place to rest our troubled heads, didn't we lads?" Chuckling agreement rose from the other five ruffians, converging on their leader as he strutted toward Theodren. Confidence in the superiority of their numbers kept any fear from the face of the bandit leader as he stood only a couple feet from Theodren's towering form. "Seemed a shame just to leave it here unused when it could bring much needed relief to the boys and me!" justified the greasy bandit with a grin.

Anger smoldered in Theodren's chest as the understanding that he was supposed to be intimidated by the smaller man set in. He sighed, seeking a breath to control his ire. Fighting this many men would require using his Vitae, and while he was confident in his own ability, brawling against this many men while also defending Reina and Theviana and making sure that no one escaped to tell the tale of his strange power, was a gambit he wasn't willing to risk. "We don't want any trouble, just give us our horses and we will be gone." He grumbled.

The greasy bandit cocked his head to the side as if surprised at his answer. "What a reasonable fellow you are! And here I thought I'd have to take you down a notch." From beside him Reina snorted derisively, shooting the bandit a haughty look of disdain.

Annoyance flashed across his face for a moment before a cruel smile slithered across his lips. "In fact, leave us the woman, and we'll let you take both horses. The boy's and I have a little more relieving to do that she could be of great help with." A deep sickly pink and red of lust and violence filled the souls of the bandits who chuckled at their leader's suggestion, some of them already making lewd gestures toward the pretty woman at Theodren's side. The anger that smoldered in his chest erupted into an inferno of rage.

Smiling, he placed his hand on the greasy bandit's shoulder, who taking it as a gesture of agreement, grinned even wider.

Theodren's large hand clamped down on the man's shoulder. "I'm going to hit you now."

"What does -" CRACK! Theodren held the bandit in place, good and steady for the fist that plowed through the bandit's face, pulverizing bone and cartilage alike.

The ruffian fell to the ground with a gurgle, all guile and grins forgotten as his face slammed into the dirt. Theodren pulled Retribution from his sleeve as he roared a challenge to the five remaining men who looked on in shock. "Everybody listen up! I'm handing out judgement one at a time." He pointed the hammer at the nearest bandit who drew his own sword in response. "So get in line and wait your turn."

Theodren's eyes were locked on the taller gangly bandit closest to him, when the smiling face of baby Theviana was suddenly thrust in front of his face. He blinked, in the moment of tension, Reina had snuck under his guard to stand before him. Holding the baby above her head and up to his face, she heard the whispers of rage in his soul come to a halt as he beheld the cherubic face of his Goddaughter.

"Hold this please." She said calmly, depositing Theviana on Theodren's chest as he scrambled to hold her securely, Retribution slithering back up his sleeve. "You're being very rude. These gentlemen just wanted to play!" Shadows surrounding the camp grew longer, bending and reaching out toward the bandits in an unnatural display. A wicked grin lit up Reina's face as she assumed a ready stance.

"Let's play." She leapt at the first bandit with an acrobat's grace. Landing on her hands she bent almost in half before spring boarding feet first, into the jaw of the first man, knocking him flat on his back. Reina landed on his chest in a casual pose, looking around nonchalantly as if her most pressing concern was the state of her nails.

She made a show of admiring them as the rest of the bandits shook themselves from their shock and charged her as one. Reina's hand shot out at the four approaching men, sending a shadow along the ground toward their feet.

Two of the men tripped and one stumbled, leaving the third to approach unhindered, sword and shield at the ready. Reina winced internally at the weakness of her shadow, but she pressed on.

The bandit swung low at her knees in an attempt to force her to move and move she did. Grabbing on to the man's shield, she vaulted over the sword, over the man and onto the ground behind him.

Reaching over her shoulder, she grabbed her assailant's collar. Her right leg shot back into his, unbalancing him as she heaved and twisted, using her hip as a fulcrum to throw the first bandit into the second who approached, daggers in hand. Both men went sprawling into the dirt cursing her and each other as they untangled themselves.

Reina had never been so exhilarated or exhausted in her life. Her chest heaved with every breath and her heart felt ready to explode from fear and excitement. She had never fought without her thread before, and certainly not for her life.

She had excelled at using her thread to manipulate the order of the world around her, cutting through air resistance like steel wire and pushing her physical abilities higher than anyone else. But now she felt naked. She hadn't even retrieved her golden shears from the dirt where she had dropped them. Unwilling as she was to touch the blood on their shining blades.

Now she fought only with her wits and an unfamiliar power. The two men she had managed to trip regained their feet, the first pulling twin daggers whose quality was at odds with the unkempt state of the ruffian who bore them.

"Ooh! Those are pretty!" She exclaimed, dancing out of the way of the second man's curved saber, and straight into his companions' range. His eyes narrowed at her as he threw swift and measured jabs at the woman. Each feint and strike an effort to properly gauge her speed.

Reina could only dodge, with each parry she tried to gain purchase on the man's wrists. Hoping to twist or manipulate them into releasing the daggers. But each attempt was a failure, punished with thin lines of red that wept down her arms.

"Ugh! Just stay still!" She shrieked at him, trying once again to snare him with a shadow. She was rewarded with a satisfying crunch. They both looked down to see the knife wielding bandit's foot bent at an odd angle, smothered in darkness.

His eyes shot wide at the unnatural wound. "W-WITCH!" he screamed, stumbling back on his remaining leg, causing his advancing companion with the saber to slow, a worried expression darkening his face. "RUDE!" She barked, poking the knife man hard in his chest. Darkness spread from where she touched him as he fell to the ground, knives forgotten, scrabbling at the black stain that spread through his chest.

She scooped up the blades, dancing backward to create distance between her and the final bandit. Where the other two had run off to, she couldn't be sure, opting to keep her eyes focused on her final opponent, who advanced with the measured steps of a veteran.

"I've got your measure now witch!" Shouted the bandit, sending short swings and feints at her, choosing to keep himself at a distance from her necrotic touch and newly appropriated daggers. "I am NOT a witch!" She shouted back, weaving between each strike, all while she searched for an opening.

A sneer covered the man's face. "The only thing you are is dead!" He shouted, throwing a handful of dirt into Reina's face. Her arms flew up to shield her eyes but it was too late. Her eyes closed involuntarily at the onslaught of debris. In a panic she lashed out with shadows and knives in a flurry of desperate strikes.

Her knife found its meaty target as her shadows jerked the man from his intended path straight into her blade. Clearing the dirt from her face she blinked the world back into focus. The last bandit lay in a heap at her feet, blood pouring from a wound in his chest where he had landed on her blade. Behind him lay the dried corpse of the man whose daggers she'd appropriated. Still on her guard she turned to see the two men, unmoving, being dragged beneath the earth by thick roots from nearby trees.

She leveled a glare at Theodren who merely cocked an eyebrow at her in return. "Those guys were mine!" She whined, stomping over to the knife man's corpse pulling at his belt until it came loose, sheaths and all. Prize in hand she strutted past Theodren who looked on at the carnage. "I totally had them." She huffed.

Once she was past him, Retribution emerged from the ground, crawling its way back up to its resting place on Theodren's bicep. He chuckled as he took a last look at the final bandit's corpse. Silently thanking the vineling while he wiggled a finger at the babe in his arms, who despite being out of Reina's arms for minutes now seemed as hale and healthy as she had ever been. He eyed the woman as she inspected her new blades and the sheathes they belonged to. Perhaps they could part ways soon. With Theviana no longer in need, perhaps he could be rid of Reina by the time they reached the next city. But as the sun glistened off of her golden hair he found that perhaps it was better to err on the side of caution. After all, she had proven herself quite capable against the bandits. He looked down at their bloodied forms. Such men were not worthy to share the world with his Godchild, but perhaps, Reina could share a larger part of the child's world than he had originally planned.

CHAPTER 28
BEITHIR

Theodren emerged from his newly acquired tent, groggy and unsure of the world around him. Stretching, he welcomed the warm morning sun that banished the chill night air from the world. He yawned and gave a muted grunt as he blinked their small camp into focus, only for a large and familiar mound of brown fur to blink back at him.

"Oh you've got to be joking." Theodren didn't dare move. Staring down its scarred snout at him was the young bear from weeks ago, resting by the smoldering embers of the fire. It gave a large toothy yawn as it stretched and clambered to its feet, shaking its own grogginess from a massive furry head.

Theodren looked around for Reina who was supposed to be on watch. It wasn't until the sound of a gentle nasally whistle came to his ears that he looked up to see her perched on a large branch, Theviana in her arms and head resting against the trunk of the tree. "Reina!" He hissed, eyes flickering between her and the bear that lumbered closer to him.

"Huh? Wha? I'm not sleeping, you're sleeping!" Reina jolted awake, eyes blinking fast as she clutched Theviana to her chest, panic and then relief filled her face. She craned her neck to look down at Theodren. "What's your prob... oh..."

He was not looking forward to another fight with the grizzly. He held his arm straight, palm out at the bear. "Stop! Stay!" He shouted in a tone reminiscent of his mother disciplining his fathers hounds. The bear stopped in its tracks, cocking its head to the side as it considered the man before it. A look of thoughtfulness crossed the bear's features before its shaggy rear end slumped to the ground, sitting almost like a dog.

"Huh." Theodren managed, bewildered by the seemingly docile bear. "That was the cutest thing ever!!!" Reina shrieked from her branch. She swung down from the tree, bursting with an uncharacteristic energy Theodren found offensive this early in the morning and rushed to his side. Depositing the baby in his arms, she turned and leapt at the bear. "Reina, don't!" But it was too late. Airborne and arms spread, she landed face first in the bear's chest, doing her best to wrap her arms around the massive beast.

Theodren tensed, expecting violence, a roar, a rampage. What he was not expecting was an almost human-like expression of bemused exasperation at the small human clinging to his neck. "Reina! Get off the bear! It could be dangerous!" Her head turned, showing half of a pout. "He's not dangerous, he's a friend!" Theodren released a massive sigh. "It's not a friend, it's a predator!"

Reina reached up, grabbing the furry cheeks of the bear's face, she pulled them upward into an approximation of a smile. All pink and black gums crowned with yellow teeth, Theodren grimaced.

"If not friend, why friend shaped?" She asked, further terrorizing the creature who whined in response. It was strange to Theodren to see Reina so excited. She must truly have a love for animals, he reasoned, trying to connect the city girl impression that he had made of her to the animal lover he now saw clinging to the bear's neck. It was stranger still to see a bear so tame. Especially this bear. Theodren still recalled the roaring savagery of his claws and the ferocity of his fangs as they had battled only weeks ago.

His curiosity piqued, he searched deep into the beast's soul, hunting for some kind of subterfuge or aggression hidden anywhere amongst its Vitae. The Bear's soul glowed a brilliant green, interspersed with calm blues and pleasant yellows. A tiny dull red of irritation flickered amongst the other emotions but there seemed to be no threat there. What was strange was the brilliant green of the bear's soul, it was oddly familiar in a way that he couldn't quite place. A moment passed and then it clicked.

Theodren looked down at his own soul, thrumming powerfully in his chest. As his connection to the beast became apparent, he groaned. The reason the green of the bear's soul was familiar was painfully simple. It was the exact same color as his. When Theodren had healed the creature after their fight, he was still inexperienced. Dumping massive quantities of his own Vitae, his own soul into the bear and now...

Theodren turned his eyes to the beast's annoyed face as Reina continued to fawn over it like a child with a new puppy. A piece of his soul now lived within the bear, fully absorbed into the creature's Vitae.

He ran a hand through his hair. Another mouth to feed, and a big one at that. Reina's muffled giggling grated at his ears, a sentiment he apparently shared with the bear, who groaned and grumbled at the enthusiastic woman's harassment.

Theodren sighed, pulling Reina off the suffering creature. Her giggles continued as she dangled from his grasp. "Can we keep him?" She asked, offering the best impression of a puppy dog face she could.

"I do not believe my saying no would deter you in the slightest." He said. She squealed as he lowered her to the ground. The bear stood, plodding up to Theodren, it poked him with its nose letting out a pleased huff.

"I have to name you now don't I?" Theodren grumbled. "Ooh! Ooh! What about Barry?" Blurted Reina, bouncing on her toes in excitement. Both Theodren and the bear looked at her with mixtures of disdain and disbelief.

She blinked at them. "What?" Theodren shook his head, returning his attention to the beast before him. The bear was even bigger than he remembered. Five feet at the shoulder, ten feet tall on its hind legs, Theodren had truly been a novice when he pumped it full of Vitae.

His attention wandered the bear until they landed on the intense amber of the creature's eyes. The color and hue reminded him of cold nights spent indoors gathered around the fire. His mother would read them tales of great heroes and vicious monsters, using her thread to cast shadows on the wall, illustrating her tales to the wide eyed children of his father's hall. Theodren remembered one tale in particular.

The tale of Beithir. Beithir was a great dragon who lived in the far north, removed from the world. Kings and Queens the world over would make pilgrimage to him, requesting his council or his judgement, renowned as he was for his wisdom and fairness. It was also rumored that Beithir held a vast horde of gold deep in a cave in the mountains where he lived. One day the king of a nearby land came to the beast seeking his riches. Three times the dragon rebuked him, and three times he returned. On the fourth day the king arrived with soldiers and fire, demanding what he claimed was owed to him as lord of that land.

Beithir acquiesced, under the condition that he would give the gold to the king's soldiers, and they would have to give it to him. The dragon gave each man a small fortune, and when the time came to relinquish their treasures to the king, they refused. Scattering in all directions, the soldiers returned to their families to live as lords of their own. Leaving the king to stand alone before the dragon he threatened. "A king with no one to follow him is no king at all. And loyalty that can be bought is a poor ware indeed." Was all the dragon said, retreating into its lair, leaving the scorned king to suffer his fate in the frozen north alone.

Theodren nodded as he decided on the name. The name of a wise and noble beast. Placing his hand on the bear's brow, he spoke. "Your name is Beithir."

Chapter 29
Plans and Pawns

One week later...

Piercer leaned back in his chair, distancing himself for a moment from the mountain of contracts, reports and missives that cluttered his desk. He had sent his men, Gunther, Ginter and six others, west to the small town Hardwright had described, in search of the priest of mysterious importance. Twisting his head to the side, a soft pop in his neck gave temporary relief to the tension that had been building more rapidly in the recent days.

Piercer could not stand the Cardinal. Not the man, nor the church he represented. Thirty years he had devoted to the Holy Order's legions. Thirty years of tedium and hardship interspersed with extreme violence and loss, only to be cast aside, abandoned when men of violence like him were no longer needed. Some soldiers he knew had rebelled. Demanding pay and admittance to the city they fought for. and all of those men were either taken at the hands of the Justiciars or had fled across the sea to try their luck in Grandia's more recently conquered territories.

His chin came to rest in his hand as he remembered that day. Scores of paladins in golden armor and deep hoods, emerged from the city to place his brothers in bondage, dragging them away in golden chains to a fate unknown. He would see his men, even if just their bodies returned. And the Cardinal may have delivered him the piece he needed.

The target was more than just a simple priest as Hardwright had described. Of that he was certain. The shiftiness of the man's demeanor conveyed more truth than any word the Cardinal could ever speak. That Hardwright wanted the priest alive meant he would be valuable within the capitol. Theodren Stormwall would provide the access he needed to go where no soldier had gone before, into the Conclave itself.

Stormwall... he sighed deeply as he remembered the last man he met with the name. Staring each other down across the great river. First they hurled insults, then arrows and then finally, words of diplomacy. No one had ever outmaneuvered him before or since, and when the giant Northman could have slaughtered them all, he did not. Restraining himself and his men, he chose to let the muddied, bloodied and bedraggled survivors of Piercer's detachment return with the bodies of their fallen comrades. When the capitol announced that the son of Thorn had joined the priesthood, Piercer had dismissed the lad as a cheap pawn given to the Conclave as a gesture of good will, but now... he would have to reassess the young man.

He picked up his latest missive from one of his spies within the capitol. The comings and goings of various politicians and priests was scrawled out upon the page. One particular line caught his interest. The Patriarch had stopped visiting the Academy. Gaius Lex the Patriarch had gone from his office to the Academy twice a week, every week for the last four years. But in the last three weeks, the Patriarch had not visited The Loom, as it was called, even once.

The Taskmaster squinted at the page. Whatever had held Lex's interest there had left three weeks ago. The Patriarch was not one to change routine lightly, and if it was important enough for the man to go out of his way for every week, then it was important to Piercer.

In the last ten years Piercer had painstakingly crafted a network of spies and informants. Bribes, threats and blackmail had taken him far in his endeavors until he knew the goings on of almost every institution of import, except, until a week ago that is, when Cardinal Hardwright delivered himself right into his hands.

The Golden Shears were an especially difficult nut to crack. None of their sect ever seemed to leave the confines of the Conclave unless they were on orders. Always returning bloody and silent, in a manner that unnerved all who were aware of it. But now the head of that order was sitting upstairs. Drowning his anger in the best booze Piercer could find him. With a plan to keep him placated, until Theodren was in hand and the Taskmaster could make his position clear.

Piercer lowered the parchment onto the flickering stub of his candle, tossing the page into the bin where a pile of ashes already sat. Hardwright's arrival had significantly sped up his timetable. So much so, that he would spend the next several nights maneuvering all the necessary pieces into place years before he had originally planned.

He set about writing his next batch of orders. The soldiers of Militas had gone soft and undisciplined in their pseudo retirement, taking to drink and sport to while away the days between what jobs he could find to keep them busy. He would have to reinstate a training regimen for the men. He would not allow laziness and lack of discipline to cost him another victory as it had for the weak willed officers of the northern campaign. All of them had retired to the city, lauded with medals earned by the men they left behind and telling tales of bravery that weren't their's. Piercer had gone to great lengths to consolidate his authority when the officers abandoned them. He would need it now.

Chapter 30
What's in a Name?

It was late in the afternoon when Theodren and Reina arrived on the outskirts of Oreton, riding out of the lush forest and into the acrid air that assaulted Theodren's nose as they rode to the gate. A harsh and oppressive haze hung over the city, coal and iron mixing with the unmistakable stench of thousands of people packed on top of each other. Beithir had not needed to be told to wait outside of the city. The heavily industrialized tang in the air was enough to keep him far back from the tree line. As the duo approached the gate, Theodren was envious of the bear. How people could live, stacked on top of one another as they did here baffled him, and he was loath to enter such a pile of humanity as this.

Two leery looking guards leaned against their spears. Eyes picking through the crowd of travelers, Theodren watched curiously as they jotted down notes every so often, and despite Theodren's best attempt at anonymity, they took notice of the large man and small woman melding into the crowd of other road weary travelers, took notice and scribbled once again in their ledger.

Finally through the gates, Theodren released the breath he hadn't known he was holding. Reina looked around, wide eyes over a wrinkled nose. "Not even the slums smelled like this." She whispered, tucking Theviana deeper into her chest as if to shelter her from the stench.

Theodren looked around, for shops, for lodging, for information. Anything to speed them on their way north and away from this city of squalor. Reina grabbed his sleeve, pulling him toward a wooden horse cracked with age, hanging over what appeared to be stables. Clicking his tongue, he urged his tired horse through a throng of people streaming by in a sense of urgency only important to themselves.

"Dismount there and tie your horses to the post, I'll be with you in a moment." Said a gruff voice from a stall out of sight. Theodren nodded to Reina and they slid from their horses. Theodren pulled his and Reina's packs from the horses as they waited for the yet unseen stablemaster. A large figure, broad at the shoulders sporting forearms thick with strength, rounded the corner, wiping his hand on a leather apron before offering it to Theodren. "Names Kemp, this is my stable." said the man.

Theodren shook his offered hand. "We need new mounts, supplies and lodging for the night." Kemp nodded, looking from Theodren to Reina and then the child on her chest. "You'll want a wagon. A trip north needs more than you can fit on a horse, especially for a young family like yours."

Reina sputtered. "We're not..."

Theodren put a hand on her shoulder. "First trip north with the little one. Got to introduce her to my Ma before she comes south to tan my hide for not bringing her sooner." He chuckled, shooting Reina a look. Theodren turned back to the stablemaster. "How'd you know we were going north?" He asked, unease edging his voice.

Kemp snorted, poking a finger at the outline of Retribution curled around his bicep. "I know a battle band when I see one son." He lifted his sleeve, showing a silver arm band of his own. "Got this one at the Stith, old Redbeard gave it to me himself." Theodren raised a brow at that. Redbeard had been a frequent guest of his father's hall, often carousing Thorn into drinking games and the telling of tales from the war.

The Stith he remembered, was a fort built on a promontory that jut into the Jormungand. Grandia had made a massive push for the fort, hoping to claim it to guard crossings into the north and establish a beachhead. It was a desperate and wasteful battle. Many a body in gold and white livery was washed away as their commanders drove them onward. Through sheer numbers and an almost suicidal bravery, The southern legion managed to cross into the north if only for a moment. Redbeard had been his father's foremost friend and Jarl and he would not stand for golden boots on northern land. A ferocious fighter as well as a mad tactician, He had seeded the bank with oil in the night. And when the enemy crossed, they were greeted with a corridor of fire that led to Redbeard and his warband who, to hear him tell it, held off the enemy advance single handedly.

Theodren cast an appraising eye over the stable master's soul. The colors were muted, dimmed from decades of soldiering and the simple wear of time, but they were not muddied with cruelty as the bandits or Hardwright's guards had been. This was a man who killed when he had to and only when he had to. He gave the man a genuine smile. "My father told me many tales of the fighting at the Stith, if you were there then I am glad to know you. My name is Roden, and this is my wife Steina and our child Thevi." Theodren said, saying their fake names loud and clear enough for Reina to remember.

Kemp chuckled "It is good to know you as well, I would ask a favor of you for your trip north." Theodren considered for a moment. "Name it." Kemp turned and hustled to the empty stall where a workbench sat, cluttered with an odd collection of tools, scraps of iron, ledgers and parchment. Muttering under his breath, he found one sheaf of parchment that he had been looking for and stashed it in an envelope that he sealed and marked with a red 'R'.

Kemp returned with the letter and handed it to Theodren. "When you get north, give this letter to my cousin Eric. He should still be at the Stith, runs the Wet Boot tavern." Theodren turned the letter over in his hand before tucking it away in his pocket. "I'll see that he gets it." he promised. Kemp nodded. "Now, if you sell me those two horses of yours, that'll cover the cost of the wagon and some dry goods for the trip, but I'll need two gold a piece for oxen to pull it all. Reina cleared her throat. "Cows? I thought horses pulled carriages." Kemp raised an eyebrow at her. "City girl eh? Horses are all well and good for pulling your snuff boxes in the city, but for a grueling trip north over rough terrain, you'll want something with stronger legs than that."

Reina narrowed her eyes at the "city girl" moniker but couldn't rebut it so she sniffed and turned up her nose. Theodren rolled his eyes as he dug into his coin purse, pulling out six gold from the generous collection of coins he had gained from the Mayor and bandits. "I'll need two oxen and all the dried meat this will get us." Kemp weighed the coins in his hand. "I'll need two days to get this together, but there's plenty of Taverns around here to choose from. Shouldn't cost you too much either."

Reina turned pleading eyes on Theodren. "Two nights in an actual bed!? Oh please *dear.*" she teased begging him to accept the deal that would get her a warm bed and perhaps even a bath for two nights. Theodren weighed the risk the lost time would bring them. It would take Hardwright at least another week to return to Grandia in the state he was in. It would take two more for whatever men he sent to reach the ghost town they left behind and then more time still to track them north. Two days would be an acceptable loss to their schedule he reasoned.

"You've got a deal." Theodren held out his hand to the stable master who shook it in agreement. He turned and shouted at his stable hands who were idling in the corner. Giving them orders and measurements for materials that would make the wagon they needed. Reina bounced excitedly next to Theodren as her mind was already on the minor luxury of bathing and clean linens. "Any recommendations on lodging?" Theodren asked between the man's barked orders. Kemp turned, eyebrows scrunched together in contemplation. "Anywhere but the Blue Rose." Reina looked up at him. "Why not? I saw a flyer for it on the way in, it seems nice for the price."

Kemp shook his head. "Some things that seem too good to be true, are." Theodren watched as a purple of unease seeped into the man's soul. "I've had customers go into that place and never return for the beasts they stabled with me, it's after a while someone from the city always comes to take their horses or mules or what have you." He looked Theodren and Reina hard in the eyes. "You seem like nice folk, do not stay at the Blue Rose." With that he turned back to his stable boys, barking orders as they scrambled to do his bidding.

A curious look passed between Theodren and Reina once the Stable Master was out of view. "Steina? Really?" She scoffed walking off toward the sounds of the street outside. Theodren groaned, following after her. He would likely not hear the end of that.

Chapter 31
A City of Secrets

The hustle and bustle of the crowded street grated on Theodren's nerves, but Reina seemed to have it worse. Sweat beaded on her brow and her breath came ragged and fast as she clung to his sleeve more desperately the deeper they pushed into the city.

Shouted offers from vendors and angry curses between citizens assaulted Theodren's ears. But the whispers ravaged Reina's mind. The whispers had been bearable at the gate and almost silent in the relative seclusion of the stable. But here on the street, pressed in on all sides by the irritable foot traffic of Oreton. The whispers had built up into a cacophony of human darkness. Their deepest secrets and darkest desires assaulted Reina as she clung to Theodren like a drowning woman to a raft.

Suddenly, her surroundings changed. Theodren hauled her off the street and down an empty alleyway until the sounds and voices faded away, leaving only a dull echo to bounce off the stone buildings around them. Theodren's face filled her sight as he called her name loudly. "Reina!"

Tears beaded at the edges of her eyes threatening to spill over. "They won't stop! All of them! All of their dark thoughts. All of their greed and cruelty! It's like they're shouting the worst of themselves into my ears!" She sobbed. Each panicked breath sending tendrils of shadow flailing this way and that on the alley walls.

Theodren placed a hand on both of her ears. "Listen to me." He murmured, like he was calming a skittish colt. The sound of his heart beat, steady and strong, thrummed in his palms and into her ears. Her eyes locked on his as the storm in her mind began to calm. "Don't listen to them, listen to me." He brushed a tear from the corner of her eye. "Theviana needs you."

The reminder of her responsibility broke through the turmoil in her mind as her eyes narrowed in concentration. The city was a sea of whispered secrets and dark desires. Each of the millions of people walking around with their own darkness threatened to drown Reina if she listened to them all at once. She searched the chorus of whispers for one she recognized.

There amidst the chaos of greed and fear was a whisper of familiar regret. Theodren's soul spoke to her. It told her his anxiety, his fear of inadequacy, his fear of failure after already losing so much.

Deep in his soul she heard the worst of it all. What if time dulled his rage at Hardwright? Was he honoring his friends properly? Did he even deserve to live? What if he failed to avenge them? Who did he think he was to fight the Order alone? Did losing his rage at Reina mean he wasn't committed enough to his friend's vengeance?

The turmoil in his soul was more profound than Reina had thought. Composed as he seemed to be, the idea that he second guessed himself so persistently surprised her. As she considered his darkness the surrounding cacophony of souls seemed to fade and her shadows slowed their menacing dance on the alley walls so long as she kept his soul at the forefront of her mind. Snippets of whispers were still audible, but no longer did they threaten to overwhelm her as they had before.

This was how he survived. She realized. All of his fears and anxiety were alive within him, but he pushed them to the side in order to focus on what was in front of him. She steeled herself as she did the same, pushing the whispers away and focusing on his soul and his alone.

Before long her breathing slowed from its panicked pace and sounds of the city returned as Theodren pulled his hands from her ears. "Whatever you heard in my soul... I can't imagine what it must be like to hear people's worst impulses."

She went to answer when a voice cut her off. "Oh you poor dear you look dreadful!" Theodren looked up to see an older woman walking down the alley towards them. A severely tight grey bun rested over a face coated with too much makeup and pulled too tight for the wrinkles that should have surrounded dark eyes Theodren couldn't quite tell the color of. She had the look of a woman desperately fighting off the grip of time. She shifted her wicker basket laden with vegetables further up her arm as she pulled her deep green shawl tighter around the shoulders of her sleek blue frock. "You two look as though you may collapse on the spot! Are you looking for an inn by chance?"

"Indeed we are madam, my wife and I just got into town." Theodren said, resuming his role of traveling family man. "No wonder You both look ready to drop! I run an inn just up the road from here. Follow me and I'll have a nice warm stew and fresh blankets for you two." Reina stepped out from behind Theodren to better see the old woman, shifting the babe in her arms to a more comfortable position.

The old woman's eyes locked onto Theviana, asleep in Reina's arms. "And an adorable child to boot! You really must come with me." She laced her arm into Reina's, guiding her deeper into the alley. Reina looked back at Theodren confused. He could only shrug and follow along as the old woman led them down a twisting route of back alleys and side streets all while she asked them where they came from, and if they knew anyone in the city.

Theodren and Reina answered as vaguely as they could, doing their best to keep their fabricated history synchronized. "You two really are a lovely couple. I'll set you up in a delightful little suite. I dare say you may never want to leave!"

As they rounded the final corner, one building stood out from the rest. Where the rest of the buildings were of stone construction, this building was made of wood. Two stories tall and narrow, there could not be more than a handful of rooms from the look of it, but it seemed well maintained. coated in fresh lacquer and decorated with dark blues of varying shades. Hanging from a sign post over the door, was a blue rose painted on a wooden sign that creaked softly as it shifted in the wind.

Theodren froze in his tracks. "What did you say was the name of your inn?" The old woman turned back to him as she continued marching Reina forward toward the blue door. "How silly of me, did I forget to say? My name is Dahlia Black, and this charming inn of mine is the Blue Rose."

Chapter 32
A Dark Soul

Reina disappeared into the gloom beyond the blue door as Theodren stood rooted in the street. The hairs on the back of his neck stood at attention for reasons he could not immediately explain. He shook his head. Reina was in there now, and besides the Stablemasters cryptic warning, there was no reason to distrust the Blue Rose or the woman who ran it. Setting his jaw, Theodren followed after them into the dark tavern.

Reina was sat in a high backed chair by a roaring fire, holding Theviana close to her bosom while her eyes wandered the room. Theodren could sense the unease in her soul as she fussed over the child. "I'll have your stews ready in a moment dear!" came a voice from the back of the common room. The floor creaked beneath his boots with every step he made toward Reina. Sitting down in the chair across from her, he sent his vitae sprawling across the floor, searching for souls beyond the three he already knew about.

Reina looked up at him. "You're scared of this place." Theodren sighed. "The stablemaster has me spooked. Did you hear any whispers from the old woman?" She scoffed. "She has a name Theodren." He stared at her silently waiting for her answer. She relented, shoulders falling. "No, I wasn't listening, not since the alley. You don't know what it's like." Theodren nodded. For a moment his focus was lost in the dance of the flames in the hearth. For all his unease, there was little that soothed him quite like the crackle of a fire. The way the light danced, pushing darkness aside even if only for a moment. It was not unlike life itself in that way.

A brief spark of energy that needed to be nurtured until it can sustain itself. Consuming fuel and air to survive and shine brightly, bringing warmth and light to those around it until it eventually burned out, returning to ashes and silence.

Theodren's brow furrowed as he stared deeper into the flames. It really was like his Vitae. almost as if on instinct he reached for the flame with his mind, probing. The energy within the blaze was there, just out of reach, if he could only...

"Here we are! Two hearty bowls of stew for my road weary travelers." Theodren returned to the present with a blink and a deep inhale as regained his awareness. Theodren looked up into the face of the innkeeper and almost flinched. The grin on her face was uncomfortably wide and toothy for a face as wrinkled as hers. Light from the fire danced across the topography of her face but not her eyes. Even as close as she was, Theodren could see no color to them, only darkness.

"We are most grateful for your hospitality Madame Black, this stew smells delightful." He managed. And indeed the steam coming off of the bowl smelled rich and savory, paired with a loaf of bread that was soft to the touch. Reina broke off a piece of her loaf, dipping it daintily into her stew, scooping bits of meat and vegetable into her mouth to sample the meal. Eyebrows climbing her head, she turned to the woman. "This is wonderful! The meat is so tender, what is it?

The crone chuckled "Family secret I'm afraid deary, if everyone knew what makes my stew so special I'd go out of business!" Theodren ladled a spoonful of the stew into his mouth, pausing to blow on it first. Leaning back in his chair, he pushed the stew this way and that with his tongue, searching with his vitae for anything that might harm him in the food. His last encounter with Poison had been an educational one and he was not willing to swallow anything that glowed a toxic black before his mind's eye. Deeming it safe, He allowed the bite to pass, warming his stomach as it settled. "Hearty indeed." he grunted, reaching for his next bite.

Madame Black grinned. "I could hold the child while you eat. I'm sure it would do you good to have your hands free even for just a moment." She offered, holding her hands out for the child. Reina's brows came together in sudden suspicion, the hand holding Theviana held her tighter to Reina's chest. "Oh don't worry deary, I've held many children in my day!" The old woman crooned. In truth Reina's back and arms ached from carrying the child so close for so long. Surely just a moment of reprieve while she ate was no crime. Removing Theviana from the sling on her chest, she hesitantly handed the babe over to the woman who smiled all the wider.

The relative calm of the inn was shattered the moment Madame Black's hands touched the child. Theviana let out an ear piercing wail at the woman's touch. The babe's arms flailed and she kicked in protest. Reina snatched the child away, pulling Theviana back into her arms to soothe the screaming child. Theodren's attention was pulled away from Reina and Theviana when he felt an almost atmospheric shift in the Vitae around him. He looked back at the innkeeper, where before was a matronly smile now seethed a vicious scowl of disgust. Sensing his eyes on her, the dark expression was gone as quickly as it had appeared. "Some children really can't abide anyone but their mothers it seems." she said with a sardonic chuckle.

"Yes, she needs her mother." murmured Reina as she rocked Theviana in her arms, soothing the hiccupping sobs that came from her tiny mouth. "I think I'll get you both some tea." she offered, turning around and shuffling off to the kitchen before either of them could refuse.

Theodren looked back at Reina. "What was that?" he asked. "I don't know, but I don't like her, and neither does Thevi." She hissed. Theodren nodded. Something was wrong with this place. He could not shake the sense that there was a danger here that he was not seeing. He pushed his Vitae out further. Probing deeper into the Inn than he could see with his eyes.

Madame black re-emerged from the kitchen with two mugs on a tray. "My famous Blue Rose Tea! just the thing you poor dears need to relax after a long journey on the road." She placed the cups down on the table in front of them. Black earthenware mugs filled with a milky blue tea that swirled lazily in the cup, topped with a blue rose just like the one above the door to the inn. "Now don't waste a drop! and when you're done I'll take you up to your room." She looked down at Theodren, whose eyes had not moved from her since she had returned from the kitchen. "Everything alright dear?" Theodren shook himself. "Ah, no, I was just wondering if the other guests would be joining us." She chuckled. "I'm afraid we're alone here dear, You're the only guests I have in this place." She said, walking away toward the stairs.

"She's lying." Whispered Theodren. Reina leaned in closer to him. "How can you tell?" His eyes turned to the floor beneath their feet. "Our souls aren't the only ones here." Her brows shot up at that. "You can see them? Where?"

He nodded. "There are eight of them, down in the basement and three aren't moving." She looked down at the bowl of stew. "Do you think Madame Black put something in the food?" Theodren shrugged his shoulders. "Or Maybe the tea." he guessed, searching for anything still active within the brew. There within the tea was a sickly blue vitae swirling along with the current in the Tea. "Don't drink it, there's something alive in it, something from the rose." He hissed, the souls in the basement worried him, he wanted to investigate but he would not endanger Reina or the baby to do it.

Reina looked down into her mug. "Alive?" She dipped her finger into the drink, stirring it. Theodren watched as the lazy blue energy soaked into her finger, leaving the drink entirely. "That was..." Her eyes began to flutter, interrupting her sentence with sudden exhaustion. "Reina!" he hissed, grabbing her hand, shoving Vitae into her skin as quickly as he could before she passed out completely. Her eyes flew open. "Ow!" she snapped back to awareness, rubbing her hand where Theodren had touched her, a tiny red mark left behind by the heat of the Vitae flooding into her. "You fell asleep." He whispered. She shuddered. "But did it work?" Theodren looked back down at her tea. No longer swimming with the sluggish blue energy he saw before, he nodded. "Should be." She handed him the mug. "Here. Now let me do the other one." Theodren nodded, placing a hand on hers, clearing the poison as quickly as she consumed it.

Both mugs clear of poison, They drank it quickly, finishing just as the Madame landed on the last step. "Wonderful you finished your tea! Now if you'll follow me, I've got a room all set for you two." Theodren and Reina stood to follow her, single file up the narrow stairs. As Theodren stared into her vitae, he realized he had never seen a soul so black.

Chapter 33
Lost Soul

Theodren and Reina left the warmth and glow of the fireplace behind as they followed Madame Black up the stairs. "I'm sure you two are just exhausted. So I've prepared a nice warm bed and a bath for you both." She purred, guiding them towards the room at the far end of the dimly lit hall. The pair gave each other worried looks as they followed the innkeeper into the room. A simple four poster bed was pushed against the far wall of the room, set with clean looking blankets. It looked almost as inviting as the large wooden tub filled with warm and soapy water, sending coils of steam into the air to catch the firelight.

Theodren turned to her, affecting a facade of polite gratitude. "This is a splendid room, I'm not sure we can afford such generous hospitality." The innkeeper waved away his concerns. "Not a trouble at all dear, having you here is all the payment an old woman like me needs." she chuckled. "Now you two settle in, and I'll have breakfast ready when you wake." Theodren nodded. "Thank you madame, The food was just what we needed, I feel I may sleep for days."

A malicious smirk flashed across her face for only a moment before she turned to Reina. "Have a lovely rest now you two." she said as she made her way out of the room, closing the door behind her, The latch giving a soft click as it locked into place.

Reina turned on him. "We are NOT staying here." She whispered. Theodren looked at her quietly for a moment, a plan forming in his head. "No, *we're* not." He agreed cryptically. "What does that mean!?" She hissed.

His shoulders set. "That woman had the blackest soul I've ever seen. Even darker than Hardwright's." Reina's frustration turned to a quiet anger. "She's not our monster to slay Theodren." He stared at her as she continued. "This isn't your town and these aren't your people. We can't risk exposing ourselves just for strangers we don't know.

Her logic was sound. Their best course of action was to sneak out the window and find a new inn somewhere more reputable. They had a purse full of coins and no need to embroil themselves in someone else's trouble. But before he could agree with her, he felt a change.

Vitae began flowing into him. He looked around for a source but there was nothing in the room with them, he examined the feel of the Vitae, like a tailor examining cloth before it merged with his own spring. It was... young, vibrant. Untainted by the burdens of a life long lived, but what he saw at the end of the length of Vitae was a white bolt of terror. This was the essence of a child.

As he looked around, his eyes went still at the floor. Though he was two floors above them, he could still see the forms of Vitae in the basement. The black form of the Madame was visible in the basement alongside the others. But where once was eight, now sat seven. The littlest one, was now absent.

The fire in the small hearth grew to an inferno as Reina shielded her eyes from the sudden light. It was as though a massive wellspring of fuel was dumped on the blaze. Reina blinked the spots from her eyes to see Theodren's shoulders heaving in rage.

"Does no one but me, know the fucking VALUE OF A LIFE!?" He snarled. Darkness retreated from where he stood in the room, as if not daring to enter his presence.

Reina winced. The relative calm of his soul was gone, replaced by a vicious thirst for violence, for punishment, for retribution. His rage was overpowering with the names of his slaughtered friends joining the whispers that assaulted her mind.

She fell to her knees as they called for vengeance against the old woman, vengeance against Hardwright, and... vengeance against her. Her shadows lashed at the room around her while fear filled her soul. She clutched Theviana, crying at the disturbance into her chest as her eyes rose to find Theodren, Retribution in hand, stomping toward the door.

"No. Wait!" She cried, throwing out a hand that would never reach him , but her shadows did. Darkness flew at his back but parted around him as if deflected, slamming into the door instead, driving it shut.

He glared at her. "That woman deserves justice." He hefted the hammer in his hand. "And I'm going to give it to her." Reina relented with a shout. "Fine! Kill her! Bash her head in you great oaf!" Theodren paused at her sudden outburst. "But what if there's more people? Who's helping her? Why is the city collecting their horses?" All of these questions fell from Reina's mouth and landed on Theodren like hammer blows.

She was right. There were too many things he didn't know. She rushed across the room, shoving Theviana into his arms. "She needs us to keep our heads on straight." Retribution changed from hammer to budding vine in an instant, gently placing a suckling peach in the baby's mouth to soothe her cries. "Now." she looked him dead in the eye. "What will you do?"

Theodren's face was screwed tight in a grimace as he waged war within himself for the self control he needed. Ultimately, reason won out. Theodren gave a great sigh like the sound of air being pushed out of a bellows.

"I'm going to let them take me." She blinked at him. "You can't be serious." He sighed once more. "She killed a child, Reina." She took a step back as he continued. "Just now, I felt it. She was... terrified."

Reina considered this silently for a moment. "So we tell the city guard, get them down here." Theodren shook his head. "If they're not complicit they're at least aware of it. How would they know to get the horses the victims left behind? No. What's happening here is evil and I will not stand for it." He handed her Theviana and their shared coin purse. "Go. Find somewhere nearby to hole up. Come tomorrow..." his fist clenched. "There will be punishment."

Chapter 34
Willing Captive

Theodren stared Reina down as she tried to come up with an argument. She knew he was set on this path. She knew that he wouldn't be shaken from his moral code, but to willingly let himself be taken? She shook her head. Ice cold anxiety filled her chest. "This is a stupid plan."

He grimaced at her as the footsteps of multiple people creaked along the hallway floorboards. "Hide." Theodren collapsed back against the bed, feigning unconsciousness. Reina looked around for a place to hide. There was no space under the bed and no wardrobe that might hide her. In a panic she backed toward the window. She fumbled with the latch all while the footsteps got ever closer.

The metallic click of the door handle sent a shock of fear through her soul and she jumped to the darkness of the corner, trying to make herself as small as she could. Her timing could not have been any closer. Just as she came to a halt, the door creaked open.

Madame Black stood in the doorway, hands clasped together as she strode into the room. Theodren didn't dare to move. Keeping his breathing as even and slow as possible. "Tsk tsk tsk. Falling asleep without even bathing. Poor form indeed." Madame Black chided as she looked around the room. She froze. "Where's the girl?" She hissed, looking around the room for Reina, who shuddered in the corner. The innkeeper's eyes betrayed a terrible fury as they searched the room for Reina and the baby.

She stopped when her eyes landed on the window latch Reina had managed to pry open just seconds too late. "She went out the window!" She hissed, spinning around to face the two men still waiting in the doorway. Unnaturally long arms crested emaciated torsos wrapped in ragged peasants garb over sallow skin. "Find her. I WANT that child!" She screeched. The two men nodded dumbly, shambling off toward the stairs in search of Reina who remained in the shadows.

She turned her attention to Theodren who remained still on the bed. "At least I'll have my consolation prize." She smirked. Grabbing Theodren by the collar, she yanked him from the bed with surprising strength. It was all he could do just to stay limp in her grasp. Like a misbehaved puppy, Theodren was dragged from the room by his scruff, Madame Black barely struggling with his weight as the door swung shut behind her, leaving Reina and the child, alone.

The silence boomed throughout the room as Reina slid to the floor, hyperventilating. That damnable man had gotten himself captured! And that woman! Theodren was a truly massive man, to be picked up like that woman had done would require an unnatural strength.

Reina heard the thudding of Theodren being dragged down the hall. She cursed, rising to her feet she tiptoed to the door. Cold and shaking hands gripped the handle as she opened it as quietly and as cautiously as she could, just in time for Theodren's boots to disappear from the top step of the stairs.

The shadows still wrapped around her in a way that she could not explain, enveloping her in the surrounding darkness, muffling her steps. It was the only reason she was not also in the Madame's grip.

Finally at the bottom of the stairs, the innkeeper dragged Theodren to the kitchen, just barely out of sight from where Reina hid. The sound of rusted hinges rang out along with quiet commands that she couldn't make out.

Reina eyed the stairs. The memory of each creaking step filled her with trepidation as she planned her escape. Reina's eyes turned to the banister, calculating the distance between the railing and the floor below, she nodded to herself and leapt over the side. Leaving her free hand outstretched, she caught the bottom of the railing post, slowing her descent before landing on the tavern floor in a crouch.

Reina winced at the barely audible sound of her feet hitting the floor, and she waited for a minute that felt like an hour before she continued her path to the exit. The sound of the kitchen door swinging open met her ears just before her hand grasped the front door. "There you are." Barked Madame black from behind Reina. She turned in place, eyes wide with fear as she clutched Theviana to her chest.

Madame Black pulled a shining silver carving knife from the carcass of whatever it was that she had added to their stew. "You're never where I need you." She chuckled, turning back toward the swinging door, cleaning the knife with a clean rag as she went. The Madame paused as something out of place caught her eye. The front door was open, Swinging carelessly in the faint evening breeze.

Chapter 35
Parts or People?

THUNK! Theodren was tossed unceremoniously down the rickety wooden stairs to the basement floor below. Unsure of who was watching and where they might be, he remained limp even as his head and spine paid the price. He lay there in a heap for only a moment before strong hands grabbed him wordlessly and dragged him to a cramped cell of iron bars buried in the stone walls and floor of this subterranean prison.

The scrape of iron on iron echoed off the walls as the door to his cell slammed shut, leaving him well and truly trapped. Daring the risk, Theodren cracked an eye, doing his best to get a layout of the space through the spots that filled his vision from the fall.

The stone walls were lined with sconces that lit the room in an almost painful brightness that drove the shadows from the room. There would be no hiding here. The room itself was about the size of the tavern floor itself, filled with what appeared to be work stations lined with glassware, scales, and instruments made of shining sterile metal that Theodren shuddered at the sight of. What unnerved him more however were the jars.

Shelves of them. They lined the room for as far as Theodren could see, each shelf bearing a label. [Adrenal Glands: age 5-12], [Liver: age 10-25] he kept scanning the room, sickness building in his gut. [Eyes: age 15-25], and at the end of the line of shelves stood; [Heart: age 12-25]. There was a numbness in his soul as shock, terror, and a deep sadness mixed within his heart.

The sound of the basement door grinding open shook Theodren from the horror on the shelves in front of him. The black soul of the innkeeper was making her way down the stairs and he would have words with her.

***

Reina sprinted down the darkened side streets and moonlit alleyways of Oreton, panic filling her soul as each breath came ragged and fast. Where she was running to, she couldn't say. All she knew was that she had to get away from that tavern and that woman. Rounding a corner she found the sign she didn't know she was looking for. A sword held over a scale. Hope filled her heart at the sight of the Holy Justiciar post aglow in the dark of the city night. Pounding on the door she shouted. "Help us! Please!" her eyes darted about searching for any sign of the long armed ghouls the madame had sent after her.

She froze. There in the mouth of a nearby alley lurked a man with long arms. There was something abhorrently wrong with the man that she could not describe. He did not move, he did not speak, he merely stared at her with lifeless eyes as she continued to beat on the thick wooden door that finally swung open on silent hinges. "Who goes... OOF!" The moment she felt the door open Reina launched herself through the door and into the Justiciar office.

"Young lady! Just who do you think..." Reina slammed the door shut behind them. "You have to help me! The woman! She took my... My husband! She drugged him with something and took him away! We were only looking for a place to stay the night but she did something to him!"

Thick black eyebrows creased together in a mirror of the holy guard's mustache, pulling a piece of parchment and quill from the desk behind him, He began taking notes as Reina rattled off the events of the evening that saw Theodren captured and her on the run. When she got to the name of the Tavern, the sound of the Justiciar's quill scratching on the parchment came to a halt. "Did

169

you say you came from the Blue Rose?" He asked suddenly. Reina's eyes narrowed. "Yes I did, weren't you listening?"

He stared at her for a moment before standing. "Wait here please." The Justiciar Reina had mentally named "Mustache" stood abruptly and walked deeper into the hall of offices, looking around for someone Reina couldn't see. At the third door down he stopped abruptly, casting a glance back at Reina before closing the door behind him.

There was something about the way the man's demeanor changed when she said the name of the tavern unnerved her. She shifted Theviana in her arms as she tried to settle the hairs that stood on end at the back of her neck.

Making a decision, she grit her teeth as she opened herself to the whispers once more. This late at night, There were fewer people walking the streets. But in the dark, the whispers grew louder. The torturous whispers of people lying in bed with only their thoughts bombarded her mind as she grimaced through the whispered self doubts and troubled nightmares of the sleeping city.

Grinding her teeth she wrenched her focus by sheer force of will to the Justiciars gathered in the office hidden from her sight. "She'll fetch a high price." Was the first whisper she was able to differentiate from the rest.

She blinked at the sudden clarity, pressing on, she redoubled her efforts. 'The ones with kids are the worst. At least the payout will be good.' 'Have to take them back before the long arms come.' Her mind reeled at this new information. Justiciars were supposed to be a Holy Order of justice. Beholden to none, save their oaths and their honor, but there was no doubt in her mind, they were conspiring with Madame Black.

The wrongness of it all infuriated her. Was no one truly decent? If even the Justiciars could be bought, what then was the value of the Order? She looked down at Theviana who slept peacefully in her sling. They were going to sell her. Sell them both, to the Madame. They had made the decision as if she were mindless cattle to be handed off for a price. Her blood boiled at the assumption of helplessness by the Justiciars.

As her anger roiled, the solid wooden desk before her snapped under the weight of shadows that grew longer and deeper as she stewed on her anger. Since she was a child, no one had given her any choice, any agency, in where she would go and what she would do.

Her mother had sent her to the Conclave. The Conclave had sent her to Hardwright. Hardwright took her to the village and now Theodren had taken her here. The only person that had given her any choice at all was Nihila, and that choice came with consequences. She flexed her hand watching the shadows respond. Fixing her eyes on the door the Justiciars were plotting behind, she marched forward. From here on, no one would decide for her.

Trying the door as silently as she could, she found it locked firmly. Glaring at the door handle as if it had personally insulted her, she searched for a new angle. The lock itself was simple, made of worn brass sporting an unassuming key hole that, to Reina's delight, was filled with shadow. She pushed and prodded at it, puzzling her way through the lock all while the conversation between the Justiciars continued on the other side of the door.

"Think she knows we have her yet?"

"I couldn't say, nasty woman has those things everywhere. They could be on their way here now."

"Well then we need to get rid of her! I'm not going to be the one telling the Bishop why Madame Black's not happy."

"No need to fuss sir, we'll just haul her and the child back to the Inn, collect our reward and everything will be right again."

"I suppose the peasants have a use after all, even if it's just as bounty."

"Indeed sir, Old Dahlia pays top dollar for littluns. Got this belt with what she gave me for a kid three weeks ago."

"Why kids?"

A hushed tone came over the room as Reina continued with her efforts to push out the locking pins on the door.

"I heard tell she sells em. Makes good money down at the docks, loads em on river boats, never to be seen again."

"Nah, it's parts I think."

"Parts?"

"I heard the Bishop had a sick liver, all that drink. Then he goes to see Madame Black and he's right as rain! It's parts I'm tellin' ya. She strips em for parts."

"It doesn't matter what she does with them. We are not paid to know." If it keeps the riffraff off the street and we get paid then that's all that matters."

The click of the lock releasing its hold on the door made all four of the men turn. Standing in the doorway was a nightmare from their darkest dreams. A woman, shrouded in a black mist that whipped about with tendrils of ice cold shadow that seemed to engulf the room. She glared at them with lightless eyes as she drew two long wickedly curved daggers from her belt.

"You are a sickness." She hissed shadows lashing at the men who cowered away from her. "And I will cut you out."

CHAPTER 36
THE WOMAN IN THE DARK

"What in Weaver's name!?" Shouted Mustache. A tendril of black smoke slammed into him before he could say more, pinning him to the wall, legs flailing in a fruitless struggle for stability. Reina blanketed the room in her shadow, giving in to the emotions that made them strongest. She had worked hard these last weeks on the road with Theodren to understand and control her new power, but here, in this moment, she neither needed nor wanted control.

The weight of her darkness buckled the knees of the remaining Justiciars, sending them sprawling to the floor before they could even react. Glaring into their hearts, she searched the rotten pits of their souls for what secrets she could find. Fear flooded them, she could feel it through each tendril of shadow that bound them to the floor. "What the fuck are you?" screamed the youngest of the four. She looked at him, disgust blanketing her face as she stared them down without answer.

Since she had received her power from Nihila, she hadn't known what to do with the river of Acher that coursed through her soul. But now that she had her shadows bound to the very hearts of the men prostrated before her, She had an idea. She blasted Acher deep into their souls, engulfing and inflating each pit of fear in their hearts until it consumed them. Unhinged screams filled the air, echoing off the stone walls in a chorus of tortured souls. As they shrieked, the Vitae flooded out of them, like a bowl once filled with water, now flooded with oil, driving the life water from the vessel.

One mind was more difficult to crack than the others. Mustache hung from the wall, silently terrified but not overwhelmed as the three withering men on the floor were. Curious, she turned her attention from the screaming soldiers and stalked toward the Justiciar who remained, pinned to the wall, panicked, but otherwise unharmed.

Looking closer, she tsk'd. "Priest." she spat, noticing the thread that coiled around his heart.

He blinked, as if remembering that he was not entirely helpless. "Witch!" he shouted, lashing out with his Thread. Clearing away the shadow, he dropped to the floor, cursing as he fumbled for the club strapped to his belt. Reina leapt at him. Daggers held in front of her in a ready guard, she advanced in a curved line, seeking to unbalance the Justiciar who now finally had his weapon in hand.

The air hissed as her daggers flew out in exploratory jabs and slashes, testing his defenses. Each attack missed him by inches. Her brow furrowed, a film of gold light seemed to radiate off of the Priest, pushing both her shadows and her daggers away at the moment before impact.

He laughed as her attacks pinged harmlessly off of him. "Your foul magic will never pierce the armor of the Weaver!" Brandishing his weapon above his head, he bellowed a challenge, driving the golden club down at her.

Like a leaf in the wind she danced around his blows, furiously searching for a gap in the golden aura that protected him. "You don't deserve his protection." She snarled. He faltered, if only for a moment as the whispers of Reina's words lingered in his soul, continuing his assault he shouted. "What would you know, witch? I'm Odrain's champion! I was chosen for his grace!" The club smashed into the wall, inches from where her head had been. He cursed, swinging wilder and faster hoping to reach her with a lucky blow.

She had struck a nerve, she thought as a wicked smile lit up her face. She searched his soul for confirmation, and was rewarded with whispers of inadequacy buried so deep, he likely wasn't aware of them. "You've never worked hard for anything have you?" She laughed, Acher infusing her voice.

"Bitch!" He screamed, lashing out with thread only to find open air where her head had been a second ago. "This office is mine because of me! I deserve it more than anyone else!" He screamed. But his whispers betrayed him. In his heart of hearts, he knew that he had only gotten to where he was due to his father, some lofty bureaucrat Reina had no interest in knowing.

"I'm sure that's why daddy dearest gave it to you." She snickered. The golden glow that surrounded him flickered. "How do you know that!?" He snarled, swinging his club and a lasso of Thread at her midsection, forcing her to throw herself backwards out of the way and into a wall.

Her back slammed into the stone with a grunt that knocked the air from her lungs. Sensing the advantage Mustache launched forward bellowing a challenge as he slammed his weighted club down at her head.

Sparks flew at the meeting of Thread-imbued club and shadow-covered blades formed in an X above her head to catch the blunt instrument at the base, just above his hand. Dropping the daggers, she maneuvered his wrist into her grasp, twisting as she pulled his arm, palm up, over her shoulder.

She was rewarded with a wet crack and a howl of pain as his elbow broke. Throwing her hip back, she pulled with all her might, sending the man toppling over her shoulder and into the wall. The force of him hitting the wall sent Reina stumbling, heaving ragged breaths into tired lungs.

He groaned, propping himself up into a sitting position against the wall. She slammed her mass of shadows into his chest, pinning him to the wall. He grunted, but gave a broken laugh. "You can't kill me, you can't even touch me. I have the Weaver on my side. You're just some witch. And when everyone finds out about you. You and that brat on your chest will be torn to pieces." Reina glanced down at Theviana who merely stared at her with surprisingly calm eyes. She was insulated by a mass of shadows surrounding her like a dark blanket, blocking out all sound from the babe's ears. Reina was glad for that as the Justiciar's threat rang in her ears.

She snarled looking back up at the broken man before her. Though he spoke with bravado, she could see that the fear welling in his heart was written across his face. The pain in his arm must have been distracting him because the gold aura that had been surrounding him, sputtered a dull glow. She squeezed tighter with her shadows, hoping to crack his infuriating shell with brute force.

"I don't have to kill you, it's not as if anyone listened to you to begin with." The pits of fear in his heart responded to her words, growing larger. She grinned pushing what Acher she had left into her voice, speaking truth to the fears that only she could hear.

"You could tell everyone you know and no one would care because no one cares about you." He flinched back as if struck. "You were placed in this tiny office on this nameless side street because no one thinks you worthy or capable of more than to be hidden away in an alley."

"Shut up!" He barked, but the whispers weren't done. "You've ruined every opportunity you ever had because you thought you were smarter than everyone else. But I'll tell you a secret that everyone knows but you." She leaned down next to his ear as he struggled against the shadows that bound him. "Everyone knows that you are as useless as you are incompetent. They only pretend to be amicable with you because of your father and even he is ready to disown you."

"Don't..." he pleaded. but she continued. "Soon you'll be forgotten, alone, cast into the gutter where deep down you know you belong, right next to the peasants you spit on for years. Not even the Weaver will want you." She looked down into his eyes, red with pain.

"How many women and children have you sold to the Blue Rose?" The whispers of a buried and broken conscience shouted out to her. A cacophony of varying numbers between thirty and fifty filled her ears.

Her disgust for him only grew. "You don't even know?" She sensed a hidden shame flicker through him even as he sneered. "Urchins and peasants finally finding something useful to do with themselves, even if it's just as parts." He spat. His words at odds with the shame buried within him.

"What does she do with them?" She hissed, squeezing her shadows tighter. "I don't know." He wheezed, darkness tightening its grip on his ribs.

"Liar!" She spat, as his whispers told her everything. Those long armed men were no men at all. They were golems comprised of flesh. Odds and ends sewn together onto a mentally broken victim. True man made monstrosities created by some dark science of the Innkeeper.

But that was not the worst of it. The Justiciar had known about the organs she sold. Most of the nobility knew of her medicines designed to keep those who could afford her services, young and healthy.

It was only after he became a Justiciar captain of the Iron Quarter of the city that she had approached him, offering substantial bribes for whatever subjects he could deliver to her. The younger the better. After all they were only peasants, oftentimes they were even petty criminals, he had justified their demise as punishment for their crimes, but deep in his soul he knew this was not justice.

Her nostrils flared as her eyes locked back onto his. "You are a monster." She whispered, shocked at the callousness of the man. He opened his mouth as if to give some retort, but Reina would not hear it. She slammed her hand over his mouth. Pushing Acher down his throat, past the weak aura that protected his body and into his soul.

Icy cold Acher coiled around his heart, pumping him full of fear. His wide and wild eyes bore into hers as his muffled scream filtered through her hand. His heels beat on the ground in a frenzy, like he was trying to run away sitting down.

"Death is too kind for you." She snarled. Her Acher filled every pit of fear in the man's heart. Each one screamed out his personal nightmares, but one in particular caught her attention. A new fear emerged, blossoming as she watched. It was her. A vision of a woman cloaked in shadow.

"The Woman in the Dark." his heart whispered. She pumped frigid power into it, until all that filled his brain was her. His mind cracked under the fear and the strain. Babbling incoherently as Reina released her dark grip on him, allowing him to slump to the floor, mumbling about the Woman in the Dark.

Reina stood tall admiring her handiwork. Three of the Justiciars were shriveled husks, terror etched across their faces for all eternity. The Captain she had left alive, babbling on the floor to suffer in his madness for all the victims he had sacrificed for his greed.

She checked on Theviana again to see her sound asleep. She marveled at the tiny child strapped to her chest. She was a prodigious sleeper to be sure. She thought back to Theodren now trapped at the hands of Madame Black and her golems.

She sighed, turning on her heel she marched out of the devastation she had made of the Justiciars office. Resolving as she walked, to give Theodren a piece of her mind. Once she rescued him of course.

Chapter 37
Deadly Medicine

The sharp snap of heels on stone reverberated through the basement. In the relative darkness of his cell Theodren kept one eye cracked open, observing the severe figure of the innkeeper sauntering through the cellar. "Such a pretty face." she crooned speaking to someone laying on the table just out of sight. Theodren searched for any Vitae he could find in the room besides his and the Madame's. There were a handful of weak souls packed away in large crates with breathing holes so small he almost missed them. Terror, pain and misery clouded their souls, but what really grabbed his attention were the chaotic patchworks of Vitae that stood but did not move.

There against the far wall were two forms standing eerily still. No matter how hard he looked he could find no light in their eyes and no color in their souls. They were the long armed men that had stuffed Theodren in the cell but they could hardly be called men at all.

A mismatch of limbs and odd scars made up their beings. A hunched stature concealed an imposing height that Theodren had missed at first glance. Long arms that reached down past bowed knees and a face as slack and empty as the unnervingly long fingers that hung at their sides. But what puzzled Theodren most of all was their Vitae. They each possessed great pools of bluish grey. There were no patches of color or shifting hues. There was only that constant pallid blue.

"I know you're awake." Theodren's breathing stopped. "Most people don't know this, but breath..." she grunted, cutting through something tough. "Is the essence of life." she finished. The sound of heels on stone drew closer. "And your breath is just brimming with life isn't it?" Theodren knew his charade was over before the click of her steps stopped in front of his cell. Rising to his feet he squared his shoulders at the woman who inspected him from outside his cage like she was already selecting which cuts she would make on him first.

The facade of a matronly innkeeper was gone. Replaced instead by a severe woman slicked with blood from hand to elbow.

"What have you done with the people who were here?" He growled. She narrowed her eyes at him. "Figured that out, have you?" she purred, dragging bloody fingers along the bars of his cage. "I put them to better use." she answered dryly, walking back to the table she had been working at.

In her moment of inattentiveness, he urged Retribution into the ground behind his feet. It burrowed into the cracks between the stones like a weed, disappearing into the earth below.

"All of these people, wandering the world with no purpose, no drive, no passion! They're no better than mongrel dogs feeding off the scraps of society." Theodren craned his head at the edge of the bars, trying to see what the Madame was doing. "I take the poor dears and I find them a way to matter."

A loud POP! Echoed off of the basement walls and drove an ice cold nail into Theodren's heart as he recognized the sound of ribs breaking. The innkeeper turned around, holding her prize in her fist. A small heart that could only belong to a child, dripped blood down to her elbow. "This lovely little heart will go to much better use in a person that matters don't you think?" She dropped it unceremoniously into a jar filled with the same blue liquid that filled the hundreds of other jars that lined the walls.

"MONSTER!" he roared, throwing himself against the iron bars that creaked but held firm. She merely gave him a disinterested look as she turned back to the body of the child whose death Theodren had sensed earlier. "I wouldn't expect some country bumpkin to understand the nuance of higher Alchemy." She sighed, continuing her dissection. Theodren silently urged Retribution to work faster. Somewhere beneath the stones, he could feel the vineling's Vitae as it dug and scraped at the earth holding the walls of his prison in place.

"I am simply making use of the tools Odrain gave us." she said, holding up a blue rose for Theodren to see. "Did you know that in the Eastern Isles they use these for medicine? They use the entire plant from roots to petals." She returned attention to the body in front of her. "The petals when hydrated and subjected to heat, make a natural sleep elixir more effective than anything they're making in the capital. But even the Islanders don't know what this specimen actually does."

Between sentences more and more organs joined the heart in jars on her work table. "The blue rose slows cell activity almost to near standstill. Which means..."

"They're still alive." Theodren gasped. He stared hard at the jars surrounding the room. A dull glow of Vitae flickered in them, fear staining each one through and through. "That's correct." Purred the Madame toweling the blood off her hands. "I find the well-to-do of this city will pay *anything* for the extra years, fresh young organs will get them. After all, why shouldn't they? If they can afford it they deserve it." She strutted closer to the cell where Theodren seethed. "Their youth makes us strong, a byproduct of younger blood in more experienced bodies." coming to a stop just out of reach of his cell she sized him up. "Older donors like yourself might be less lucrative, but I believe everyone should have a purpose, willing or otherwise." Theodren snarled at her.

"As slaves?" he guessed. She smirked. "Correct again. A shame that clever little mind can't be put to better use. But alas a body like yours would be wasted as anything else but muscle." Turning to a separate work station filled with glassware and pestles, She prepared a syringe. "Once my golems return with that lovely wife of yours I might find a use you two could share." She smiled at him with not a hint of warmth. "The child however I want for myself."

Theodren bristled. "You're not even fucking human anymore are you?" he growled. Her grin grew wider. "Who can say?" she giggled. "Children that young, when properly utilized make a fascinating series of elixirs that I've found reverse the aging process by years. She ran a hand through the grey of her hair. "Just a little more and I may even pass for forty again." she said with a dreamy grin.

"For now." she returned her attention to Theodren. "I think we should get you good and ready for your new use." Holding the syringe up to the light, she pushed on the plunger till a fine jet of deep purple sprayed from the needle. "Mule, Cow, Please restrain our guest so I may administer his medicine."

The two golems that had stood silent and unmoving lurched forward. Theodren readied himself as they unlatched his cell door, fists rising to his jaw in a guard drilled into him for years of his youth. The Madame scoffed. "Oh I wouldn't do that dear, I'm afraid they're much stronger than they look. You may hurt yourself."

Theodren snorted. The two behemoths lumbered into his cell, dull eyes betraying nothing. Almost faster than he could react, two long scarred arms flew at him, grasping for his wrists. Theodren leaned back, just barely avoiding the reaching fingers. He wouldn't be able to avoid them that way again. He could feel the cold of the stone wall seeping into him.

If back was not an option then forward was the answer. Their speed and reach had surprised him the first time, but he had their measure now. Ducking under the grasping hand of who he assumed was Mule, he shot forward. Driving a shoulder into the man's gut, he wrapped both arms around his legs and heaved to the side, gritting his teeth at the surprising density of the golem in his arms. Slamming the golem to the ground he had no time to breathe before the next pair of lanky arms was upon him.

Cow had circled around him when he had wrestled Mule to the ground. Snaking his long appendages around Theodren's neck, yanking him backwards, and off balance. Almost immediately a fist from Mule slammed into his gut driving the wind from him.

He doubled over, trying to suck air back into his spasming lungs while he wrestled the arms from around his neck. Even his prodigious strength was no match for two of these monstrosities, he thought, as he continued his desperate battle against the flurry of snake-like limbs. Their pools of Vitae were massive, almost as deep as his own, and unlike him they seemed to feel no pain or weariness. A cold fist struck his jaw, hard.

Buckled knees met cold stone with a CRACK! As he clung to consciousness only barely. Mule and Cow piled onto him, holding him down with their dead weight. Stars flashed before his eyes as he reeled from the blow. He was only vaguely aware of the Madame's heels announcing her approach.

"Really now, what did you think would happen?" He felt a cold prick of pain on the back of his neck as she drove the needle home. The hands that held him down released their icy grip and he leapt to his feet. Or at least, he tried to. Cold flooded his veins, spreading from his neck to the rest of his limbs. Within his mind he roared and railed against the prison of his lethargic body that now lay limp on the stone floor.

"I think we'll let this one sit for a little while." she purred as the sound of her heels followed by large shuffling feet retreated from the cell. He could feel the foreign Vitae invading his system, overwhelming his body. With what strength he could muster, he grit his teeth. Pushing his own wellspring of Vitae at the flood of poison that threatened to overtake him.

He wrapped his brain in a blanket of his life force, hoping to at least keep his mental faculties intact. The sluggish blue crashed against the wall of Vitae protecting his mind. Crashed, and then receded. No, not receded, absorbed. His Vitae was conquering the poison, metabolizing it and making it his own, albeit slowly. Hope filled his heart as his worst fear fell away. Now relieved of the fear that gripped him, a silent rage took its place. The *injustice* that these innocents should suffer at the hands of such a callous and unfeeling monster as the Madame lit a fire in him. A fire that in his current state Theodren had failed to notice was draining his vitae. Preoccupied as he was with fighting off the poison and plotting his captor's retribution, he was entirely unaware of the vitae that drained away to a deeper part of him as the question rattled through his mind. What truly was *Justice* in this world?

He had no idea how long it would take to clear the poison, or how long before Madame Black returned, but he would not waste a second.

***

Glassware clinked and knives gleamed in the lantern light of Madame Black's laboratory as she brewed her latest formula. The man in her cell was a mountain of muscle all on his own, she'd hardly have to alter him at all to add him to her collection of golems. Those organs of his however, there were many of her benefactors that could put them to better use. Her golems shuffled past her as she worked, almost oblivious to the muffled sobs and groans that came from the large crates Mule and Cow were loading on rail carts deep in the gloom of her workshop.

Her hands flew over practiced movements and measurements all while she preened over the efficiency of her enterprise. Long decades had she devoted to the science of alchemy. Longer still was the time she had spent in service to her master who had taught her the arts she used to steal life with the power of the mysterious blue flower.

Once she had been little more than a local healer; daubing poultices and ointments on every day afflictions. But her master had been the first to see her true genius. She grinned to herself as she recalled the lean young Doctor who had offered her the expertise and knowledge she had so craved. He had shown her the miracle of the Blue Rose and its ability to steal life. He had given her the tools to rise and she wasted not a second on pity for her test subjects. Once he had shown her the ways of alchemy, he had moved on to Weaver knew where and left her to develop her own enterprise.

The Justiciars alerted her to quality subjects whether they were vagabonds or simply travellers who wouldn't be missed and it was a simple matter then to guide them to her inn where her concoctions would close the trap on her unwitting prey. Sitting in her cell was a new liver for the local lord who had drank his to decrepitude. There was a new heart for the Baron who some believed did not have one of his own and a myriad of other odds and ends for those who could afford it. The majority of the cattle that came through her cells ended up in crates like the ones her golems were pushing down the tunnel out of her workshop after only losing perhaps an eye or a kidney. They would need to be healthy to survive the next leg of their journey to the mines and shipyards where they would spend the last of their days.

Madame Black gazed back at the lifeless desiccated body of the young girl on her operating table. Odrain had blessed her with two prime specimens and when her golems returned with that woman and most prized of all, the babe, she would finally have the ingredients for another elixir. She frowned at the lines and gray hairs that spoiled her visage in the mirror behind her station. She had lost track of time at some point. Years had become decades even as she wound back the clock on her own mortality, but each time she clawed her youth back from the bottom of an elixir, she found that she needed younger and more potent ingredients. It was not enough for the subject to be young. Youth was in no short supply among the vagabonds and travellers of the kingdom. What truly made the ingredients effective was the adrenaline that fear mixed within their blood. She had to admit, she did not entirely enjoy the screams, the wailing or the tears required to prime her subjects for harvest. She shook her head as she thought about it. "So unnecessary" she chided the lifeless girl on the table. But the results spoke for themselves, the blood from the girl would be potent to say the least, but it would be nothing compared to what she would squeeze from the baby.

A distillation of the young woman's heart and adrenalized blood from the child would do much to smooth her face and darken her locks. She smirked into the dirty mirror. She would be beautiful again.

CHAPTER 38
STOLEN SOULS

A lone figure stalked the alley. Though she walked in moonlight, she remained in the dark. The shadows of the stone city seemed to almost reach out to her as she passed, but Reina noticed none of this. She was, instead, focused on the conundrum of the Blue Rose.

Theodren had allowed his capture. Presumably in search of answers that only captivity could provide, and that left Reina alone, with only her thoughts for company. Theodren was strong and resourceful, she knew that under normal circumstances, no man should be able to best him. But something about the long armed men that she had seen in the Madame's employ...

She shuddered. They frightened her. Not only her but the Justiciars as well. They were scared of them, she could feel it.

As if summoned by her thoughts, two figures rounded the corner ahead of her, shuffling footsteps echoing off the stone walls of the otherwise silent city street. Long arms hovered just inches from the cobblestone as they lumbered toward Reina, and behind her, she could hear the same rough steps of a third.

She grit her teeth. She had been hoping to avoid any further violence this night, but violence had found her. Setting her eyes on the leftward creature, she listened for his soul. Listened and was overwhelmed. Her knees buckled under the weight of the cacophony of tortured screams that came from the twisted collection of souls housed in that one monstrous body. It made no sense, it should not have been possible to possess more than one soul, yet here in this creature lumbering toward her was a multitude.

Once the screams of the golems tortured souls filled her ears there was no shutting them out. Gasping sobs racked her frame as she tried and failed to regain control. The lumbering features drew closer. Her nails dug bloody gouges in her palms as her own scream joined theirs. She needed to get up, she needed to run, she needed help!

In the depths of her heart she pleaded for salvation from the horrors that assaulted her mind. And from the depths, a darker horror answered and time stopped. **"What could a Daughter of the Dark have to fear in the moonlight?"** Nihila's voice slithered through her mind, clearing away the chaos that had overwhelmed her.

Relief flooded her as the silence of the night returned. Reina opened her eyes, looking for what form the dread goddess would take this time, but there was nothing except for the three long armed golems that had closed in around her. **"Up here daughter."** Chuckled Nihila.

The flapping of wings rang out as a raven soared out of the shadows on the wall. Black feathers that seemed to almost shine in the moonlight, and a long sharp beak, gave the creature a distinguished look. Reina was transfixed by the thing as it strutted toward her. Cocking its head, it fixed her with a mocking stare. **"Death isn't only for humans, you know."** Chuckled the Raven.

Reina struggled to find the words for how grateful she was to simply not see the talking corpse of her victim. Nihila strutted past the cloth foot wrappings of the golems to perch on the top of Reina's fist, still clenched from the tension.

"What vexes you child?" The goddess asked, staring at her through the beady eye of the raven. Reina blew a heavy sigh. "I can't do this. I can't stand all the whispers! It's like they're screaming in my ears and I can't make it stop!" She whimpered, ashamed at her weakness.

Nihila hopped up her arm to her shoulder, pecking at her cheek. **"Did you think that death would be an easy discipline to master?"** Reina shook her head.

"You don't understand! My mind can't take it! Just listening to these creatures makes my head feel like it's going to split open!" Nihila cocked her head at her. **"creatures?"** Reina scoffed incredulously. "These three! These men! There's something wrong with them!"

Nihila went silent, as if seeing the golems for the first time. Reina continued. "I thought I was getting better, but it's like there's hundreds of souls in them and I can't hear them all at once!" Reina waited for her goddess to speak, but neither encouragement nor admonishment came from the raven. There was only quiet.

Reina stared at the bird who only had eyes for the golems. **"What is this!?"** She hissed with a vehemence Reina had never heard before. **"Who would do this to a SOUL!?"** Nihila screeched. Acher leapt out of the bird, coalescing into a figure cloaked in a darkness Reina could not even comprehend. Shadow raged throughout the alley, like waves in a storm against a stone beach.

Walls cracked under the goddess' fury, whatever was wrong with the golem's souls they had angered Nihila and Reina was afraid. Shadows latched onto the long armed men. Wet pops and sickening cracks rang out as the golems were disassembled piece by piece, until they were nothing but bloody components scattered about the alley.

Even after the massacre at the village, Reina had never seen such vicious carnage carried out so brutally. The goddess' attention turned to Reina. **"Daughter."**

Reina swallowed through the dryness in her throat. "Y-yes goddess." The figure seemed unstable, shimmering in the moonlight as if the bounds of its form could not quite decide where they should be.

"Bring me who is responsible for desecrating these souls. They have stolen from me and I will have my payment." Nihila seethed. Reina shook before the true form of the goddess. An older woman wrapped in a cloak made of a night sky shrouded in clouds. From her hip hung a silver loop sporting a single key of thick iron. It knocked against the lantern topped staff she held as she strode closer to Reina.

The goddess placed a gentle hand on Reina's trembling chin. **"Be not afraid, daughter, not of me."** Reina looked up at the otherworldly woman. **"Be afraid for the souls who won't reach my door."** Reina could still see the anger in the goddess' eyes, but there was a sadness there too. Reina knew that what Madame Black had done was evil, but to upset the goddess of death was an extreme she hadn't thought possible.

Nihila nodded as if reading the thoughts straight from Reina's mind. **"Now take me to this Madame, she owes me a great debt."**

CHAPTER 39
MAN HUNTERS

Hooves broke the silence of the night as eight men, weary from their haste, trudged to the stone stable. Ginter rode straight to the door, too impatient to dismount, he swung an iron shod boot at the stable door. BAM! BAM! BAM!

Gunther sighed, shouldering his brother's horse out of the way, his tremendous bulk displacing the horse just before the door swung open with a loud; "I will slap a saddle on the next man to..." Kemp blinked a weary eye at the second man to match his height in recent days.

Taking advantage of the momentary silence, Gunther jumped in. "Pardon the intrusion Stablemaster. These gentlemen and I would like to put up our horses and cart for a few days and we are hoping that you would be amenable to our lodging them with you."

Kemp's brow furrowed as he attempted to square the rough and scarred appearance of the man's face with the eloquence of the words that came out of it. Giving up, he shrugged, holding the door open for the parade of rough looking men.

"You're a big lad." Kemp said matter of factly. Gunther gave a tired smile, as if the frequency of such a comment wore at him. "Aye, our mother was a Nordlander, father was a Grandian trader." volunteered Ginter, patting his much larger brother on back.

The stablemaster looked from Gunther to Ginter, searching for some resemblance that would mark the unlikely pair as brothers. "Your father must've been a brave man." He chuckled, drawing up a lodging ticket. "It's been years since I've seen another Nordlander, and now two walk through my door in as many days. Gunther and Ginter shared a look. "Another Nordman you say? Did he happen to have a woman with him?" Gunther asked as casually as he could.

Suspicion twitched at the edge of the stablemaster's eye. "Someone you know?" He asked. Gunther shrugged, attempting to affect an air of indifference. "Cousin's actually. We were supposed to meet up at the gate, but we got waylaid on the road."

The story sounded plausible enough, but something about the band of ragtag soldiers rubbed the Stablemaster the wrong way. "Tell us where they're staying." The little brother demanded, just a hair too forcefully. Kemp raised an eyebrow and Gunther shot his brother a look. "Just to check on em, that's all." Ginter blurted.

"It would be good to share lodging with my brother and his wife." Gunther offered quickly. Trying to distract from his brother's eagerness. The stablemaster gave the men a second look. Chainmail peeked out from the rough edges of their cloaks, the youngest of the eight had shed his cloak entirely as he removed satchels and saddlebags from their horses, revealing a padded gambeson, patched many times over with many different color fabrics. The youngest mercenary unloaded their packs into the large sturdy cart before handing the horses over to Kemp's stable hands that took them with bleary eyes and yawning mouths.

These were manhunters. North or south, it made no difference, Kemp could spot the soldiers of fortune anywhere. "Must be hard, sharing lodging with a young couple and their bairn." Kemp said as he handed the lodging ticket over to Gunther, whose eyes narrowed just slightly at the mention of the baby.

"Aye, little brat just wouldn't quit his wailing while we traveled together. Had to send them on ahead just so we could get a night's sleep." Gunther shot his brother another warning look and Kemp was certain. Roden was a hunted man, and if he was in danger, so too were the woman and child. While Kemp was not one for keeping other's secrets, betraying a fellow Nordman in his hour of need was not something he would stomach.

"So, think you might tell us where they're lodged?" Gunther asked, a hint of steel underlying the man's polite tone. The Stablemaster could almost feel the shift in the mercenaries attitude as the big man gave just a hint of menace. No weapons were drawn, none had to be. The message was clear enough to see for those who knew what to look for.

Their hands all rested casually, almost lazily, on the hilts of their weapons. Spaced evenly amongst the stable hands throughout the place, the soldiers each had a perfect area of range, so that they could attack freely without interfering with their compatriots' swing.

In his younger days he might not have even perceived such a threat, and if he had he would have likely responded with immediate and reckless violence. But his younger days were well behind him, and cleverness would see him through.

Praying that the young couple had heeded his advice he gave his answer.

"You might find them at the Blue Rose."

CHAPTER 40
THE FIRE OF CREATION

Theodren seethed. It had been hours since Madame Black had poisoned him with her twisted alchemy. The rough stone of the cell floor pressed into his cheek at an uncomfortable angle, sapping the warmth from his face as he fought against the last of the poison that had threatened to destroy his mind and tyrannize his body.

Being forced into the tedious and drawn out battle within his own body gave him time to analyze the dark blue Vitae of the poison. While Madame Black may not have known she was doing it, she had managed to manipulate the plant's Vitae on a crude level. Preserving the plant's chemical defense and redirecting it in a way that benefited her and harmed her victims required a subtlety and skill that Theodren loathed to admit in the woman.

Still, to defeat one's foe is to know one's foe. As his father liked to say. As he pushed and burned at the poison with his own Vitae, he wondered what Polly would think of the plant. No doubt it would have found its way into her bag of remedies-for-poor-behavior. He gave a soft chuckle tinged with sadness at the thought. As the sound left his throat he tensed.

No sound came to answer his, not the click of Madame Black's heels or the shuffle of the Golem's feet. They hadn't noticed. From where he lay, he could see little beyond the stone in front of his nose but as his eyes returned to focus, the stone wiggled.

Small green shoots sprouted around the brick in front of his nose, Retribution pulled itself from ground, reaching out for

Theodren. It latched on to the torn collar of his shirt, sliding back to its resting place, coiled around his arm. Whatever it had done in the hours he laid there had clearly taken its toll. Theodren could feel the exhaustion coming from the vineling. Curiosity overtook him as he compared the Vitae of the blue rose coursing through his system to the green glow of Retribution.

He pushed the poison toward his arm, curious what the vineling would make of it. At the first touch of it, Retribution recoiled, surprised by the foreign Vitae in its master's system. The vineling uncoiled from his arm, raising the head of itself almost like a snake watching a mouse.

Pain brought tears to his eyes and he struggled to stay silent and motionless as Retribution struck, burrowing into the flesh of his arm, just deep enough to reach the blue Vitae beneath his skin. Breathing through gritted teeth he almost laughed out loud at the relief as the vineling began siphoning the poison from his blood.

Like a leech with sickness, it pulled the dark blue Vitae from his flesh. Theodren watched fascinated while Retribution devoured the poison. Devoured it, and metabolized it. Alarm built in him as the blue vitae grew stronger in the vineling, but it seemed not to care. Growing stronger off of it, changing.

Having drawn the last drop of the poison from its master, Retribution pulled itself from his skin, settling once again around Theodren's arm. Blue Vitae slowly disappearing amidst the vast green of the vineling's own life force. He breathed a sigh of relief as the wound closed with the speed he had grown accustomed to since Yggdrazil's appearance in his life.

His fingers twitched as he regained control. His strength was his own once again. Upstairs he heard the entry bell of the tavern's front door ring out. Keeping an even and slow breath, He waited.

An exasperated sigh preceded the scrape of a stool against the stoney ground and the click of heels as the Madame passed his cell. His heart beat a frantic pace in his ears when her footsteps paused in front of his cell, but she pressed on, climbing the stairs.

The sound of a trapdoor creaking open and then shut was all Theodren needed to hear. Pressing his fist into the ground he rose to his knees and finally his feet. The cell was barely tall enough for his height, but soon that would not matter. Feeling still returning to his limbs, he trudged toward the door.

Across from his cell the Golem's only stared at him. Unable to move without instruction and completely incapable of initiative of thought, they watched as Theodren grabbed the wall of his cell and pushed. Retribution had done its work well. Just holding the bars, he could feel the give in the stone below where the bars had been well anchored hours earlier.

Theodren yanked and shoved. Working the bars this way and that until finally the scrape of steel and stone signaled his victory as they came free in his grasp. Placing the bars as gently as he could against the wall, He turned to the golems who stared back at him wordlessly.

Pity welled in his heart as he considered the broken creatures before him. Glassy eyes devoid of life and mismatched bodies covered in puckered and angry scars. Who they might have been was long gone, what remained was a pale imitation of life and a cruel one at that.

Neither creature moved as he placed a hand on both of their heads. He wasn't sure how he knew, but the souls in these creatures were beyond saving. At first he had thought them empty, but looking at them now he could see how wrong he was. Their vitae was as scarred and as thrown together as the bodies that housed them. These were not the souls of two people. There were perhaps as much as ten souls bound together with horrific pain in each golem.

Even if he could find a way to heal their minds from the effects of the poison he had only barely broken free of. He could never restore their souls, and he shuddered to think what ten souls in a single body would do to a human mind. He sighed as he steeled himself. There could be no salvation here, only mercy. He pushed Vitae as gently as he could into their brains. Grabbing hold of where he remembered the core of their mind should be from his tutors at the Conclave, he flooded the bundle of cells there with Vitae, forcing them to grow. Grow until they could no longer and finally, they burst. "Be at peace." he murmured as their immense Vitae flowed into him.

Theodren killed them as quickly and as painlessly as he could. He could not bear to see them suffer any further pain, not from him. Cow and Mule slumped to the ground soundlessly as he Guided them as gently as he could to the floor in perhaps the only position of rest they had enjoyed since the Madame gave them their cruel names.

He gave a silent prayer to Yggdrazil and even to Nihila for their souls as he turned to face another horror. There on the table was a young girl, or at least, what remained of one.

Curly brown locks turned golden from the sun lay still on the head of the desecrated child. Tear stains were still visible on her face, streaking from eyeless sockets that had been robbed by the Madame. Below the neck the child's chest was splayed open, an empty cavity where organs should have been. Instead they sat in jars surrounding the girl. Her heart, still waiting to be labeled and stocked like some miscellaneous product. Just one of hundreds already tucked away.

The callousness of it all stoked a fury in Theodren. The likes of which he had not felt since the village. Rage seethed within him as he stared down into the girl's face still marred with fear. He memorized every detail he could see, no matter how painful she was to look at. This pain was his penance for his failure to act sooner. She had been robbed of justice because he was uninterested in her suffering until it was too late. The more he stewed on her fate the more Vitae seemed to drain from him, still unnoticed, focused as he was on the injustice before him. He refocused on committing her features to memory, from her lashes to the slightly crooked teeth in the mouth that hung open in a ghastly and permanent moan, he would remember it all. It seemed as if the light in the cellar grew brighter, and as the image of the child's tortured face burned itself in his memory forever, he realized that it had.

The fires in each sconce burned a brilliant red. Suffused with a Vitae that confused him. As far as he knew, fire was not a living thing, it should not, it could not possess Vitae, and yet as he stared deeper into the heart of the fire, he realized that he was wrong.

At the heart of each miniature blaze, was an ember of Vitae. To call it life seemed not quite correct to Theodren, it was more akin to a concept of creation. It was said that at the beginning of time Odrain had gifted fire to humanity as a means to sustain life and create civilizations. And as the flame mesmerized him he understood. Life was more than just creation, it was also destruction, and rebirth.

Fire had been a part of man's life since its inception, and thus it was his to command and he knew just what to do with it. Pouring his vitae into the fires of each sconce along the walls, they erupted. Brilliant flames shot forth from them, bathing the room in light and fire that licked out at the shelves and workbenches surrounding the room. Even with the mysterious drain on his pool of Vitae, he had received enough from the two golems that such an expenditure of power was merely a drop in the bucket.

The supernatural flames spread quickly, devouring everything in their path, shattering jar after jar on every shelf as the flames boiled the sealed containers into bombs of pressurized liquid and glass. Theodren retreated from the blaze, covering his face with his sleeve to shield his lungs from the acrid smoke that quickly filled the space. As he blinked his eyes through the haze, he noticed a door he had not seen from his cell, shrouded in shadows now banished by the blaze.

His heart chilled as he remembered the two other souls he had seen through the floor hours ago. "They must be through that door!" he coughed to himself. He tried to push through the flames but the heat was intolerable. He grit his teeth as he took step after burning step through the blaze, determined to see what was beyond the door. The cracking of stone and the groan of overburdened support beams halted his progress.

Retribution had done its work well in loosening the foundations and support of his cell, perhaps too well. The destabilized earth and blazing fire shattered what support remained in the cellar, sending beams and debris down in a shower in front of the door, blocking Theodren from the mysterious tunnel beyond it with a pile of burning rubble.

A roar of frustration leapt from his throat as he was forced to retreat once more, rushing for the stairs leading him up to the Tavern and away from the inferno below.

CHAPTER 41
A TALK WITH DEATH

Reina walked silently down the twisting maze of alleys back toward the Blue Rose. A soft coo from the bundle strapped to her chest reminded her that Theviana would need to eat and soon.

She cursed Theodren silently for perhaps the hundredth time for his scheme that separated them. Behind her, Death chuckled. **"Quite rash even for him."**

Reina harrumphed in agreement. By now she simply assumed that Nihila was privy to her inner thoughts and didn't question it. What did confuse her was the change in the goddess's demeanor. She seemed almost an entirely different person from their first meeting.

Nihila drew alongside her, staff clacking against the cobblestone with each step. **"Everyone has their own understanding of death, daughter, and it can change as people change."** The goddess spoke with the voice of a teacher Reina couldn't help but trust.

Nihila continued. **"When I first offered you my gifts, what did you think of me?"** Reina thought back to that terrifying moment in the village, death smiling at her through the lightless eyes of her most devastating victim. She shuddered. "You were terrifying." Reina whispered.

Nihila placed a weathered hand on Reina's shoulder, giving her a comforting pat as she continued on. **"To the unprepared The End and The Unknown can be terrifying."** She glanced out the side of her eye at her mortal protege. **"And now?"** Asked the goddess. Reina's brow creased together. To her eyes now, Nihila was a weathered albeit matronly crone. Her staff held a lantern to light the way. And her cloak, while made from the stuff of shadows, seemed worn from time that Reina could not begin to fathom.

"You're not evil, you're…" Reina struggled to find the words. The curve of Nihila's staff brought the word forward in her mind. "You're a shepherd," she concluded.

Nihila snorted. **"A shepherd, indeed."** The comparison seemed to amuse the goddess but she didn't refute it. **"Every soul that splits from their Vitae departs from their bodies forever. As the keepers of the Black Door, it is our responsibility to guide these souls that seek us out to our step and once they're ready, let them through."**

Reina puzzled over Nihila's words. "But you're more than just death." Reina said, a question hiding in her statement. **"No, I am not just death. I am the lacking of things, I am entropy, I am the absence of creation and most of all daughter"** Nihila stopped to look Reina in the eye. **"I am the End and the Unknown."**

Reina swallowed hard as she tried to consider the magnitude of the being beside her. The only god too powerful for Odrain to bind, holding dominion over death and beyond. "Why do you just watch?" Reina found herself asking. "You control so much, you can do so much, why do you let people like Hardwright, the Church, Madame Black, get away with all of the terrible things they do? There's so much suffering! You could stop it all but you don't! Why!?" Reina found herself shouting, surprising herself with the depth of her feeling on the subject.

Nihila turned to her. **"You wish I had killed you back in that village before you hurt any of those people."** The goddess spoke with a clarity that struck at Reina's soul. **"I took no part in the weaving when Odrain made this Tapestry. I wasn't there when he made man kind and I was not there when he gave man souls. Millennia ago I might have told you he was a fool. I've certainly watched man work enough evil for it."**

Nihila gave a sad smile at a child's chalk drawing, proudly scrawled on the side of the building they passed. **"I have also** seen the good and wonderful things they are capable of if they are allowed their better natures." She turned her attention back to Reina. "Life is for the living, dear. For good or ill, your soul is yours to do with as you please." Nihila sighed as she seemed to lean heavier on her staff. "Over the eons I have heard so many excuses from so many hollow souls for why what they did was never their fault. I trust you will hear them too when the day comes."

Reina was baffled by Nihila. Every sentence she spoke upended her precarious grip on what she knew to be true about the world.

"And this charming place must be the Blue Rose." Nihila mused. Her words turning the very air to a chill fog with the ire in her words. Reina opened her mouth to answer when the goddess cut her off.

"The last time you were here, you left the souls within to suffer." Nihila said, less an accusation than a statement of fact. "I didn't know what she was doing yet, I was just trying to keep us out of trouble." Reina reasoned.

The goddess was unmoved by her answer. "I brook no excuses daughter, when you accepted my gifts, you accepted a duty as well, and that duty is to the dead, and many there are from the Madame's schemes." Nihila seethed, eyes boring into the door and the darkness within. "Remind the Madame that she is not beyond my reach."

CHAPTER 42
THE LIGHT IN THE DARK

<u>"One more thing dear, before you go."</u> Reina turned, just inches from the door, midway through recovering from Nihila's admonishment and steeling herself for her confrontation with the Madame. Nihila had somehow made it soundlessly onto the steps behind her. From the depths of her robe she pulled a small lantern. All rosy glass and ornate wrought iron, it gave a deep red glow, like an ember in a dying flame. As she handed it to Reina, the warm glow of the tiny flame within danced with the sway in Nihila's grasp.

Reina took the lantern with a confused reverence from the goddess. "What is it?" She asked breathlessly, feeling the weight of a gift she did not quite understand. Nihila blinked at her. **<u>"It's a lantern, dear."</u>** She answered, amusement pulling at the sides of her wrinkled mouth.

Red flared in Reina's cheeks as she hurriedly hooked it to her belt. "Oh." she mumbled, eyes glued to the floor in embarrassment. Nihila chuckled. **<u>"It does what lantern's do best. It lights the way."</u>** Reina's brow creased at the goddess' cryptic explanation, but Nihila had already turned, walking away into the darkness until all Reina could see was the bobbing glow of her lantern swaying on her staff, and before long, that was gone too.

Reina shook her head as if to clear the strangeness of the encounter from her mind. Turning back to the blue door, she set her jaw. She would not run again. The door creaked open at her touch, clanging the bells above the door that echoed into the gloom of the dark, but far from empty tavern. Reina had almost missed them, as faint as their outlines appeared in the shadows, she felt, more than saw, that she was not alone.

She reached for the lantern that glowed dimly against her hip. She raised the thing to eye level, squinting as her eyes adjusted to the new light, and suddenly, she felt a pull. There in the gently dancing flame of the lantern she felt a hunger, perhaps a need for something. On a hunch she channeled the Acher from her soul to the tiny red lantern in her grasp. The flame leapt at her gift soaking up the icy power like fuel and growing from it.

Reina's breath caught in her throat. She was surrounded. The room was packed with misshapen forms. Grotesque cadavers shuffled, limped and hobbled about aimlessly, most missing body parts or sporting cavernous wounds where organs once were. Every ghost among them was horrifying, but worse still were the children. They cried from empty eyes, stumbling about with outstretched arms for a parents comfort they could not find.

These were the souls she had left behind. Reina's grip on the lantern tightened till her knuckles were white. Whatever the madame had done, she had decimated not only their bodies but their souls as well, mutilating them somehow until not even their soul was whole. They were lost, crippled, broken things whose torment had not ended when their lives did. All thanks to the barbarous cruelty of the Madame.

The sound of a trap door creaking open in the kitchen drew Reina from the horrific scene before her. "You'd better have the girl and that babe in one piece or I will..." Madame Black paused mid sentence as she pushed through the door, shocked into silence to see Reina standing alone in the dark, cloaked in black. Holding a red lantern that illuminated her pale face, streaked with a silent tear. "Welcome back darling! You had us worried sick disappearing like that. Don't you know it's dangerous after dark?" The mask of the matronly innkeeper returned to the Madame's face, doing her best to recover the facade, unsure of how much Reina might know.

The gall of the woman to behave so innocently even as the ghosts of her cruelty circled at the edges of Reina's vision, infuriated her. "You don't see them, do you?" Reina asked, emotion shaking at the edge of her voice. The madame stared at her. "I'm sorry dear, see who?" Black asked, eyes shifting to each corner of the room.

Reina lifted the lantern higher, pouring as much Acher into the flame as it could take. "Them." Reina spat. As all the spirits in the room were illuminated by the angry red glow of Reina's lantern. The Madame jumped back with a scream, bumping into yet another desecrated soul behind her. She whirled around with wild eyes at the impossible sight of her victims still haunting the tavern. "What trick is this!?" she screeched, arm flailing about with her cruel knife still in hand. She sliced at the arm of a man with an empty chest, but the wound was not felt for there was no blood to be spilled. The undead creature merely stared at the Madame. Dahlia Black had spent lifetimes studying, dissecting and reconstructing the bodies and body parts of those unfortunate enough to find themselves beneath her blade, but never once had she allowed herself to consider the state of the souls that lay within.

Reina forced her way into the darkness of the Madame's soul. She weathered the wave of callousness and cruelty as she searched for the pits of fear buried within her rotten soul. Finally she found it. A kernel of fear that all of her work had been for naught and that she would not be remembered for her contribution to science she placed above all else, even her soul. "Reina bared her teeth under the strain of using so much Acher all at once. That paired with the stress of delving into the Madame's dark soul sapped her of much of her strength, but she had enough to finish her task.

Reina straightened her back, staring imperiously at the Madame whose eyes still flew in every direction as she tried to rationalize the horrors that she was seeing. "You are a murderer. You murdered all of these people!" Reina shouted. The Madame's wild eyes focused on Reina. "It wasn't anything so mundane as murder! It's research! It was for a higher purpose!" She screamed back, rationalizing her actions as much to Reina as to herself.

"Your excuses mean nothing. You are nothing more than a cut throat." Madame black shifted back at that as if struck. "I'll have you know *darling*." she said mockingly, affecting a coolness that the whispers of her soul betrayed as false bravado. "I have the greatest mind in the entire city, no, the empire! Nobles come to see me from lands you've never even heard of for my work! I solved mortality! I conquered death!" She screamed, her voice filling with anxiety as she noticed that the horde of shambling souls had all as one been inching toward her.

The arrogance angered Reina further, that a cruel and monstrous woman like her would dare to think that she had conquered death. Reina barked a mocking laugh at the woman who backed further into a corner, seeking as much distance as she could from the shuffling mass dead that pursued her torturously slowly. "You haven't conquered *anything*." Reina spat. "You're just a petty thief who accidentally stumbled on prizes too big to understand and my mistress wants them back.

"Your *Mistress*?" The Madame asked incredulously. Reina could feel the last of her Acher slipping by, it was time to bring this to an end. "You don't get to talk about her." she hissed. Holding the lantern as high as she could, she spoke. "Dahlia Black. You have stolen the bodies and lives from these people, and souls from their rightful path to the Black Door. In the name of Nihila, goddess of death, I declare your soul forfeit, and your life at the mercy of these victims gathered around you. In the name of Nihila. You are condemned."

Reina pushed the last of her Acher into the lantern, and it blazed an almost blinding light as moans rang out from the crowd of undead gathered around the Madame and they lurched forward, grabbing at her with hands as cold and hard as death itself. "NO! GET OFF ME! I"M BETTER THAN THIS!"

Reina could hear the tearing of clothes and gnashing of teeth as the horde assaulted the woman responsible for their suffering. "NO! PLEASE! IT HURTS! I'M NOT SUPPOSED TO DIE!!!" The Madame's cries of defiance turned to pleading, then screams and finally to gurgling silence as bits of her were ripped from her person.

First her arms, torn at the joints, disappeared into the crowd, followed by her legs, leaving the Madame a flailing, screaming stump as her body parts were claimed by the same people she had raided for resources over decades of her cruelty. Then her jaw was ripped from her face, gurgles replacing the tortured screams of the woman who had tortured them. Finally, her chest was broken open. Organs ripped from her body haphazardly as the light finally left her eyes.

Reina felt her strength wane as Madame Black's gurgling finally stilled, but she grit her teeth. These souls deserved more than just vengeance. She wasn't sure what she needed to do, but Nihila gave her the lantern for a reason and she wouldn't quit yet.

Holding the lantern still higher, she screamed from the pain of a will almost spent, but her effort was rewarded. In her chest, forgotten since receiving it, the tattooed door swung open. She looked down at the blinding light that poured from her bosom as all the souls in the room turned to her.

Sweat ran down her face from the effort of holding the lantern aloft, but she didn't dare lower it. Here was a purpose that was hers. Since her world had been turned upside down in that nameless village she had been lost, aimless guided only by Theodren and his relentless march north, but this was a purpose that was hers and hers alone. These souls needed her and she would not fail them.

The souls nearest her disappeared into the light, followed soon by the souls behind them, and those even further back, until the room was empty once more.

At last the door swung shut, the last of the crippled souls gone from this world, and her arm which felt to her like it was cast in lead fell, lantern hanging limp in her grip as she too began to fall.

"Easy, easy." Said a comforting and familiar voice as she fell into the strong arms of Theodren. He checked on Theviana, still bundled tightly, if a little low to Reina's stomach, and then he checked on her, clearing a stray hair from her face.

"When did you..." she began to ask, but she was gone, unconscious, before the sentence could be finished. "You did well." He murmured, hoisting her in his arms.

Smoke was beginning to gather in the room, spreading from his destruction in the cellar. Theodren looked around at the bloody chaos of the room, but save for the remains of the Madame spread about the room, they were alone. "Time to go." He grunted, settling Reina and the child more comfortably in his arms as he made for the door.

CHAPTER 43
BARELY FREE

CRACK! Smoke billowed out through the splintered remains of the blue door as Theodren, unwilling to spend the time searching for the handle in the smoky dark interior, slammed a large boot into the door. rocking the thing off its hinges, and sending it clattering down the steps to the stone street beyond.

Theodren sucked down lungfuls of the comparatively fresh city air, hacking out the slick tasting smoke from his throat. Eyes still watering, he barely made out the crowd of boots standing before him.

"I'll be damned." said a nasally voice. Theodren stiffened, trying to make sense of the men surrounding him in the dark. "Father Stormwall, I presume?" asked a much deeper voice. Theodren managed to gather himself enough to take a better look at the men gathered around him. Eight men, all wearing similar pairs of iron shod leather boots popular with soldiers, cotton pants and padded jerkins. The uniform was the same for all of the men except the two in the middle.

Where one was small and lean, the other was a giant, about as tall as Theodren himself and just as big around. The smaller of the two had a wicked glint in his eye that shone over a crooked nose, and the larger was a scarred man, rippling with muscle, and while he should have cut an imposing figure, there was a jovial sense of good-naturedness about him. If these men were sent by

Hardwright, they were not what he expected, and certainly much earlier than he anticipated.

Theodren coughed and spat. "Name's Roden. And I'm only father to this one here." He lied, shifting Reina in his arms to make the baby more visible. Ginter gave a snort at Theodren's deception. "Nice try dickhead, we've been tracking you since the village, you and the lovely set of narrow foot prints you got sleeping it off there." Ginter laughed.

"Please allow me to tell you how we know you are the man in question." Gunther added, striding confidently past his brother. Theodren took a step back, half of his foot coming to rest awkwardly on the broken door behind him. "Our client claims you massacred the village and his men and these gentlemen and I have been tasked with returning you to him forthwith so that you may face judgement. Now your tracks from the village lead north, and there's only one place north and that would be the lovely city of Oreton. There's only one stablemaster at the southern gate and he directed us here." Gunther grinned, examining Theodren from crown to foot. "Where the only other Nordlander within two hundred miles came stumbling ass over tea kettle right into our hands." Crowed Ginter.

Theodren had barely listened, his efforts to plan an escape thwarted by the shock of being accused of the slaughter at the village. The gall of the Cardinal to accuse Theodren of massacring his own friends enraged him. The injustice of it pulled at his sense and strangely, he felt it pull at his vitae as well. A great store of his Vitae was being pulled for some task that he was unaware of and he could not spare the attention he had trained on the soldiers but the slow drain on his Vitae concerned him still. "Hardwright can take what's left of that leg and shove it up his ass. I didn't kill the villagers." Theodren spat.

The grin spread wider across Gunther's face like a man who had just planned the winning move of a chess game. "While I do appreciate you confirming the identity of our employer, and thus yourself, the truth of the matter is that our opinion of the matter is beyond even the Cardinal's purse." Theodren cursed his foolishness for outing himself, though it seemed the deceptively intelligent brute before him would never have been convinced of anything else. "Now before you think of any brave and daring escapes." Gunther continued.

The scrape of swords leaving scabbards rose from the men around him, all pointed at him and the sleeping forms in his arms. "I'll have your hand as a new ball scratcher before you can blink." Ginter threatened, drawing his own curved short sword.

He couldn't fight them, not with Reina out of commission. He sighed, "They aren't a part of this, let me put them down somewhere and I'll go with you. Ginter barked a laugh. "What so you can have your hands free? I think the fuck not, my large friend."

A low chuckle rose from the other six men before Gunther cut them off. "The woman and the girl play no part in the contract. Once she wakes up, they are free to go where they wish, until such time however..." Gunther began conversing with the two men closest to him, who nodded smartly before sheathing their swords and running off toward the stables.

"We have a rendezvous beyond the city." Gunther finished. Theodren growled in frustration but allowed himself to be herded along amongst the mercenaries. Just before he was pushed around the corner, he felt the drain on his vitae stop and a new sensation filled him. The weight of strange eyes landed on his shoulders and he struggled to turn to see where the gaze was coming from.

There in the flickering shadows of the burning tavern was a young girl standing alone in the street. Curly brown locks turned gold from the sun covered her head in a way that cut all resistance from Theodren as he was hauled away by the mercenaries.

It was the child on the table. Every feature was exactly the same down to the empty eyes that pierced his soul in a way that he had never felt before, it was as if every deed, good and bad were laid bare before her hollow eyes. They were fathomless pits that drank in the firelight around her. Theodren wanted to stop, wanted to shout, wanted to ask what she was, to beg for her forgiveness but the soldiers dragged him around the corner, and she was gone.

Theodren was shuffled through the dark and narrow alleyways, until the open gate of the city stretched before them. A cold prick of pain lanced his back as Ginter discreetly pressed a dagger into Theodren. "No funny business now." the smaller man hissed, as Gunther distracted the guards with charming conversation. And as the band of men slipped past with Theodren in tow, he felt a tug in his mind, as a beast with familiar Vitae caught their scent.

CHAPTER 44
BAND OF BROTHERS

The moon hung low over the black skyline of trees as Theodren and his captors made their way into the forest. Large manacles now shackled Theodren's wrists, placed upon him by Ginter who chuckled to himself as he pocketed the key in a pouch at his belt. Theodren barely noticed, shaken as he was by the specter of the young girl that promised to haunt his nightmares for the rest of his days. She seemed so real in the light of the burning tavern, was she a product of his guilty conscience? What was that drain on his Vitae?

Theodren's musings were cut short when large boots filled his vision. "We are going to rest for a few hours." Gunther stated simply, staring Theodren up and down as if he was still trying to get the measure of him. "Will I come to regret tying you two together for the night?" Theodren didn't answer, staring back at the scarred face as he tried to assess him as well.

"We could always find her *other* sleeping arrangements." Gunther threatened casually. "She stays with me." Theodren growled, holding her closer. Gunther held up his hands in mock surrender before one of the men handed him a length of thick rope from his pack. "

And does the child have a need for anything this night?" He asked, uncoiling the rope as he planned the length and the knots he'd need to keep Theodren secure. Theodren looked down at Theviana. The babe had slept most of the journey, only waking here and there when startled or for brief feedings before returning to slumber. Theodren was no expert on child rearing, but even he felt that they had gone through fewer swaddles than was probably normal. Theodren craned his neck down, taking a sniff at the sleeping child. A sour smell wrinkled his nose and he sighed. "I'll need to change her."

Gunther chuckled, as he deftly removed Theviana from the wrap around Reina's stomach. Theodren cursed, struggling against the chains on his wrists until he felt the cold prick of steel at the back of his neck. "Easy there ya giant fuck, my brother's doing you a favor." Ginter chuckled.

Theodren cast his mind's eye over the group of men. He looked feverishly for any malice or cruelty that would warrant throwing caution to the wind and risking everything to tear through his restraints, but there was none to be found among these soldiers, soft blues and greens made up their souls, muted by the exhaustion and relief of a trail hard traveled and a quarry found. For now, all he could do was trust that he was simply business to them.

The larger brother strode to where his men had settled into more comfortable positions propped against trees or rocks "I require your canteen Mr. Shellberg".

"Why my canteen?" asked one of the men propped against a tree. "Because yours is the only canteen here filled with actual water Mr. Shellberg." Laughter rang up from the crowd of men and the figure Theodren assumed was Shellberg snorted and held up a canteen. Another figure held aloft a length of passably clean linen. "For the littl' un sir."

Gunther reached down, grabbing both offered items. "Much obliged gentlemen." He chuckled. Theodren watched with a feeling of curious panic as Gunther pulled the dirty swaddle from Theviana, tossing it into the hastily set camp fire. The scarred mercenary lowered himself to a kneeling position. Placing the baby gently on his raised knee, he slowly poured the canteen of water over her torso and bottom, washing away any filth leftover from the soiled swaddle.

Satisfied with his efforts, Gunther quickly wrapped Theviana in her new swaddle, before she began to fuss, gently bouncing her and patting her bottom softly with leathery hands that looked at odds with his gentleness. Gunther hummed a soft tune as he walked her back over to Theodren who watched with a baffled expression on his face.

"War orphans are commonplace in our line of work Mr. Stormwall." Was the only answer Gunther gave to Theodren's look of surprised confusion as he placed Theviana gently against the rise and fall of Reina's chest.

"You're an odd bunch." Theodren grumbled, still coming down off of the panic he felt when Theviana was pulled from him. Ginter snorted. "You're one to talk. I didn't know they let bears join the conclave." he chuckled, finishing the last knot that bound Theodren to the tree behind him. More laughter rang out from the men, and Reina stirred against his chest. "Huh? Wha?" She mumbled, eyes still pinched closed as if opening them was an affront to her senses she could not bear.

Theodren shushed her. "Shh, Reina. We've been caught. We're outside the city now." Reina's eyes flew open and her hands scrambled at her chest until she found Theviana asleep once again in her arms. Her eyes fluttered closed once more as she recovered from the momentary shock. "Oooooh my head." She moaned as her eyes screwed even tighter.

"Reina, We have to get out of here." Theodren hissed. Reina only groaned in response, tucking herself tighter into his chest. As she moved, Theodren caught sight of the red lantern now hooked to her belt. His brow furrowed at the thing that last he saw, had been dangling from her hand back in the city. The flame sputtered within it. A tiny thing devoid of any of the Vitae he had sensed in other fires. Instead, where the Vitae should be he sensed a withered spring of cold deathly energy, tied at its root to Reina's soul.

Theodren gave an exasperated sigh as the soft whistle of Reina's snoring reached his ear. He turned his mind instead to the still approaching ball of Vitae somewhere out in the dark of the forest. The bear had refused to go near the foul smelling pile of humanity that was the city of Oreton. Not that Theodren could fault him, but he had grown fond of Beithir, and the bear had grown fond of them.

While he could tell that Reina's constant fussing and cooing over him and his red colored fur wore on the beast's nerves, there was a begrudging affection for the small blonde woman who fed him extra morsels any chance she got. There was no guessing which direction Beithir was coming from, and no telling what the largest bear Theodren had ever seen would do when he saw them bound at the mercy of strange men.

Theodren's teeth grit together as he considered the odds of six men, including the oddly well-spoken Gunther, against one bear. Even with as massive as Beithir was and the casualties they might endure, a disciplined group such as this one could still triumph.

Theodren scratched at the cold iron of the manacles around his wrist as he subtly tensed his muscles against the rope that bound him to the tree.

The rope gave a creak as he tested his might against it but the iron had no give at all. The strange girl in the city had drained a large portion of his Vitae and while he still puzzled over her and her eyes that were framed even now within his mind, there were more immediate issues at hand, and despite the girl's drain on his Vitae, he still had enough that he had taken from the golems Mule and Cow that he was strong enough to break through his bonds, the manacles however were another matter.

Daring a glance at the brothers who stood discussing their plans some yards away he caught the larger man's eye. "Ah if you're puzzling out why your Thread won't work in your bid for freedom, I invite you to examine your manacles." Gunther said loud enough for his voice to travel. Stretching his arms out as far as the rope would allow, he frowned at the metal binding his hands.

"Lead alloy, I'm afraid." Gunther continued. Can't have you priests working your little blessings!" Ginter cackled, both men turning back to their conversation.

Theodren couldn't help a small smirk from taking a hold of his lips. He was not a priest. And he didn't need Thread. Searching with his mind, he gave a gentle nudge to Retribution coiled sleepily around his arm.

As his mind brushed against the consciousness within the vineling, he felt it stir. A feeling of disgruntled curiosity pushed back at his thoughts, as if to say; "haven't I done enough today?" Theodren pushed some of his Vitae toward it. Offering an apology and a request as he fed it an image of the keyhole on the deceptively plain looking manacles.

A long moment passed as the Vineling considered the image Theodren presented. Finally, he felt a squeeze around his arm, before Retribution released its grip, uncoiling itself as it slithered from his bicep to the lead manacles.

A sigh of relief escaped his lips as he felt the vineling begin its work. But his relief was cut short. Movement through the bushes pricked the ear of every man present and even the sleeping soldiers leapt to their feet, swords in hand.

Something was coming.

CHAPTER 45
BEITHIR'S BATTLE

Theodren's chest felt fit to burst as he refused to part with a single breath until the rustling in the brush made itself known. "Easy lads! Don't need you stabbing breakfast now do we?" said a tired sounding voice from the road. Soft cheers went up as the men sheathed their swords. Rushing into the brush and emerging with two soldiers, one the oldest of the group and the other appeared the youngest, carrying packages of smoked meats bound in strings.

Ginter whooped excitedly. "Where the hells did you find those!?" The youngest soldier shouldered his way through the press of excited men. "Nicked em from that stablemaster! Just had em layin' there by this wagon, figured I'd throw em in ours instead." The young soldier boasted. A groan rose from the men as their excitement turned to ire as one of them cuffed the young soldier. "Damn you Boyle! You just can't keep your fucking hands to yourself can you?" Ginter spat. The older soldier held up his hands. "It's alright lads, left some silver for em before we left." Boyle looked to the old soldier confused. "I didn't know you left your coin for em, Mr. Cane." The young soldier said, embarrassment replacing his earlier excitement. "That's cuz I didn't." The old soldier chuckled, tossing an almost empty coin purse to Boyle. "I left yours, you great walnut." Laughter roared from the men as Boyle's ears turned a deep shade of red as he pocketed the coin pouch.

Before the laughter could continue, a deep rumbling growl shook the clearing. The reason why Theodren had been unable to determine what direction Beithir was coming from was because the bear approached from the one direction he could not see. Behind them. Shouts rang out as the men wasted no time pulling themselves into a line of sword points and heater shields.

Beithir's massive head loomed at the edge of Theodren's vision. The great bear lumbered forward, sniffing at Theodren and Reina. Hot breath ruffled the hair on Theviana's head as Beithir assessed them in his own way.

"Fuck! It's huge!" Ginter shouted, adjusting his grip on the short sword he held pointed at the beast over his shield. Gunther barked orders at the men as they got on line. "Our client isn't paying for bear food, gentleman! As one! Advance! READY! STEP!" From his barked order the men responded with war cries as one. "RAH!" Gunther called again. "READY! STEP!" and the men answered "RAH!" once again.

Beithir turned, assessing the wall of sharp swords and sturdy shields that closed on him. Turning from Theodren, the beast rose on its hind legs, branches poking at the ends of its ears as it glared down at men who stood at only half his height.

Theodren watched as fear clouded, but would not overtake their souls. Finding courage in each other, he saw determination harden their faces. Theodren mentally urged Retribution to work faster as the gap between Beithir and the men began to close.

With a mighty roar Beithir slammed a massive paw into the formation. Denting shields and tearing flesh with his giant claws, the men stabbed back at the bear, exacting their own pound of flesh for each clawed haymaker they suffered.

Boyle, the youngest and least experienced, buckled first. He fell to a knee under Beithir's assault, blood pouring from a deep gash on his shoulder where a claw pierced the shield wall.

Theodren cursed his helplessness as Beithir and the men bloodied each other relentlessly. Gunther roared a challenge, standing tall above his men, lashing out with his long sword at the bear's chest.

Blood poured from the wound where his sword buried itself in Beithir's chest, but the bear felt it barely at all. Thick ropes of iron clad muscle coursed beneath Beithir's fur, infused with Theodren's magic. He was a beast beyond compare.

Beithir swatted the sword from his breast, sending it flying into the darkness, he then turned his attention on the large unarmed man before him. Beithir lashed out, slamming a paw as large as a man's torso into Gunther's chest, sending him flying into the coals of the fire behind him and coming to a violent rest in a bloody heap against the rough bark of a tree.

"YOU GIANT COCK WAFFLE!" Ginter screamed, leaping forward from the broken wall of soldiers. Throwing down his shield, the smaller brother drew a second short sword. Brandishing it in his off hand, he roared obscenities at Beithir who paused almost stunned at the small man's display of hate. "Bring me that mouth of yours ya fuzzy fuck! I'm gonna make me a new shit pot!"

For a moment, everyone in the clearing, Beithir included, grew quiet. Mentally shaken as they were by Ginter's slew of obscenities. Theodren, still reeling from the same shock, almost didn't notice when the shackles binding his wrists gave a soft click, before falling away into the dirt.

The chaos resumed in the form of Ginter launching himself at Beithir, who reacted almost too late at the twin swords with madman attached, flying at his throat. Beithir blinked at the man, before opening his toothy maw wide, catching Ginter around the midsection.

Teeth met chain mail as Beithir thrashed. Swinging Ginter from side to side, who only screamed more obscenities, slamming the pommels of his swords into the bear's face.

Theodren, now free of the manacles, leaned himself forward as far as the ropes would allow, until he could gather his feet under him. Gritting his teeth, he held Reina and the baby closer, sheltering them from the force of the rope pushing back against his shoulders as he pushed with his legs.

He was rewarded with a loud SNAP! as the rope gave way to his strength. Now free of his bonds, Theodren placed Reina and the baby, as gently as he could against the tree. Turning to the chaos of the fight that continued without him, he slammed his palms into the ground, and got to work.

CHAPTER 46
IRON FAVOR

Theodren's palms slammed into the ground as he sought out the roots of the trees around him. Beithir was covered in the blood of several shallow weeping wounds, given to him by the remaining men who fought bravely but in disarray. While Theodren was not inclined to remain their prisoner, he had no desire to kill them either. The men had shown consideration for Theviana and Reina and their banter reminded Theodren of times past in his father's hall listening to the warriors cajole and make merry.

No, these men would serve him a better purpose. Theodren's probing fingers of vitae brushed against deep roots lying in slumber beneath the ground. Pushing his own vitae into them, he was rewarded with movement.

The soldiers all froze in their tracks as the clearing began to shake. The creak of hundreds of trees moving at once sang out through the woods, as if they danced in the gale force winds of a storm, but there was no storm. There was only Theodren. The men shouted in surprise, struggling to keep their feet as the ground erupted beneath them. Roots as thick around as a man's leg shot from the dirt, snaring each man still standing and raising them into the air where their legs kicked in a fruitless search for solid footing.

To their credit, the soldiers did not allow the fear Theodren saw swimming in their souls to cease their fight. Each man responded with curses or shouts as they hacked away at the roots that held them hostage. Ginter, still in Beithir's mouth, landed a lucky hit at the bear's eye, causing the beast to roar in pain, subsequently dropping Ginter in a heap of bloody and broken bones.

Battered as he was, Ginter let loose a laugh through bloody teeth, dragging himself with one arm back toward the bear that pawed at his wounded eye. "ENOUGH!" roared Theodren, another root erupted from the ground, lashing Ginter in place. There was only one way to stop the fight without killing them but Theodren was loath to use such a tool.

Gritting his teeth through the distaste in his mouth, he fed the trees around him a different kind of vitae. Blue flowers bloomed throughout the clearing, transforming the dark and bloody expanse of trees into a flowery paradise at odds with the carnage laid before him. A sickly sweet scent pervaded the air, wafting over the soldiers and Beithir as well. The cloying scent invaded the nostrils of every man still standing and in an instant, battle cries turned to yawns as their eyes rolled back in their heads and they staggered to the ground.

One by one the men's adrenaline was overcome by the blue rose. Not even Beithir was left standing, slumping to the ground with his massive head coming to a rest on Ginter's bloody but unconscious back like a pillow.

A symphony of snores was the only sound remaining in the clearing as Theodren climbed to his feet. Theodren nodded, assessing the space. Eight men, all wounded but none dead and Beithir with a score of shallow wounds along with a bruised and bloody eye. Theodren would have his work cut out for him.

Theodren walked to where Gunther lay propped up against a tree. Shallow breaths came hard and fast as he held a hand over a large gash in his neck. "You're not a priest, are you Mr. Stormwall?" Theodren flinched, surprised at the large man's consciousness. Perhaps the scarred soldier was far enough from the center of the clearing and its new bloom of flowers not to feel its effects. Theodren came to a squat in front of Gunther, watching bright colors of Gunther's soul flicker with each passing second as the blood flowed through his fingers.

Theodren didn't quite know how to answer that. "It's complicated." he shrugged. Gunther only chuckled, sending more blood through his fingers. "I'm going to heal you, you and your men, am I going to regret it?" Theodren asked, fixing a hard stare on the mercenary captain. Hope flickered in Gunther's soul. "My men." Gunther coughed, blood running down his chin. "My men first." He wheezed. I swear on any honor I have left, I swear an Iron Favor."

Theodren had heard those words before. A soldier saved, owed an iron favor to whoever saved him. There were many who owed his father such a favor and many his father owed in turn. An Iron Favor was not something to offer casually, and Theodren knew that Gunther meant what he said.

"Your men will live without aid for a few more minutes. You will not." Theodren responded firmly, pressing his palm into the bloody wound just above the man's collar bone. Pain greeted him immediately as Gunther's wounds screamed into his mind's eye, a grimace cracked his face but he breathed a disciplined breath and got to work. Theodren pushed vitae past the gushing blood, mending bone, skin and muscle without overfeeding the cells as he had done when he was less experienced.

The wound closed and color returned to Gunther's face, Theodren turned his attention to the decimated ribs next. His brows came together as he pushed and pulled with his vitae until the ribs were back in their original shape, Gunther hissed through gritted teeth at the pain as he set the rib, spending only a minimal amount of vitae to begin the healing process.

Now free of any life threatening injuries, Theodren stepped away from Gunther, nodding to himself as he searched the man's body for any injuries he might have overlooked, and examined his soul for any subterfuge he might have missed as well. Finding none, he moved on to the rest of the soldiers, leaving Gunther to pant through the pain of his recent healing still against the tree.

The roots Theodren had used to subdue the soldiers deposited the men in a line before him. He grunted as he dragged Ginter's mangled form out from under Beithir's shaggy head and deposited him still snoring next to his comrades.

Theodren sighed, rolling up his sleeves and squatting down before the line of men and their multitude of wounds. Each would need individual attention and each would need their share of Vitae. Resolving himself to his task, he placed his hands on the youngest soldier's shoulder. As the first streaks of dawn began to light the sky, Theodren began his work.

CHAPTER 47
LITTLE VICTORIES

Theodren rocked back on his heels, thudding to a seat in the dirt from where he had been crouched over the last of the injured men. Beithir released a great yawn that echoed Theodren's own exhaustion. He leaned back into the wall of Beithir's fur, enjoying the warmness of it in the early morning sun.

"What in Weaver's fucking wang hit me?" Ginter groaned, clutching his head as he sat up. Blinking the world into view, he stared dumbly at Theodren resting against Beithir who stared back at Ginter.

Ginter blinked, Beithir blinked back. "Fuckin hells!" Ginter shrieked scrambling to his feet as Theodren waved away the noise that was wholly inappropriate for his level of exhaustion.

Ginter scrambled to retrieve his sword from his belt, spitting a scream of curses as fumbled for the weapon that was not there. "That's quite enough brother." Gunther said reassuringly, clapping a large hand on his brother's shoulder.

Ginter whirled around, staring up at his brother's face that had one extra scar to add to the collection. "I thought you were fucking dead!?" He barked, confusion elevating his voice. Gunter only chuckled. "Not just yet, I'm afraid."

"So loud." Reina groaned from where she still lay beside the tree. Theodren looked to Gunther. "Just bring him up to speed, I'll be right back." He climbed to his feet even as Ginter was still struggling to grasp the situation. "Oi! You!" But Gunther had already pulled him away. "An iron fucking WHAT?" was all Theodren could hear as he walked to wear Reina lay grimacing beneath the tree, sheltering her eyes from the sunlight that leaked through the leaves by holding the bundle of Theviana just over her face.

"Good morning." Theodren grinned, amused at the creative means of shade that Reina had created for herself. "Hnnngggg." was the only answer he received. "You have five minutes." He said softly. "Then we need to be moving." She groaned again but cracked an eye. A promising first step to being awake. "The tree." She croaked. Theodren's eyebrow raised slightly. "Tree?" her other eye popped open. "It's still alive!" She shouted as loud as her whisper-like voice would allow.

Theodren looked up at the tree Reina was laying against, and true enough it stood tall and lush, with not a hint of death or sickness to be seen. "So it is." He said, already puzzling at it. "Hurray for small victories." She mumbled, still delirious from her over exertion of power.

Theodren scooped her and the baby up in his arms, carrying them as gently as he could to the cart the soldiers had brought with them. It was a sturdy thing, unremarkable except for the thick iron rings bolted into the floor of it, presumably for unwilling guests. He placed her softly on a pile of what should be clean canvas as she murmured herself back to sleep.

The groans of poorly slept men and the rustle of chainmail told Theodren that the rest of the soldiers were regaining consciousness and soon their feet. "To me gentlemen!" Gunther called, cutting off his brother's expletive laden rant.

"What the hell happened captain?" Boyle yawned, stumbling with the rest of the men to join their Captain. "We were beaten gentlemen." Gunther answered solemnly. Grumbles of disbelief and discontent passed through the men. "That we still breathe the sweet air is thanks only to Mr. Stormwall here." He waved an arm to Theodren who now stood next to the cart, arms crossed as he watched the proceedings quietly.

"He has done me an Iron Favor, keeping us all alive. And so I owe him a favor in turn. I will not hold any of you to my agreement, but I am postponing our delivery of Mr. Stormwall to the client." The men looked around at each other. "So... we're still taking him back to Militas?" Boyle asked, his hand half raised. It seemed that there was no question about sticking together with their Captain.

"Yes, Private Boyle, we are merely making a detour." Gunther grinned at the lad. "Detour where cap'n?" Shellberg asked, still idly running a puzzled hand over the spot on his torso where a bloody gash should have been. "Good news and bad news on that front I'm afraid." The men quietly waited for him to continue. Watching him chew the inside of his cheek to find the words.

"The good news, gentleman, is that where we're going, we'll find the best beef and beer, the likes of which they don't allow even in Militas." A hesitant cheer went up at that as the road weary men each had their own fantasy of hot beef and cool beer. "The bad news however..."

Ginter spat. "The bad news is that he wants us to go to fucking Nordland." The men stared at Ginter incredulously in their silence. Theodren cleared his throat. "I'm going north to leave the child with my father. What I have planned is no place for a baby much less the only survivor of Hardwright's massacre."

The men all looked between each other. Remembering the blood and viscera sprayed throughout every home in the village, and the mass of freshly dug graves Theodren had left behind. "And why the fuck would we take you there?" Ginter snarled, pushing past his brother and storming over to where Theodren stood beside the cart.

"Far as I can tell. That massacre was your fucking doing, you and that bitch in the cart." he spat jamming a finger into Theodren's chest. "I don't give a fuck about any favor and I'm certainly not going weeks out of my way for your fucking field trip you murderous shit."

Green light erupted from Theodren's eyes as Retribution gathered itself in all of its vicious glory in his fist. "I will say this only once." The calmness of Theodren's tone made a startling contrast with the fury on his face and the unnatural booming volume of his voice. "You are alive because I allow it." The shadows grew longer as the trees they followed, groaned and seemed to reach inward toward the group of men. "I spared you and your men because I repay kindness with its like and cruelty with the same." He raised the hammer with a single hand, the shadow of it making Ginter flinch as it passed over his eyes.

"You are not *taking* us anywhere." Theodren slammed the head of the hammer into the ground, by Ginter's feet, the impact shaking the earth strong enough to make the smaller man fall backwards with a shout. "You will follow." Theodren slammed the ground again, keeping Ginter too rattled to stand. "You will leave." He brought the hammer down again. "Or you will die."

He glared down at Ginter's soul, watching the man's vitriol turn to disbelief and then to fear. Despite the look of defiance still on Ginter's face, Theodren knew that he would think twice before provoking him again. He turned to the rest of the men, still staring at him with a mixture of fear and confusion. "My name is Theodren, son of Thorn." His voice boomed across the clearing as he hardened his resolve. "Heir to The Gnarled Throne."

Confusion and recognition filled the souls of the men as he made his proclamation for the first time since leaving his father's lands. "Your Captain owes me an Iron Favor for your lives. As such he will aid me until that debt is paid. Retribution is owed to the Cardinal Hardwright and I *will* deliver." Locking eyes with each man, he took their measure before finally landing on Gunther who looked on at his brother, hand still gripped tightly on his pommel in concern even as he tried to maintain an air of collectedness and calm.

"I leave your choices and your lives to you. But your captain and I..." Theodren turned away, looking down into the cart where Reina still slept, holding Theviana tightly to her chest. "We are going north."

To be continued.

THE TENETS OF THE TAPESTRY

JKL Parker

Genesis

In the beginning, there was everything. The whole of the universe not yet formed, it existed as a great sea of chaos. The facets of reality thrashing against each other as there was no one to guide them. But then, there was Order. Odrain the Weaver, holy father of all creation, took hold of the chaos, and bound it to his will, enacting order upon the wilds of the ether and crafting the fabric of reality into a cohesive cloth, the Tapestry. Under the Weaver's immaculate wisdom, the earth was separated from the sky, and the ground was made separate from the sea. Night was made separate from the day and the seasons were ordered into flow. Through this, unruly chaos was brought to heel and the world was born, perfect and fruitful. It brought forth life, and all who lived upon Odrain's Tapestry knew that he was the one and only god, and his church was to be the authority most high throughout the land.

Excerpt from the Bible of Holy Order, Edition #5.

(All previous editions are to be returned to the nearest church. failure to relinquish unauthorized holy texts will be punished severely.)

THE TRUE GENESIS

In the beginning...

There was everything.

The whole of the universe, not yet formed but there none the less. It existed in condensed forms of essence. Concepts of a thing not quite real... yet. For all of these concepts knew no shape. Every concept and facet of reality were merely threads tangled together in the vastness of an empty universe. Until, there was Order. Ordain came into existence as a being of no power of his own, sustaining himself only on the power he attained from others. It was his union with Yggdrazil, the goddess of life that created mankind, and with the birth of man, came a need for the order that Odrain promised. With the help of Yggdrazil, the other facets agreed to assist in the creation of this ordered existence, lending their power over their facets of reality to Odrain so that he may create a world in which mankind could live. Suddenly every thread had a place and a purpose and Odrain bound them into the great tapestry of the universe. At the end of the tapestry, the gods were to be freed from Odrain's control so that they may all bask in their creation together. But they had been deceived. Odrain stripped the divinity from each thread and killed them, binding them as they thrashed.

for the weaver had a singular purpose. To rule over all the colors of the tapestry. To guide its many threads into its own image. For a time there was quiet. For the people who sprang from the tapestry, there was only one God, Odrain the Weaver, the God of Order. For how could it not be so? There were no gods who survived to be mentioned.

Excerpt from the Book of Life

Odrain the Weaver: The god of order, a divine tyrant believed by all to be the only god to ever exist. Odrain's authority over the tapestry is nearly absolute and as such his divinity and right to rule creation has been above reproach since the dawn of man, until now.

Yggdrazil the Tree of Life: God of life and creation. Goddess of all life, and of beginnings. Where there is the spark of creation, you will find her light. The union of life and order was what had initially created the first man, and as their divine mother, she could not allow them to die. Without her encouragement the The Tapestry would never have been made, and the other gods would never have died.

Nihila, keeper of the Black Door: A goddess not only of death, but of nothing. She governs the very absence and end of things. She was the only god that Odrain feared to interact with as he knew that she was the end of all things, himself included, and where his tapestry ends, she begins. She spends her days entertained simply by the goings on of the Tapestry, watching kingdoms rise and fall, enjoying the tiny dramas of each life as they strut across the world and when their stories end, she collects them, shepherding each one carefully to her black door.

The Holy Kingdom of Grandia: A holy land believed to be bequeathed to the Church by Odrain himself, It consists of the southern half of the continent of Terrus. Its records stretch back to time immemorial, and is believed to be the birth place of the first man. Once a small theocracy, it has expanded steadily over the centuries as it seeks to establish its manifest destiny of bringing order to the entirety of the continent, and then, to the world at large. Its expansion was only halted mere decades ago, when its forces were summarily routed at the battle of the Stith by Thorn the

Stormwall, who held the only known passage across the Jormungand for years while outmanned by the Grandian forces who threatened to overwhelm his position if not for his fierce defense of the Stith, a river fort that overlooked the Jormungand river, a vast body of water that separated north from south.

Nordland: A collection of nation states that encompasses the northern half of the continent of Terrus. Cobbled together as an alliance between smaller kingdoms to defend against the encroachment of Grandia, the many kingdoms became one under the guidance of Thorn the Stormwall who gained fame for his defense of the Stith and his brave incursions into Grandian territory to harry supply lines and disrupt the attacking force. The country now exists as an oligarchy headed by Thorn, who was elected king by the other lords unanimously after the battle of corpse bridge, and ultimately the end of the war, for the time being.

The Holy Capital: The largest city in the south of Terrus, and home to the Conclave. a Holy City within a city, dedicated to the church and used as a religious college for the Holy Order as well as a bastion of religious and political power throughout the south.

The Holy Order: The major church that governs the whole of Grandia, its dictates are the law of the land and are enforced by priests stationed in every village, town and city in the land and beyond.

The Nameless village: A small hamlet several leagues north from the Holy Capital, it is a modest place, made up of humble folk who simply wish to live quietly away from the larger cities. Some move there to escape their past, others simply to disappear. The people are generally distrustful of strangers and travelers but always look out for each other.

Militias: Once a military garrison, it has expanded into a large city north west of the Holy Capital. At the end of the holy war for expansion, Grandia's soldiers were forced to remain there as a means of maintaining readiness for the moment that the Holy Kingdom was prepared to wage war again. It has been over two decades since the end of the war, and the soldiers there have grown a resentment toward the holy city that has robbed them of their freedom. A growing motto among the resident soldiers is "Always recruiting, never discharging." They keep themselves busy working as mercenaries for the garrison commander who maintains their readiness and their loyalty for his own ends.

Oreton: A harsh city of industry in the north of Grandia. It serves as both a hub of trade for material wealth and a mining city that pulls minerals from the earth and contributes to the grime and haze of the city of stone and metal.

Divine Thread: The divine power of the Weaver that allows the wielder to order the fabric of the universe to heed their will. This power is wildly varied and unpredictable in how much and to whom it is bestowed. While there is some belief that it can be inherited, this is not a proven fact. The way that a person's thread is expressed through their power largely matches their personality and requires a great deal of study and discipline in order to use it proficiently. Any person who manifests Divine Thread in the kingdom of Grandia is mandated to study and serve the Conclave where they will be trained in the ways of the Golden Order and made into a priest in some capacity or other. While there are some in the Nordlands who manifest their own Thread, the people of the north resist the notion of order and bureaucracy that the church represents, and so their thread is expressed not in external power but rather physical strength and resilience.

Vitae: The Life Water of creation. While it can not manifest new sentient life, it can prolong, preserve and improve any existing life that it is applied to. However, too much Vitae can cause the cells within living creatures to become cancerous and grow out of control. All creatures are born with a limited amount of vitae that they can not control. Theodren however has his own font of Vitae which allows him to produce increasing amounts of life essence which he can use to heal himself and others. While vast it is not inexhaustible and requires time, rest and food to replenish. There is one way to recover Vitae quickly, and that is to kill another living being and absorb their life essence like an ultimate predator. Being possessed of Vitae also enables the bearer to see the colors of Vitae that exist within a person's soul and to an extent understand their emotional state. This is a power of untold potential that grants its wielder authority over not just life, but the spark and light of creation itself. It is a power that will take Theodren years to fully understand.

Acher: An icy river of death magic that gives the wielder power over death, shadows, and the dark whispers of the soul. This power is not easily controlled as it seems ironically alive and seeks to consume any and all life that comes into contact with the wielder. As an acolyte of Nihila, the goddess of death, nothing and the end of things, wielders of Acher have authority over the absence of things, and with Reina's understanding of shadows as the absence of light, she wields them as deftly as any weapon. And with the lantern given to her by her patron goddess of death, she can feed Acher into its deathly light to reveal the world of spirits and call them forth.

Theodren: Born a prince of Nordland to his father Thorn Stormwall and his mother the Lady Morgana, Theodren was raised with the expectation that he would be responsible for the burden of authority over the people of the north, though he found what time he could to slip away from his lessons and training on the arts of statecraft and war to admire the blacksmiths whose fires and warmth filled the Northern capital of Troenhold. His mother had been a necessary part of the treaty for peace signed by his father. A simple non-aggression pact in exchange for keeping a high ranking priestess within his court. It didn't take long for the Lady Morgana to woo the warrior king into a marriage bed, and their child Theodren was a source of pride to both of them. When Theodren began showing signs of possessing his own Divine Thread, his mother began telling him stories of the opulence and wondrous extravagance of the Conclave and the southern capital. Much to Thorn's dismay, Theodren had been convinced to join the church of his enemy, robbing him of both a son and an heir. Theodren learned quickly that his share of Divine Thread was meager to say the least, and any privilege he held in the north was nonexistent within the conclave. But he was a young man of earnest conviction, and devoted himself to long hours of study that stretched into the dull dawn of morning. He graduated from the Conclave on sheer creativity and will power as his thread was not up to even the most basic of tasks without deep knowledge of what was required. He was disheartened to find himself relegated to the nameless village at first. He had thought this was perhaps a practical joke of some kind as his orders contained no name next to the location, only a map with a line that ended in seemingly nowhere. But Theodren made the best of things. He quickly made friends with Eleina, a spirited woman with fiery red hair matched only by her personality, and he learned to do the best he could to serve the people of his village with integrity and quiet determination.

Reina: The daughter of a well regarded courtesan, Reina was trained from an early age to excel at everything she set her mind to, or face harsh consequences. As the daughter of a woman of influence, there were many who sought to gain her favor, and by extension, her mother's, by lavishing a young Reina with praise and refusing to admonish her for any wrongdoings. Reina was a sheltered young woman raised more as an ornament for her mothers vanity than as a daughter. When her massive potential for Divine Thread manifested itself, Reina was promptly shipped off to the Conclave where she tried to find the belonging that she so craved, but never received from her mother. Here it was her power and skill that gained her influence and opened doors and not her relation to her well connected mother or her shadowy unknown father. When she was finally faced with the consequences of her actions for the first time in the nameless village, her life came crashing down around her. Were it not for Nihila's intervention, and Theviana's reliance on her for survival, she would surely have cracked and been destroyed under the weight of her crimes.

Lusis Hardwright: Cardinal, and head of the Order of Golden Shears, Lusis Hardwright is a cruel and conniving man who learned to claw his way to influence by manipulating and scheming his way to the top, often at the cost of the people around him. Like Theodren had little power of his own to speak of, but he excelled at using his thread to gain influence over the minds of others and bend them to his will. His bitterness at his lack of personal power leads him to abuse those he deems lesser than himself either in power or authority. He despises those who hold any power over him and will resort to any method to gain leverage over them.

Gaius the Patriarch: Leader and supreme authority of the Church of Holy Order, not much is known about the man and his origins beyond rumor. All that is known for certain is that while few have seen it for themselves, there is no one possessed of as great a length of Divine Thread as the Patriarch himself.

Richard Piercer: Commander of one of the largest outposts of Grandia's military, He spends what should have been his retirement maintaining order and discipline among aimless soldiers with nowhere to go and scheming plans known only to him. He keeps the men fit and employed by dispatching them as mercenaries throughout Grandia and beyond. Whatever plans the Commander has in store, it will become clear that the Conclave has made a grave error in forgetting about the soldier sons of the Holy Kingdom.

Gunther: A large and scarred soldier, He is without question the Commander's favorite. Charming and deceptively intelligent for his size and strength, he has devoted his life to serving the Soldier Sons and rose quickly to authority and status throughout his years fighting in small wars and disputes outside of the Holy Capital. Quick with a joke and slow to anger, he is a master tactician and a born soldier.

Ginter: Twin brother to Gunther though his short stature is a point of disbelief to most people. He is the opposite of Gunther in almost every way. Despite that he is fiercely loyal to his brother and the men under the command he and Gunther share. He is short tempered, often rude, and perhaps the most skilled warrior that the Soldier Sons has ever known.

DEDICATION

Since the dawn of time, mankind has gathered together to tell and share stories, and I am beyond honored to be someone who gets to continue that tradition. But I could not have done it alone. Not without an amazing group of people who believed in me and my story. I began writing this story when I was working long hours at the hospital to support my fiancé who was the first to encourage me to keep writing. Then there were my parents who pushed me further to expand on the world I had created. And just when I thought I was finished, Dr. Cheyenne Marco changed everything. She believed in me, my story, and my ability to turn it from a novel to an epic fantasy. She devoted her time and her expertise to my story and I could not be more grateful. So to all of you who cheered me on... Thankyou, this world of mine would not exist without you.